HALF-BLOODS RISING

THE ROGUE ELF #1

J.T. WILLIAMS

DWEMHAR REALMS

THE REALM OF URLAS

1

THE SACRED WOODLANDS

Not idly do the Blades of Urlas guard the sacred realms of the world. A shimmering shadow descends, as unseen specters shout from the dark places of the world while others barely break the silence. As in all whispers, there is a truth beyond mere words, secrets to the shroud of what moves both seen and unseen. Beneath a starlit sky, in the hidden woodlands of a sacred realm, there is but one that awakens from the darkness of mere consciousness. A once sleeping soul, a powerful splinter within the fabrics of creation meant to disrupt the cataclysm of a darkness reaching its hand out to devour that which does not expect it. The rogue elf has awakened.

He tasted the tinge of blood in his mouth. Kealin spat and moved his elven blade into an angle behind him. His master called this a guarded stance. He studied his adversary, watching his breathing, his footwork, his subtle movements, and his slight nuances that hinted at his next moves. His opponent moved forward and spun, slashing low before jumping into the air. The blade swung toward his head. He dodged it, sidestepping to the left before kicking his opponent's knee. He moved his hand along his hilt, spinning the blade to strike, only to parry another blow meant for his shoulder. The shadowy form of an elven warrior recoiled, and now it took a guarded stance.

Gravel sliding under his feet as he shifted his weight, Kealin ran forward. His opponent, taken by surprise in his agility, faltered. He struck him twice. His bare chest was chilled by the night air, but the half-elf did not mind. His blood was hot, and he was eager to fight.

Two more opponents, greater in size than the first, rushed him. He jumped, slashing one across the chest. The second one was more determined, but through a series of careful parries, he too fell. Now another one approached. This one was larger, and the half-elf knew he must be ready.

All around him, the trees of the great elven woodlands were alive with the songs of night. A faint glow of the moon was on large green leaves that rustled with a strong wind. The larger man was upon him. He worked to disengage, moving to the left, but the swordsman moved with him. He had played fair until now. His master would be happy with his work so far, but he was not one to rely on mere teachings.

He reached behind his back, drawing a second blade, and rushed his opponent. He struck repeatedly with the first blade. With a careful twist of wrist, he forced the man's sword upward. He locked the man's blade high. A split moment later, he buried the second sword deep in his stomach.

He smiled as the man fell to the ground.

"Kealin, your skill with two blades is exceptional. If only you could do such tasks without two blades. I am impressed but cannot approve of this. Your brother will not approve of such either."

The voice was that of Blade Master Rukes, and his tone was less than approving.

"Then you can tell Taslun of my folly," Kealin replied.

"There is no need, little brother."

Kealin turned to see his brother approaching the arena grounds. The collapsed forms of the phantoms he had faced vanished in a flash of sand. His brother approached just as the last one was blown away in the winds.

"The Blades use one sword, not two."

Taslun was the epitome of what Kealin knew Master Rukes wished to produce in a swordsman. Fearsome in many regards, he was also tall and slender. At all times, he had a long curved blade strapped to his back. He had spent many years learning his craft, and the lineage of their father was with him. He had pointed ears and blond hair he kept long down his back.

"I cannot expect a brother of mine to have such disregard for order."

"Then be sure Calak knows so he will not disappoint you. He is closer to you in blood; the elf side of him is strong. I must make up for that. Besides, Master Rukes is who gave me my second blade after he realized my proficiency with the cruel one I used to have and surprise you with during our duels. Again, I will do what I must."

"What you must do is come home now. Master Rukes is done with your disappointing practice."

Rukes confirmed his brother's words. "Tomorrow, young one. We will further your sword work. And, while I did approve of your use of two blades, you must understand the limits that places on you within Urlas."

"Of course, Master. I have not forgotten."

Kealin bowed to his master and followed Taslun away.

They walked in silence from the arena. Under towering pine trees and beside the bank of the great Lake Eldmer, they passed over the white stone bridges that connected the cobblestone paths running around the length of the ancient waters of their realm. These were the Urlas Woodlands. A sacred island, an entire world away from troubled lands. They were on the edge of this place. A large sea encircled their lands, but none normally left their shores. They were all safe here. It was an enchanted realm that only those of elven blood could find and dwell within. It was also a purist elf domain, but his family was allowed admittance. His father was a renowned Blade, the warrior class renowned for their blade work learned over hundreds of years. His father had earned his place in this sacred realm of the elves from fighting in wars long ago. But when he came, he brought his wife, a human.

Kealin was the younger brother to Taslun, and older brother to Calak, who teetered between his stalwart eldest brother and Kealin when it came to his own desires. Taslun was a step from joining the Blades of Urlas. He was just awaiting his final trials and the christening of the Blades.

"YOUR MOVE into your high guard was slow," Taslun said. "And when you complete your trials for moving from tenth degree to the eleventh, witnessed by the Eyes of the High Council, you will not be able to use two blades."

"I'm not too worried of that," Kealin said, putting both his hands behind his head as they walked. "It's been made clear that no one cares for one like me training to become a Blade. I doubt I'll ever be observed by the council for admission to the higher tiers. Thankfully, our father has three children to be proud of. His eldest, soon to be a Blade, his daughter who even the greatest archons say rivals her pure blooded rivals, and Calak, the young one no doubt to follow his 'elder brother', and they don't mean me."

Calak was hastily coming up and was like his brother Kealin in every way, but still not of the skill that he had obtained. In fact, Kealin was on track to surpass that of Taslun, but he believed he could never serve as a true Blade. His blood was not elven enough; he, like his sister, Alri, had taken after their mother. It wasn't like they didn't look like the other elves, but the council had deemed their blood not as pronounced. Alri was lucky in some regard. She was a mage, and fortunately for her, the mages did not have the same standards as the Blades. She, like their mother, was under the direction of High Archon Oaur, and was trained in many forms of spell craft. Though she was the youngest, she was not the type to be ignored.

"Did you go watch Alri, too?" Kealin asked.

"I did. Just a bit though. I can only take so much of repeated staff movements and incantations. It looks good from afar with all the flashes and snaps of the spells but up close I just think of how I could dodge the fireballs and break her staff."

Kealin laughed, "Well, this is Urlas. I don't see any of us having a chance to ever truly fight something beyond shadow warriors in the training area."

They crossed over a large stream that flowed from the higher hills of the south down into the great lake that was in the center of their woodland home. Several fairies sitting on the banister, floated between the two of them as a trio of priestesses moved down the path. Taslun and Kealin both bowed their heads, stepping out of their way.

"Hail Etha, young ones of Urlas," one of them said as they passed.

"Etha be praised," Taslun said.

Kealin remained quiet and simply looked at his brother as the priestesses passed.

They began to walk again, moving between the

massive pines of Felkras woods, one of the farthest reaches outside the capital.

"You know, you might need the blessings of Etha at some point in your life," Taslun teased, "You'll cry out and Etha will simply think back to all the prayers she has heard and go, 'Kealin never prayed to me, I guess I cannot help him now.'"

Kealin nodded, "If I am in need of a goddess to help me, I would have failed the teachings of Master Rukes. I need only my blades dear brother."

Taslun looked at him and smiled, "Too bad father told me to assure you didn't go off on a random hike; otherwise we would have tested your skill with dual blades against my own."

Kealin shook his head. "Why must we do that? Do you not believe your skill to be enough? We have ended that duel in a draw every time."

"I would like to show you what it means to be a real swordsman. You cannot claim a draw when a duel turns into you rolling around on the ground like an animal, kicking dirt in my eyes."

"But that is a duel in honor you speak of. In combat, it would be warranted. You can train for duels. I expect to use my skill for more than that."

"That would only be by the blessing of Master Rukes, which you will never get using two blades. Perhaps he will look over your half-elf blood if you will simply embrace his teachings."

Taslun spoke to him like their father, and that annoyed him.

"I do not disregard his teachings; only, I feel that

they can be added to. The confines of the Blades restrict our actions."

"You cannot add to the traditions of our ancestors. One day, you will understand what I say."

Kealin stopped. "And one day you will all understand that I do not stand for our ancestors as you do. You and I are the same. Half-bloods. But you were deemed 'pure' by the council while I was deemed less."

Taslun turned. "I don't care if you stand as I do, but it is time we stop bickering as we do every day. We have no control over the council. Besides, our father was restless earlier. I've never seen him like that. There has been news from the outside world, I'm sure of it."

"Outside? Since when does news come to us?"

"The High Council is always in some contact with elves in other parts of the realms but never have I seen it and— I don't know. I will not give thought to what I don't know yet. It will be revealed soon enough. I think that is why father wanted to assure you were home before moon rise."

Kealin could sense something from his brother's words, he was nervous. A quality that Kealin never associated with Taslun. He was curious of what news his father would bring.

"CONCENTRATE!" Archon Oaur shouted.

The archon training grounds of Nidea Archo were alight in the fires of a young mage who was one of the prized pupils of Oaur.

Alri held her staff out in front of her. The two stone pillars before her were wreathed in blue fire and the great gate between the stone shook with each ramming strike. From behind it, her master created a specter of flame, a familiar of some kind of beast from beyond their sacred realm.

Alri tightened her grip, energy flowing from the center of her skull down her arms and curling out of her fingertips. She focused her thoughts into the staff, her powers accented by the Yula wood and the ruinite crystal at its tip.

The gate shook again.

She continued her spell. The mental formations of patterns, seeing the work of her own mind in engorging flame, twisted in the ethereal space visible to archons. She knew her spells but this was always the part she failed in previous exercises.

The gateway broke. The beast charged.

Alri released her right hand, ceasing the spell she had been holding on the gateway. The ground of Nidea Archo rumbled as the creature charged the young archon mage. She sidestepped, bringing her staff around in a circle, forming a ward just as the creature was within range.

It struck the ward, rolling off to her side. She held her grip, even though the creature was immediately up again, slashing at her with its fiery paw.

Her ward broke and she slid down to one knee. Summoning her energies again, she exhaled, lifting her staff to her foe.

Focus, fracture, fade. I will not fall again.

She drew up the ward a second time, held it against another advance, and then drew back the erratic energies into her form again. The raw energy wrapped itself into her core and like fire, it burned within her. But she had conserved the spell. She hated this part. This entire test was not a trial of any one skill, it was about endurance. A skill all of its own that could make the difference in a battle. Archons did not have the renown of Urlas Blades, but few archons left witnesses to their atrocities. A bleeding corpse with a missing head was not the trademark of those that came out of Nidea Archo. Archon Oaur, a Grandmaster of the Archons, had trained her for the last twenty moons to move into yet another level of arcane skill. For the past 100 years, she had trained under him starting with the basis of magics of sparks and snow to the point she was now commanding both defensive and offensive attacks at a level beyond what most of her age could do. Already, she was excelling where other purer elves struggled.

She knew she was his favorite. Just like her mother. Something that had further pushed her away from the other archons. They questioned her powers, how one that was of the race of men and elves could ever dare look upon the fires of Nidea Archo and not collapse in the trials of the first year. She had fought to be where she was. A fact that drove her to be even better.

Focusing again, she formed her ward. She could feel her energy waning but as the creature came again, she deflected it again, fracturing her own ward and veiling herself in the crackling explosion.

Alri broke the cycle, slamming her staff upon the creature before the creature vanished and only Archon Oaur stood upon the training grounds.

She was no match for the archon but it didn't stop her from trying.

He had taken the form of a Rusis, the elemental casters of the world beyond their protected realm. Her brothers fought specters but she trained against other magic users, and Rusis in particular were a deadly enemy.

Oaur summoned a spell of ice and fire, his small wands crackling with energy as he jumped toward her, freezing the ground and forcing her to either advance or retreat before he would strike with fire. She fell back, casting an eruption spell, splitting the ground with a solid black stone and shielding herself from the flurry of fireballs that came flying towards her.

Explosions rippled around her and the archon jumped upon the now solitary pillar of stone.

"You are slow, Alri! I have pulled back my attack. I have the ground above you. You have lost the advantage."

Alri smirked, but her hands trembled. Her energy was waning. They were beyond the lesson on endurance. But sparring was her favorite part of her training. She could not match her master's elemental prowess and he did hold the high ground. There was no chance for her to surprise him with a crackling bolt of lightning or an icy shard, no, elemental magic would not work here.

She stared at the grounds beneath her master and

knew what her master would not expect. Archons were not known for this. But something deep within her connected her to an older world, an older magic. Beyond the skills of typical high elves. Her master had seen her use such magic but it was sanctioned in their lands.

Alri had never limited herself to what was sanctioned or not. That was the boundary of a first moon archon. Her master pushed her. She would push back.

She aimed her staff at the ground, the energies flowing from her to the ruinite crystal shifted. The glowing blue orb on her staff darkened and she spun the spells within her mind, linking with the lower energies of her body, grounding herself. Unlike the beauty of ice spells or the dancing lines of fire magic, this magic weaved from her into the soil.

"Alri!" her master shouted.

He leapt upon her, but she ripped her staff upward, drawing up a specter of soil and bone to shield her from her master.

The summoning grabbed her master and she fell back, bringing her staff up. Her necromantic creation was a grotesque form of broken elven bones and dirt, a dead high elf, both unholy and deadly. Its eyes burned with purple fire and hissing, it slashed at her master. Suddenly, it exploded towards her Oaur in blind obedience. A moment later, the creature burst into white fire.

Her master gripped its neck, turning his head as he withdrew a dagger of the Goddess Etha, a bane of the undead. It was an artifact from his travels outside of Urlas.

He threw the creature down as it quivered and burned, turning to ash.

Alri lowered her staff and waited for the scorn of her master.

Her master looked at her, raising his eyebrow. He wasn't angry, not like last time. That was five years ago and was one of the last trials where she worked directly with other students. She did win that duel though.

"Necromancy. You were quick in your engagement but your form is poor. Your creature, though of elven blood, was like a beast. A necromancer would be able to make at least a somewhat sentient being from one of our brethren."

Alri shook her head, "This is not the path of an archon."

"No," he said, "Not as the High Council would see it. But you are not like my other pupils and thus I try to keep that in mind. But I did not reach my place in Urlas following every single rule. Necromancy is limited, it requires death. That is why Archons focus on energy and of that, I consider your work today prior to our duel of the most importance. In our realm, the dead are rare. If Urlas was assailed, it would be energy based spells that would be the shield of the elves, not necromancy."

ALRI AND OAUR retired to the temple on the sides Nidea Archo. Like all buildings in their land, this structure was built into the trunk of a large tree but had two long wings of stone that went out following the path of the sun as it passed from East to West over the encircling mountains.

Alri had never been permitted to go beyond the outer sanctum but as she understood it, there were statues to many of the gods of the North. While the likenesses of Kel, the god of war, Wura the mischievous one, and Dimn, the god of winds were hidden from her, there was one she was allowed and encouraged to look upon. It stood on the edge of the Outer Sanctum. A place she had spent many hours in and expected to still spend many more hours of her time while training under her master.

It was here, after walking through several granite pillars, that she could wash her face in a sacred fount before bowing once to the goddess. Crossing before the goddess to a bare but ornate floor, she would rest beneath a grand statue of Etha, the Goddess of Starlight whose form was so tall, her head was above the ceiling of the temple. It was said she watched over the training grounds and the actions of all future Urlas Archons. Alri had always loved the statue. For a creation carved from stone, Etha appeared to be a fair woman, with flowing raiment, and her hand outstretched to the sky. She was a patron goddess of the elves, within Urlas and outside of the sacred realm. Some of Alri's first meditations had taken place in this very spot. She could never forget those first feelings of energy awakening from their dormant state within her.

Alri bowed before the statue, as did her master,

centering her energies as was required to attune herself back to normal regeneration. She clutched her Archon Stone, a necklace containing a similar material as was in her staff but one that even as a young pupil, she was taught to focus her powers into. For archons, their connection to the arcane wells within the realms of greater magic were an important connection to build. In the case of her stone, this was her connection if ever she was without her staff and needing magic. For none of the elven race could use magic without a channeling device.

Her master took her away from the meditation area and to their typical place for drinking tea, a small balcony off to the side of the temple where her Master kept several books and frequently where she could find him if he wasn't in the training grounds himself.

Oaur tended to a small kettle of hot water kept warm by a stack of crystals.

Her master preferred tea both before and after training sessions.

"Where do the dead come from if we live in a protected realm? There have been no wars in our borders."

Oaur looked at her with an uncertain glare, scooping tea leaves into their cups.

"Fallen warriors, from a time well before now. At one time, Blades of Urlas, like your father, would train against Archons. Accidents did happen. But without risk there is no real lesson, at least, that was what we said."

Alri considered her master's answer but her

exploratory use of necromancy, learned from her own studies in the library of Urlas, had led her to feel much more dead beyond that of the training grounds.

"But what about the others. Near the grand lake?"

Her master poured water into their cups.

"You attempt to peer into the past? Does your mind really wander so far beyond my teachings and the teachings of an archon?"

"I can't not see what I feel. There was much death here. An unbalanced emotion deep within me, veiled just beyond my understanding. I could not concentrate as I needed for my summoning earlier. Perhaps, that is why it was not sentient as you say."

He pushed her tea to her. "Alri, I will not entertain questions beyond necessity regarding this. There is much of Urlas, of the world in general, that makes me question my own memory. There has been death here but to speak of it would bring more scorn upon you than the impurity of your elven blood."

So there was death here beyond the training grounds.

High Elves, such as those in Urlas, did not die from sickness or age. It took mortal injury or arcane poisoning, to kill an elf. Death was told to be rare and Alri had never seen an elf that had died or been killed. But still, she could sense death in her homeland. A quality that was not a typical characteristic of her class of study.

Oaur was staring at her now. She sipped her mint tea and trying to ignore him but he sighed.There was more to his thoughts but she had already questioned enough and she knew it.

"The High Council must contend with enough already without the wandering mind of a young archon such as yourself. There are workings in the lower world, far to the South. Changes come to some things but we will work through them. Do not let yourself be troubled. Embrace what you know, seek what is pure, do not let your mind be occupied with the darkness of unknowing ramblings."

That confirmed it. Her master would not speak further of this.

She continued to sip her tea, trying to do as her master said. Now she wondered of what went on in the South. Urlas never concerned itself with dealings outside its realm but even that had seemingly changed.

I must do as my master has said.

She took a deep breath and focused her thoughts on her tea.

The rising moon over the archon training grounds signaled it was almost time for her to head home.

KEALIN AND TASLUN had stopped near the lake near the edge of their own grove. The moon had just begun to rise above the edge of the encircling mountains. The waters of this place had always brought him comfort be it weariness from many bouts with Master Rukes, or just a need to return to the primordial waters of their creation. It was said by his people that this lake had special meaning to them, a place where their race began anew when the sacred realm was founded.

Regardless of its origins, this was home. Urlas was all of their home. Beside a bridge that led over a narrow portion of the lake, they both sit on the railings and watched the stars of their people beginning to show in the dark skies. It was here that they normally waited for Alri before heading home.

Their youngest brother joined them. Calak, an elf built in the same image as Taslun but with Kealin's own wild mind had spent time at home working on the most laborious portion of Blade training, reading of the past Blades and their many deeds. Kealin remembered being in Calak's place and he hated it. Calak seemed indifferent about it. He both loved his place as a student of Master Rukes and to occasionally break the formal rules. He was a true blending of his older brothers.

"How did your time with Master Rukes go?" Calak asked.

"Taslun is most displeased," Kealin said, throwing a stone across the surface of the lake, sending it skipping several times.

Taslun shook his head and looked over to Calak, "Displeased? No. Surprised, no. I hope at least you will follow after our father with a more proper interpretation of Urlas Blade appropriateness, Calak."

The winds shifted strangely.

Kealin sensed it, looking around. The winds never changed in Urlas, not this early, at least.

Thunder rumbled over the mountains that surrounded them.

Taslun stood up tall, looking behind them as the winds blew over them again.

It was cold.

"Why is the wind cold? It is not that time of the year." Calak said.

Taslun and Kealin looked at one another.

"Do the archons practice their ice magic you think?" Kealin asked.

Taslun sniffed the air and looked behind them again.

"No, the air has changed," Taslun said. "Calak, go home."

"What is it?" Calak asked.

Kealin noticed Taslun's hand was on his hilt.

"Not a matter for you. Go home."

Kealin felt a cold breeze again. He heard snaps in the distance. The trees around the lake began to shift with gusts that made the upper branches sway and crackle.

"There's Alri." Calak said.

Kealin saw his sister some distance away moving quickly towards them.

A horn call went out. The horns of Urlas never sounded at this hour.

Taslun drew his blade.

Calak did the same, clearly not listening to his brother's wishes.

"Something approaches Urlas," Alri shouted.

Clouds rolled over the lake, blotting out the view of the stars and the moon beyond. The air turned icy cold.

Kealin could hear more snaps. His hand was on his hilt but he had not drawn his own blade. As Alri joined them, she unslung her staff from her back. The tip of her staff began to glow as sparks shot out across the sky above them.

"This is a protected realm, the outside world cannot reach us," Calak said.

"This is something else. This isn't from the outside world," Alri said.

Dazzling orange and red flashes shot up from across Urlas. In the clouds, small circles began to spin in place but just as they did, spells from the ground slammed into them. There were more snaps, more circles, and even more spells from the woods. The archons in the capital were at work.

Horn calls went out again and across the Urlas Woodlands, towers of black stone erupted from the tops of the tallest trees. At the top of these many towers, large crystals began to spin creating a haze of fog that spread out over the lake, to the encircling trees, and out to the great mountains.

"They restore the magic protecting our realm, the archons have pushed back whatever it was," Alri said. She lowered her staff.

"Praise be to Etha," Calak said.

Taslun sheathed his own sword and looked to Kealin.

"Let's get home. Mother and father will be looking for us. They will know what has actually happened. I have never seen what has transpired here. Urlas may indeed be under an even greater threat."

2

A GROWING SHADOW

THEY FOLLOWED the path from the bridgeway, through a series of glades that led towards the southern mountains and to a wooden structure built into the large pine trees of Urlas.Their house itself was built into the tree, with interlinking platforms and structures that rose up in small towers, blending into the foliage above. This was their home and was one of the few places in Urlas Kealin knew better than others. Though, he did not do the things he did in his youth. He no longer needed to sneak out between the loose boulder in the lower part of the house or the one spot he could squeeze through on the Northern wing. Both of those spots had served him well when he wanted to get out and explore outside of the watch of others. That said, he now knew that the owls and eagles that flew over the woodlands were no mere birds but the eyes of the High Council of Urlas, envoys of their will who left

Urlas on business or alerted them to young half-elves loose in the woods past moonrise.

Unlike the rest of Urlas their home had no special name or a long history of proud elves that had been birthed and reared in their halls. It was clear to Kealin that his parents neither cared or were bothered by such facts, either. A union between an elf man and a woman of the race of men was rare, even more rare was that his mother had innate powers that allowed her to be trained as an archon. While his father was born of a noble line, he had always said it was more important of the actions one takes than the name or title of a birthright. His father was many times older than all of them, having served in the last great war against the orcs as a Blade of Urlas; his actions had earned him some of the highest honors in Urlas. But he didn't speak of them.

Kealin brushed his hand against the stone lining the lower level of their home, noticing the wooden walls reaching up around the massive white pine and taking note of the height chart that had been in their doorway since he was less than a year old. Though the first thirty years of an elf's life is but a miniscule part, given their lifespans apparently, this was something that non-elf families did outside of Urlas. His mother always smiled while they were still growing, making a notch in the wood to show how much they had grown between one year and the next. He felt a strange sense, looking up to the rest of their house. Though they were forced to live in the outskirts, due to his father marrying a woman that was not of pure elven blood, some would say they ended up in a better position. There were no other structures around them, no random chanting priestesses or boisterous drinkers as was not too uncommon in the principle city near the center of the island.

TASLUN HAD ALREADY RUN through the house looking for their parents but they were not there.

"I'm sure they are dealing with whatever it was that came into our realm," Calak said, already opening up one of his notebooks.

"Do you really think you've read something about an unknown force assailing our realm?" Alri asked.

"No," Calak said, thumbing through the pages, "But I did note the times where Urlas had been breached in our recorded history."

"At least one of you cared to study," Taslun said, making a jab at Kealin.

"You didn't." Kealin said. "I've never even seen you step a foot in the archives!"

"I did. Before you were born and when you were still in rearing within the home. But I'll admit, Calak spends more time there than you do training with the swordsmaster."

Calak nodded along, moving his finger down his parchment. "That's so I can know the things you two don't."

He tapped a spot, "There have been only two breaches in the history of Urlas. One, was only noted as a 'Blight Angel' a creature of the old world. It made it to the center spires of the capital before it was bound by multiple archons and it's head was severed by Grandmaster Vadu, Master Rukes' grandfather."

"That must have been 10,000 years ago," said Alri. "Before the orc wars. Vadu and his son fell fighting beside King Suvasel of the southern Kingdom."

"Right. The next time was prior to the arrival of the Shaman, as it is written here. But there are few details. I might have misread or not copied down what I needed to."

Taslun patted him on the shoulder, "Well, there's time for that later. Regardless, we shall know soon of what transpired today.

"CHILDREN," a voice said. It was abrupt, and caused Calak to jump as they turned towards the doorway.

Kealin turned to see their father and mother hastily moving into their home. His father was in the silver armor of their people, and their mother held her wooden staff in the crook of her arm. She smiled at them.

"You are all well?" he asked them.

"We are," Taslun said. "We were upon the Southern bridge when it happened. What have the Masters said? What was it?"

"Something we did not expect. A creature from another realm, the realm of spirits."

"But Urlas is protected." Alri said. "We cannot be found from the outside."

"Yes," their mother said, "But this was not from the outside as you understand it."

"Come," their father said. "We will speak of it upstairs."

Following each other up a wooden stairwell, they joined their parents along an open-air balcony. The sights of the woodlands and the lights from other dwellings were easy to see from atop their own home. The dark woods contrasted to the starlit sky where fairies fluttering in the upper boughs of the trees looked at first like falling stars if you did not expect them leaping from branch to branch. Even far away from the other elves, they could hear flutes playing on the wind.

Kealin took a seat with the others. He and his siblings stared, waiting.

"We are leaving and we depart tonight."

"Leaving?" said Calak. "Where to and why can we not come? It is so sudden. Where is the enemy? No one else prepares."

"They do. A great host is assembled but it has been mostly in secret. It was for another cause but now…"

"It is an old enemy," their mother continued. "Alri, you have read of the realms, the living, the dead, the one of the gods, and even alternate realms of life where events are altered ever so slightly. We draw some of our arcane energy from these places when using healing powers, correct?"

"Yes, the arcane wells."

She nodded, From the living realm, our world is safe. But others are not so well. The gods of the northern world are faltering in their war against those we call the Itsu, the malevolent southern gods. Though the Itsu supposedly cannot enter these realms themselves, their actions are felt in the greater cosmos. Those of magic are under a direct assault, and we were preparing to respond. But tonight, that war came here. The Itsu somehow found a way into our sacred realm."

"They have called all elves to the lands for a great war. The gods are in need of our skill. Shaman Iouir has foreseen greater misfortune striking the lands soon. The one called Kel has sought us Urlas Blades in particular. We, with others, go to the calling of the gods."

"Then I will prepare my blade and leave with you," said Taslun.

"I forbid it."

"But I am trained as a Blad—"

Their father stood, lifting his hand up, "You are still a pupil in need of further training and more summers behind you. Until the Blade Master decrees, you are not to depart these lands, nor will any of you others. Kealin, that means you, as well."

His father focused his eyes on him and Kealin inhaled, nodding.

"Of course, Father," he replied.

Kealin respected his father more than he let on to the others, and his father's trust and respect meant much to him. It was one of the few things that did.

"Mother, why must you go? Surely the pure elf

archons are enough. But if they breach Urlas again —-" Alri said.

"I know what I am, Alri. But I am trained as an Archon Mage; my powers will be needed. I have lived safely here for many years, and my life has been extended beyond that of normal length many, many times. I have been blessed by the elves, and I must repay that debt."

Alri did not seem convinced or calmed by their mother's words. She was red in the face and sniffled.

"Your mother and I regret this happening, but know that you are kept well in the Urlas Woodlands. Trouble will not befall you here. For the first time since the founding of Urlas, the Masters raise the encircling towers around Urlas. Our entire realm will have another layer of defense, meant to keep out both physical and ethereal threats. Rest, eat, and train yourselves, for the time may come when the bloodshed requires you to take part, but we hope that is not for many more moons."

Kealin didn't like any of this. His parent's abrupt departure coupled with the attempted invasion of their woodlands was quite a lot to think about when just this morning he was only concerned with parry patterns with his blades.

As his mother and Alri went to the upper balcony to get a better view of the stars, their father began preparing the family's meal.

Taslun and Calak sat in silence as Kealin looked out across the woods, tapping his foot. Their father was chopping several vegetables, a rhythmic sound that broke the monotony of silence. As he lit a fire in the stone oven and poured fresh water into a cauldron, Kealin felt for a moment that nothing was changing. This was like a typical night. His mother and sister frequently spent time staring at the constellations and meditating. Calak would read through his parchments, and Taslun would oil his blades on the balcony. It was a comfort to him like none other.

"I will leave this cooking," their father said.

Taslun and Kealin both looked up.

"I need to go to speak with the Masters."

Kealin's comfort fled from him. His father never left at this time of night. Though, any security he had wasn't going to be around for long as it was. Their lives would never be the same after this night.

HE DID NOT WANT to leave his children but this was of the utmost importance. He did not know where the wars of the South would take him or his wife, but Jalin wanted to speak to those who would be looking after his children. Though there were no better in all of Urlas to guide his children, but he already knew that Kealin and Alri had showed a peculiar regard for powers not quite elven in nature and of that, he had to speak to the two who knew them best

There was a small tavern of sorts on the coast of Lake Eldmer, a place not too unlike the outside world where he and those he was meeting here had visited in their travels outside of Urlas. It had been about thirty five years since his last small excursion to the outside world and though Urlas has everything an elf could need, there was something quite relaxing about having a spot where he could meet with old friends and it not feel like some committee or otherwise official council as was so prominent in elven society.

Here, on the moonlit shore, he met two of the Masters.

"Jalin! Finally, you're here. I and Oaur were wondering if you'd make it tonight, given the circumstances."

It was Master Rukes, still having a bit of soot on his face from the last few hours spent in the smithy working on new blades.

Jalin smiled, embracing both of his old friends.

"How did your children take the news?" Oaur asked.

The inside of the tavern had very few people in it at this hour both because of the preparations of Urlas for departure and nearby holy processions to the Goddess Etha that took the attention of many of the lower families of Urlas.

"They took it with the exact protests I expected. Kealin was quieter than normal. Alri looked like she wanted to roast me with arcane fire."

Oaur laughed, "Good, it'll make her training more explosive over the next few weeks. Your daughter outperforms all of my other students. Much to their and their parents' disdain."

"She's got her mother's fire," Jalin said. "You figured she would."

"If only I could say the same for Kealin," Rukes added. "The young one is fast, agile, but his obsession with dual blades is disheartening being that he is the son of a Blade with the renown of your own."

The female elf tending the bar brought Jalin his typical drink, elven draught with a thick blue cream atop a silverish brew. He sipped his drink.

"Renown? I'm in the presence of Rukes the Rumbler, how many orcs did you slay atop Demonhead? Was it not, 'enough to fill the valleys of Urlas thrice times?'"

Rukes laughed, "The scribes always get it wrong! I told them it was four, at least."

The three elves laughed.

"But," Master Rukes said, "I think it should be clear between the two of us that while Taslun and Calak are as we'd expect, Kealin and Alri take after their mother," Rukes began to whisper, "Unexpected and noticeable should they choose to follow such a path."

"Well, if the council had not already isolated them as being less than pure elf, perhaps this would not have happened?" Jalin growled. "I told you sticking some random exclusion into their minds would do nothing to engage their pride as Urlas elves."

"Urlas elves cannot naturally call up the dead as their servants." Oaur said plainly.

"Necromancy?" Jalin asked. He had not heard of this news before now.

"She is a potent archon, but considering what little she knows of that path, when challenged and fatigued, she can call upon the dead almost as if it is her true nature."

Oaur took a sip of his own small glass of aperitif wine. Jalin sniffed a hint of cherries, this was a drink he had discovered while on the island of Travaa in the Glacial Seas during their last small adventure.

"And Kealin? Dual wielding?" Jalin said looking at Rukes, "I have seen him and his brothers spar. He can wield a single blade as best as any pupil of his experience."

"You are correct," Rukes said. "He is moving quickly through all my lessons but I can't help but to embrace his abilities with two blades. He reminds me of Riakar."

"Do not compare my son to a Dwemhar here." Jalin said. "He is of Urlas, we of Urlas saved the Dwemhar thousands of years ago."

"There were less than thirty of them in that battle," Rukes said. "Riakar held the Northern Void gates with three of his kind against legions. You may not like that I compare your son to one that is not of our blood but I see the value in swordmanship of a legend of those of the Northern gods. You know what we face outside of Urlas. Given what transpired this night, it may be one like Kealin that rises up to stand against an Itsu Demon in Urlas itself. He has an old soul within him, a true reborn warrior."

Jalin chugged his beer, to hear one of his own compared more to a Dwemhar than an Urlas elf, no matter the Dwemhar's renown, was not something he wanted to hear.

"So what do we do to help them?" Jalin asked.

"Help?" Rukes questioned him, "As in that they have some handicap or sickness?"

Oaur caught on to Jalin's concerns, "I will guide your daughter towards her archon path. I will not encourage necromancy in my training grounds."

Jalin sighed in relief.

"But know that part of the charge as her Master, is to help develop her innate powers. That is the purpose of any good master."

Jalin bit his lip and stared at both of them.

"The Grandmasters of Urlas will not throw your children out because they are different than the others no more than they'd cast out others who have taken refuge here."

"Don't talk of the Shaman."

"My point in mentioning him is that Urlas is a place of protection," Oaur went on, "It was you who chose Iluri, a bride that was not of our blood. You should not be surprised that some of your children would take after her and given her powers, that is not a negative quality."

Jalin nodded slowly, finishing his drink.

"I do not know how long we will be gone. Taslun will complete his training in that time. Kealin, he still has quite a few years. Calak, even more. Alri, well, she keeps moving faster in her progress."

"Your children will be fine," Oaur assured him. "We will protect them."

"And we will guide them as is fitting," Rukes specified, "But you cannot worry of what the realms bring upon us for holding them back could do more damage than simply allowing them to be different than the standard set for you as a pure high elf."

Jalin knew what they both said was right. Though they saw each other as equals both Master Rukes and Master Oaur were much older than he was. He was confident in his old friends.

He laughed, "To think, we thought we'd have a few hundred more years before we ever had to leave Urlas."

"We, this is you and the others alone, young one." Rukes teased.

"And only a few hundred years?" asked Oaur. "I was hoping an eon would pass before I needed to leave. Watch yourself in the South, friend. Get done with the wood elves and get back here. I'm not planning on leaving but I will if I need to drag you out of some dungeon."

Jalin smiled, enjoying this last night with his old friends and confident that his children, no matter their paths in life, would be guided exactly as they needed to be.

He was about to take another sip of his drink when a winded messenger came to their table.

"Masters, you are summoned to report to High Urlas, immediately."

Jalin looked over to Oaur and Rukes.

The swordmaster chugged his drink, wiping his mouth as he finished.

"Yes, yes, we'll get to it," Rukes said. "That can

only mean one thing. Intelligence from the Southern Lands," he grumbled.

Jalin shook his head as he set his cup down. He wondered what news High Urlas had received.

TASLUN MADE a point to finish their father's cooking and served the family. Kealin noticed that their father was still gone even though it was two hours later. Their mother did not seem worried by this and instead, made a point to ask each of them of their respective studies, spending this last night with each of them.

She first spoke with Calak, who made more random mentions of facts that he had read recently from the history books than giving their mother time to talk. Kealin spent time with a whetstone, working his blades on the balcony outside their home. He did his best to ignore the truth in these random emotional bouts. His mother was always more emotional and connected to that around her. She meditated more than any archon of the high elves of Urlas yet she was the first to step up and complain of injustices as she saw fit. Once, she shattered a gateway when a purist said Alri was a 'danger to Urlas', yet, it had been a very long time since that day.

Kealin heard the door to the upper balcony open. He glanced up to where he had seen his mother and father hold one another so many nights to find Alri with their mother. He couldn't hear anything but Alri was holding a small crystal that she kept around her neck at all times.

Though he knew little of Nidea Archo and the true teachings of Archons, he understood this device was of upmost importance to any archon. He had asked Master Rukes of it and the only answer the sword-master had given him was that it was a device of immeasurable power, capable of sapping the life force of a captured archon or allowing the wielder to cast a single spell without the use of a staff.' Apparently, this was old relic from the wars against other magic users, where there was concern of a captured archon being either tortured for the sacred knowledge they held of the arcane arts, or as a way to have a last attempt to free themselves or strike without the use of a staff. An Archon Star. He never saw his sister without it and unlike many other magical items, this one did not glow and looked much simpler than even a basic circlet or bracelet. Still, for Kealin, he had his blades and without them, his fists. He had no need for an Archon Star or any other object that he was stricken to rely on in the case of dire circumstances.

KEALIN FINISHED WITH HIS BLADES, sliding them both back into their scabbards. He heard his father down-stairs but beyond a few hushed words, nothing else. His mother came out to the balcony holding two mugs of tea.

"Save me for last?" Kealin asked.

She smiled, "I don't know what you're talking

about. I just wanted two mugs of tea and this was the best spot to drink them."

They both laughed.

He took the mug from her and they both sat down looking out over the woodlands. Fairies leaped through the treetops and Moonflowers released their pollen, glowing trails of light floating up out of the woods and into the sky. Kealin smelt the sweet aroma of mint flowing from his mug and secretly, this was enough from him. He didn't need to rattle on about what he had read or anything else. Just to sit in silence was enough for him. But obviously not for his mother.

"Two blades," she said, sipping her tea.

"That's always been my preference."

"I know. I thought maybe you took my stories to heart from when you were still upon my breasts, I told you tales of Riakar and his brothers, of the wars between Rusis and Dwemhar. The stories are important, yet I've never been able to speak of them for fear of what they bring," she sipped her drink, "Not even in Urlas."

"They are just stories, likely told to the children of the lower lands," Kealin said.

"No, they are not. Any mention of Dwemhar is a hushed topic. There are some of the race of men who doubt they ever existed."

"Our family on your side?"

She sighed. "No, they believed. But part of my own induction into Urlas meant that—" she paused again, "Even in this place of peace we've made for you and your siblings, the Urlas Elves watch and listen. There is much of our past, much beyond what you've been told. Calak and Taslun, they do not get it and it is better that way but you and Alri, you are different. In one way, I wish I could take you two from here to teach you more of my family and—" she shook her head. "I cannot say more. I can say that Master Rukes teaches you well. He understands and though I know you don't like Oaur, know that he had been an ally to our family since I arrived here with your father."

"What is it about our family? Because we're not elven? Because the blood of the fifth race runs in your veins? Just because the race of men was not of the original creation, does not mean they are weaker."

"The race of men is fraught with many things. There is weakness in the blood and strength and a penchant of horrid power that makes all of us… dangerous. One day, you will journey outside of Urlas and that which you only sense partly here, will become fully realized outside of Urlas. In time, I pray, perhaps the world will not be quivering in darkness as it is now."

Kealin stared into his cup and then out to the trees of their home. He pondered his mother's words. He knew little of the race of men in general but that had never really been a concern of his. The fifth race came about well after the elves, dwarves, Rusis, and Dwemhar. They were a creation that was not strong with any kind of real magic but somehow, had outlasted and flourished in numbers in the lower lands. He had heard some in Urlas say that they were meant to teach the other races about caring for a lesser being. In this case, an infant race without the advantages of magic. He wasn't too sure about this himself.

THE NIGHT WENT ON. Kealin could hear flutes playing somewhere near Lake Eldmer and torch lights dotting the banks around the lake in the distance told him that the others of their home were not at rest.

His father came into the room behind them. It seemed they were leaving tonight. As he set multiple tunics and blankets on a table, he motioned for his mother.

"Iluri," his father said, holding her staff.

"I thought we were not leaving until tomorrow morning," she said, curious of why he was packing.

"There was another attack."

"Upon Urlas?"

"No, the wood elves have said that another vast expanse of the woodlands has fallen. Saelmark was overwhelmed. We cannot delay any longer."

As their mother and father packed their things, Kealin and Taslun stood with their arms crossed as Calak looked on beside Alri.

"Saelmark holds the largest vault of knowledge of the elven race." Calak said. "You go to defend Saelmark?"

"We go to defend all of us," their father corrected him. "Saelmark was razed. But the elves are more than just a city or holy site, we are a people and what threatens some of us, is a threat to all."

Their mother looked at them and then back to their father.

"There is more," she said.

Their father tightened his scabbard, his blade at his hip now as he stared at their mother.

"These children need no more worries."

"These children deserve to know."

There was an awkward silence between their parents before their father sighed and looked at each of them.

"A darkness is upon the Glacial Seas. Whatever moved against Urlas before is looking for a way to strike. With so many of us leaving, we hope to draw it away."

Taslun cleared his throat, "And to assail you as you journey South? Will such an act not show that Urlas is weaker? Why do you go to help wood elves when Urlas may need you here!"

"I told you," their father said, "This is but a distraction, what threatens us in the south is a symptom of a greater issue. They want us to remain isolated. We will not. Urlas will stand with our brothers and sisters."

Taslun was silent. Kealin felt the same as his brother but it made no difference to say anything else at this point.

They said little else other than goodbyes before departing. Shared hugs and swift kisses on the cheek followed. Kealin went to his father.

"Do well and be safe."

"We will, for all of you." He looked down on him

and then placed his arms around him. "I know you do not respect the ways of the elves, and I do not hold that fact against you, but remember that to use your blade for no reason but to kill makes you as the enemy yourself—senseless. Use your mind, son. It will not fail you, even if your blade does. That is the difference between you and your brother Taslun." He paused, "Remember that you must resist the path your sword will crave. I have done greater deeds with my blade sheathed than drawn."

"I will draw blood when it is necessary."

"Spoken as a Blade, son."

His father patted him on the back, and Kealin followed the others to the southern gate.

The southern gate was a sheer standing stone near the edge of Lake Eldmer. It was as large as any of the tallest white pines and this passage could only be accessed by the Elder High Elves of Urlas, a sacred gateway, that could allow the elves to move South much quicker than simply sailing out into the Glacial Seas through the Eastern opening.

A large gathering was already present on the shores.

Their parents left them, joining many others boarding silver wooden vessels destined for the southern lands.

The four siblings stood off to the side, away from the others. Their half-blood status forcing them to the fringes of society. It angered Kealin at first as he had aged, but now he embraced it. They were to be silent, as a custom, as the southern gate opened. Of course, he had no plan to.

Flutes began to play a sweet melody, and a loud horn called. The sheer stone wall split down the center and opened. While there was no natural cave to which this standing stone connected, one appeared, a portal opening not too unlike what they used in Urlas to move quickly across their realm. Through the great lighted opening the elven host would pass, arriving into the other realm and to the world of danger, where they were called. Once through the passage of rock, they would emerge through a portal taking them much farther south than if they had simply sailed out of the bay. From their exiting of the Urlas realm, they could cut across the grand seas in great time. As the ships began to leave the docks, Kealin figured it was a good time.

"For the realms of Urlas, serve us well elves!"

There were immediate glances from the other elves of Urlas. This was a moment of silence, but Kealin had never understood a reason to solemnly look on without any expression. His parents turned and smiled to him.

The great host departed with banners of leaves upon a blue standard. The flutes continued to play their melody as the host began entering into the cave.

They watched as their parents departed the woodlands with many others heading across the seas to the land across the world. The stone doorway closed.

Kealin spat on the ground and turned away from the others. In his mind, he felt that he would not see them for some time, and he trusted that to be true. He wondered if it was just an increased intuition. He could see more than most with his mind, and it was what allowed him to use his blades as he did. It was not an elvish trait, and something he knew his older brother did not possess.

As they walked back, Taslun walked beside him. "Could you not resist talking out of turn?"

"Can I ever?"

That answer was sufficient, though it annoyed Taslun more.

KEALIN SLEPT WELL THAT NIGHT, even with the news of his parents' departing. He awoke to a clamor downstairs, and to find Taslun restless, grumbling to himself. He was not so well.

He went downstairs to find his brother sitting in a chair, giving sharp glances to the corners of the room.

His brother grasped a bottle of wine and looked to him with the normal disappointing look that reminded him of their father when Kealin had done something wrong.

"What?" Kealin asked.

"I do not know," Taslun replied. "Perhaps you can explain to me why I am not good enough to answer the call to the grand gods of the North?"

"That is blasphemy, Brother. You heard our father. And why are you drinking? You don't drink."

"Yes, I heard him. But if it is as dire as it seems,

then all Blades will be needed, and I should have been needed. This drink helps clear my mind."

"Do not bother, Kealin," Alri stated from the side of the room. "I have attempted to reason with him since before the dawn, and he will not listen."

"We go to the shaman today, little brother. The shaman knows all as they all claim. If some random stranger not of our realms is allowed to have a sanctuary here, we will use him to learn more of all of this. I will not remain in the crib of Urlas, suckling the teat of safety. We will have our answer to our questions!"

"And which question?" Kealin asked.

"The question of what we should do. Rotting here is not the answer."

3

THE SHAMAN'S OMEN

KEALIN WASN'T TOO sure what his brother was thinking. Though he had the thoughts himself, he never expected this of Taslun.

Alri sighed. "I told him we were forbidden to leave. It seems with Father gone, he is not thinking clearly."

"Taslun is right," said Calak. "We need to do more. Don't you agree, Kealin?"

Kealin did not have an answer worth mentioning. He wished for a cup of tea to wake up a bit more. Unlike Taslun and Calak, he could not just sleep well and wake up fresh, another curse of his less-than-elvish tendencies.

"It is early," he told them.

"Aye, Brother, but still late in my mind. Come."

Taslun, disheveled but walking, stepped out of their home. Partially out of fear for his inebriated brother, Kealin followed, with Alri and Calak trailing behind them.

The shaman Iouir could only be spoken to at this hour. He lived atop one of the mountains in the Northern part of their home. He never journeyed outside of his 'sacred grounds' as he called them and in general, it was impossible to even speak with him except in the early morning. Much later into the day, he would be in a trance, one that he would not come out of for some time and, generally, never, if he did not wish to speak with you.

While his domain was far from their home, there was a portal system to quickly traverse the distance. Just beside the lake, there was a small stone structure with rune stones showing a map of Urlas. Taslun moved his hand over the map and then placed a single smaller stone into the region near the great falls. As the ground of the structure began to grow blue, the four siblings stepped into a glowing aura and prepared to be moved across the vast distance. The shaman had a strange relationship with their family, and this was not the first time they had sought his wisdom.

EMERGING near the waterfalls that fed Lake Eldmer, they proceeded towards the stairwell that led towards the Shaman's home. In a single line, they ascended the mountain steps that rose up with intersecting platforms that were lit by multiple torches. Though the lower parts were covered in mists from the falls, the higher they got the drier and the stronger the winds became. Further up, Kealin took note of the strange-looking wood and straw statues, created by the shaman himself, greeting them every few paces. While it was a long climb, the path was well made. Ascending higher and higher, they had one of the best views of the Urlas valley. From here, they could see across Lake Eldmer all the way to the towering spires of the capital. Beyond that, Kealin noticed the new sight his father had mentioned. These towers looked oddly unlike the rest of the elven buildings in Urlas. They were crueler than the sweeping designs of most high elf structures and instead looked almost like blackened claws erupted from the mountain tops on which they stood. At the tip of each claw was a faintly glowing orb unlike any archon spell or other magic he had seen before.

Reaching the summit, there was a single hut with a steady trail of smoke rising up into the morning sky. A red cloth covered the door.

They parted the entryway cloth and took seats before a great carpet. Surrounded by a plume of white smoke was Shaman Iouir. He rarely opened his eyes, yet it was by some power he had greater sight than all of the other elves. He had the ability to see beyond the mountain and hear unheard voices of the ethereal realms. Kealin had noticed long ago that the man was not an elf either, but he was shushed by his father when he pointed it out.

"The half-elf family has come seeking my wisdom, but I dare ask why, not that I need to know. I want to know what you will say your reasoning is."

Kealin looked to Taslun, who straightened his back to speak louder.

"Shaman Iouir, our parents have departed for

distant lands. I worry for their well-being and seek your wisdom. Our realm was assaulted last night and we do not understand all that transpires."

The shaman seemed to bow his head, and a slight grin split his lips. He reached beside him into a jar and tossed a handful of dust into a stack of wood before them. Flames leaped up, and Kealin recoiled slightly from the blistering heat.

The fire grew in size and then began to change colors. Yellow, red, orange, blue, and then at last, a soft white.

"You ask a question that would be well to ask, but not what you wish to ask. Either it is the wine you are still filtering out of your mind, or you think you can deceive me. You wish to leave to help them and drag your younger siblings with you. That is short-sighted, young elf."

"I wish to do what I have trained for."

"And what is that, Taslun of the elves?"

The shaman had inhabited these lands for some time, but there was not one person living who knew of whence he came. He had lived nearby for longer than any elf knew, and considering elves lived until they were killed, or chose to die by their own hand, he was very old.

The elder brother thought for a while before answering. "To use my blade to uphold the elves and the reputation of those of Urlas."

"Then you would do well to listen to my knowledge, for it pertains to upholding your race."

The shaman shifted his hands around several pots

in his vicinity. He mixed each of the materials in a large bowl in front of him before slowly pouring them into the fire. His voice changed as he spoke his wisdom, a custom of the shaman.

"Dey comes a time when your father and mother need you, but I feel growing darkness is upon de Glacial Seas to our north. De elves of Urlas are needed by those of the northern gods, but it is the one dey call Dimn who needs you four. Yes, I see it will be by the horned ones you will be led. You must seek the horned ones out if you elves wish to be of use to de world. Look for de horns of the sea; dey will leads you."

An image came upon the smoke from the white fire. What appeared as ripples became evident as turbulent seas and a large tornado of ice growing in size. A great fire appeared, and the tornado became water and then steam and then smoke. Next came the image of a large creature swimming, a horn cresting the water. A moment later, a great wind came through the hut and swept the smoke upward and out.

They stared at Shaman Iouir, who now rocked back and forth with his eyes closed as he hummed to himself.

"That is it, then," said Taslun. "We must take to the Glacial Seas and search out these horned beasts."

"A word of caution to you who have been made wise," said the shaman. "Though you will know how you can help those you wish to, I did not say that it was a task that assures your own lives continue. It is a dark path if you wish to disobey your father's wishes, but one that is necessary in this time of the world, be it both for the good and the terrible. A shadow grows, threatening all, and your workings, though valiant, will not be yours alone."

The shaman began to hum before raising his hands. It was the signal that he was finished with speaking for now.

Kealin looked at Taslun as his brother ducked out of the hut. He followed after with haste.

"Is that it?" asked Kealin.

"Yes."

They began a slow descent down the mountain. Alri ran up beside Taslun. "Are we going?" she asked.

Taslun said nothing to her but started to walk faster.

"Of course we are going. We didn't climb the mountain for no reason," Calak said.

"Until our dear brother speaks, do not assume," Kealin advised. "Though I will not be staying behind. Even if it is against his wishes."

"For once, Kealin, I thank you for your stubbornness," Taslun said. He turned to the others. "But I cannot have you two going also. Alri, your arcane studies are important. I would rather you be safe here than out with us. Calak, though you train well with a sword, if the wars make it to our borders, you will need to watch out for Alri."

There was a short silence.

"Then I go with Kealin," Calak said.

"And I with Calak," Alri added. "You do not know how much help you may need."

"You are the youngest of us, Alri. I do not doubt

your strength of heart, but I have three hundred years on you. Calak has one hundred."

"And I am not being left here," Alri said.

"Do none of you respect my wishes?" Taslun asked. "All the wisdom of years upon you, and you treat me as if you are mere children."

They reached the portal. Taslun once again activated it and they were moved back towards their home. Walking now South of Lake Eldmer, Kealin took a deep breath to get his brother's attention.

"What?!"

"Taslun, we are in this together," he said. " Might I also say that you are going against the wish of our parents, and that is not something I do lightly myself. Now, when do we leave?" he asked.

Taslun looked over each of them and sighed. It was clear he did not wish for all of them to go, but he knew them well enough to not try to prevent them.

"Soon. However, I wish for us to go speak with Master Rukes. Calak, go prepare one of the boats so we can traverse to the dwarven isles. It is there we will find a ship of size to navigate the Glacial Seas."

Calak nodded, and with him, Alri. Kealin and Taslun turned and headed toward the arena. The bay where they were to leave from took them from the enchanted realm too, but more directly and without a portal. Their realm sat within the far north and in icy seas. Their parents had gone with much fanfare and attention. They did not need or want that, and such small boats would likely not be missed. Taslun and Kealin headed to the arena.

As Kealin and Taslun departed, Alri looked to Calak.

"I am going to speak with my master."

"Are you sure you should? I mean, I've only met him a few times but I don't think we need to tell too many people."

Alri shrugged, "I want him to know. He has taught me since I was very young and he deserves to know. I won't be too long."

Alri headed towards Nidea Archo. Thankfully, she knew at this time that her Master would be in his study. She would have hated to disturb him in meditation and she would have thought twice of actually interrupting him.

She felt strange, looking about her homeland. Unlike Taslun, she had never left Urlas. She had no need or desire to. But as she walked towards the place she had spent so many of her days training, she felt a disconnection to everything around her. She thought of her mother and father, seeing them leave. Feeling that her connection to the sanctity of Urlas dissolved the moment they left. Regardless of the shaman or her brother's wishes, she felt drawn away from this place. Sure, not that it was easier, going with her siblings, but already the desire was within her to do just that.

She approached Nidea Archo, entering the circular gateway and taking the path through the fairy bushes outside the shrine to Etha. But her Master was not in his study, instead, he stood just outside the shrine. A fairy sat on his fingertip and fluttered away as she came before him and bowed.

"Alri, your arrival is not unexpected."

His words surprised her.

"You expected me?"

He nodded, a small grin creased his lips.

"Master Rukes and I wondered how long it would be before the Children of Jalin and Iluri decided to leave. Your father was a poor elf when it came to sticking to keeping our lines pure," he paused.

Alri stared at him. He did this sometimes. He would criticize her bloodline. Her impureness. She was used to it, in some ways. After all, his family was one of the original families to inhabit Urlas.

He began again. "But purity has its disadvantages. If I am to speak fairly besides the shrine to our goddess, I would say it is in the mixing of bloods that we find the true gifts to be had. There has been much strife between the races over pride and though I disagree with you leaving, I have spoken to Master Rukes… strange times are upon us, child."

"I will remember your teachings, the ways of an Archon of Urlas. I will assure my connection to the Arcane Wells of the Netherrealms remains strong and potent."

"Forget not that which you have toyed with," Master Oaur said.

"That is not the path of an Archon."

"Still, it is in the mixing of that which we are, taking the best of each part that makes us, that we become truly powerful. I had prepared tea for us to speak of this but, I had a foreboding. I came into the garden to clear my mind and you arrived. You go to a dark place, my child."

"Into the Glacial Seas?"

"That is not what I mean. Not the physical journey but the spiritual. You will not be the same when— if you return here. I think that is what troubles me the most."

"I must support my brothers, we must see to the path ahead."

Her Master nodded, "Yes, but even that is beyond what I see. I see your path, your journey. Please, keep your faith in the goddess Etha and do not allow yourself to be lost."

Alri smiled, "I will, Master. I will honor your teachings."

"Then, perhaps you will stay. I do not desire to see what I have seen come to fruition."

"I won't stay. I am going."

Master Oaur sighed. "If that is what you desire."

"It is master," she bowed, "I will return to you soon, we will complete our training. I will be a true Archon of Urlas."

Her master did not return the bow.

"I hope."

Alri felt sick, a sourness in her stomach that made it difficult to turn from her Master. She never wanted to let him down. But she had a deeper calling elsewhere.

"I DO NOT WISH to endanger them," Taslun told him. "I wish you would stand by my desire to not allow them to go with us."

"We are family, even if we all debate, and I already use two blades in complete defiance of elven ways. I can easily defy my brother. Especially when his decision making is marred by a bit of early morning wine."

The two brothers shared a smile.

"I am with you, Brother, as are they. We will need all of our strengths," Kealin said.

The two crossed into the arena and went to the far side. A steady plume of smoke rose into the sky from a stack just outside a stone hut. Master Rukes was garbed in a thick apron and lifted stones from a storage area outside into his smithing fire. They did not burn wood in the elven realm but used stones of the mountain that could burn and glow hot.

Master Rukes did not take time to stare at them as he went back into his hut. He emerged again with a black stone with red speckles. It was rushire ore. With a metallic tool, he stuck the raw piece of rushire deep into the burning hot coals.

"Master Rukes, do you have a moment?" Taslun asked.

"I have more than a moment." He stirred his coals and then withdrew the metal. In a rhythmic beating, he began hammering out what would become the blade of an elven sword. However, it would be many weeks of this process before the blade was finished. Rushire was drawn from the ground within the realms. It was unlike any metal used in the rest of the lands. Its use took a smithy of a certain regard, and Rukes was not only a blacksmith but an enchanter and crafter of magical items.

"What can I do for you two? Kealin is supposed to meet with me today for further training."

"He will not be," Taslun said.

Master Rukes looked up from his smithing and stared at them.

"You are the first to tell me this, that your brother will not be attending his training, yet you are the most stalwart in saying he must not miss a day."

"My siblings and I are leaving. We are needed in the Glacial Seas."

Kealin half expected their master to protest, to say something to dissuade them or to point out that they were not to leave. His reply was much simpler.

"What do you need?"

"Nothing beyond proper armor. We wished only to let you know we will not stand idly by while our parents fight a war to protect us."

"Your parents go to stop a travesty from happening. They did not go with the Blades and archons across the lands to just fight a war, but to face a single enemy, in hopes of preventing further war."

Taslun walked around to a back room within the hut and reemerged with the finest of leather armor.

"I assume your sister is going too, her Master will not like that very much," Master Rukes said.

Taslun looked at Kealin. They both donned their armor but said nothing.

Rukes snickered and smiled. "With your family, I'm

used to expecting the odd acts and random defiance. Nothing ever happens as we plan it to. Taslun, you will be a Blade of Urlas before another year passes and your brother may not fight as we do, but he can handle himself well enough. Embrace that truth."

Taslun looked at Kealin and then back to Master Rukes.

"I feel he should do as I and his brother train to do. We are doing this to protect our people; he must honor them and embrace the way of a Blade of the Urlas. But considering, if he wishes another blade in every engagement—"

"I will consider doing as my brother wants in time," Kealin interrupted. "But I will also remember that not every engagement has an honorable person on the other end of a blade. Still, perhaps, I will seek the proper path to become a Blade upon my return."

Their master looked them each over and then went back into the room. He came back with another set of leather armor.

"I admire your sudden dedication, Kealin. But I know it's not true no matter how much you claim it. Though he is less experienced, do not forget your brother Calak is not quite at the level of you two. He does look up to each of you. Perhaps that can draw you to debate less and work together more."

Taslun nodded and then bowed. Kealin did so in turn. Their master bowed back.

"If you seek the Glacial Seas, know that no elven ship can take you. Those that your parents took will not return for some time."

"We head to the dwarven isles," said Taslun. "We can acquire a ship there."

"Careful, then. The city of Corson is one that has been amicable to us, but as you traverse the northern reaches, know that the sun is hidden this time of year. Furthermore, you must watch out for one another, more so around those dwarves; it is a careful peace we have with them, and you will be beyond the blessings of the elven lands. Last night I spoke highly of both of you to your father. Though you go against his wishes, I understand such acts when the world is in turmoil. Know, you always have a home here in Urlas, I expect you both back to complete your training when all of this has been resolved."

"Thank you, Master." They both said with a bow.

Master Rukes returned the bow.

WITH THAT, they left the arena area and went back to their home. Kealin packed what little he wished to take with him, which was not much more than a thick coat and some travel meat. He walked near his sister's area and noticed her staff was gone. He quickly went to the doorway of their home and awaited Taslun. His brother had gone to find a map of the Glacial Seas. These seas were at the top of the world, and a place in legend to be barely traversable. The stories of maelstroms, beasts of the seas, and frigid waters were only some of the travesties that cursed those waters.

"I swore we had a map," Taslun said at last, coming up empty handed of any such parchment.

"Corson is not far. We can get there without a map. Besides, I have heard much of the Glacial Seas from our father, the ice and fog make it nearly impossible to easily navigate or even draw out a proper map."

"Then hopefully we can find someone who knows it," Kealin said.

They met their siblings at the bay's edge. The vessel to take them across the waters to the dwarven islands was not much more than a fishing boat good for the shallows around the lands.

Alri stood on the bank as Calak gathered up ropes.

Taslun handed him his blade. "The master sends his luck to us."

"Well, I am glad the Blade Master approves," said Alri. "Archon Oaur does not."

It was then, behind the others, the elf Alri spoke of approached. Kealin always was amazed at the way this archon looked. While they were all a bit snobbish, Oaur was a tall man, much taller than other elves. With a cloak of the woods made of leaves, twigs, and other elements of nature, he was a sight to see for more than one reason. He gripped a large piece of twisted wood as a staff but then again, Kealin had seem him with multiple staffs and each had a peculiar design.

"So it is true what your sister tells me. You are leaving."

"We must. The shaman speaks of darkness approaching a god of the North. We must go."

"Surely there are other elves who can do what you need doing? You four are young, innocent to the world, and I do not agree to Alri using her magic freely yet."

"Archon Oaur, I must go with them. We spoke of this."

"And I told you before, I do not wish you to leave. You are safe here, with me."

Kealin walked between the archon and Alri. "She is leaving with us."

"Half-Elf Kealin, thank you for your presence on the edge of the Urlas Woodlands. Do you feel well knowing that you prevent your honorable father from living deeper within the realm? It is a sad existence to dwell on the edge of the sea. At least your mother has made a good mage for us of Urlas."

"I like the sea," Kealin replied. "What I do not like is a purist pushing his will upon my sister and his foul words speaking ill of my family."

"We are all half-elves," Taslun said.

The archon nodded. "Of course, just some are better than others. Very well, Kealin, I see your mother's stubbornness and tongue in you. Watch over your dear sister. I do not wish an ill happening upon her. You do not know me, young ones," he said, speaking to the three brothers, "But I have stood beside your father many times. It is difficult for me to see you depart these lands without his blessing. But I am encouraged in my hope in what I do not understand."

"She will be well," said Calak. "The best swordsmen in the realm protect her."

Kealin had still not backed down when the archon turned and left them at the waterside. He laughed to himself as he did.

"What was that, little brother? Do you wish to insult a master mage?"

Calak laughed. "He doesn't care who he insults. It is what makes him stronger than most."

Taslun gave Calak his armor and sword.

"Archon Oaur still sometimes points out that we are half-elven," Alri said. "It is why our family must live on the outskirts, and that we all know to be true. But he is just looking out for me. He loves our family."

"It makes no difference," Kealin said. "If we were around them who dwell within the realm, we would have to deal with them. I take no insult to it now. Though, I would like to once again gaze upon the lake from the high cliffs within the woods."

"Then let us protect these woods. With respect, those of Urlas will be more accepting to our status, and what they see as weakness will fade from their minds. Let us not tarry any longer. Into the boat."

The siblings filed into the small vessel, a carved-out wooden tree of massive size. It was with great pride the elves of Urlas were as simple as elves could be. Unlike those of the South who had grand cities, Urlas elves were closer to nature in every way, from their boats and clothing to the very homes they lived in. It was only deep in the woodlands near the actual capital that you could find the large towers and ancient buildings from the founding of Urlas. But even those were far beneath the grand size of the white pines that grew in the heart of the woods. They would all miss Urlas.

They paddled from the shoreline with ease as the four of them worked together to make headway.

Kealin looked out across the water, paddle in hand; he drove it into the depths before pulling it toward him. The air was crisp, but he could taste the sea on his tongue. He had always felt at peace near the water. This waterway would take them East, directly out of Urlas and into the Glacial Seas.

"Do you know the way from Urlas?" Alri asked Taslun.

"I do but where we go is not a place of roads but of paths of ice and glaciers. Do not worry. I know the way to Corson. I've been there once."

4

THE SPICE RUNNER AND SEA DWARVES

IT TOOK SOME TIME, but the mountains and the shoreline became a further distant sight. At first, there was thick fog, but passing out of their realm, it began to clear. Kealin looked back the way they had come and no longer saw any fog or mountains, only a wide open sea.

The island Corson was a place of intersecting cultures that, although close to the Urlas Woodlands, was not much more than a haven of travelers and criminals, for the most part. Most did not come this far north anymore.

In these regions, the dwarves once ruled much of the seas. The many islands were rich in minerals and fine ores, but that goodness and honesty had become degenerate, and it was more likely a dwarf would cut your throat than offer you something to purchase. Corson would not be the friendliest of places.

"So you have been here before?" Alri asked Taslun.

"Only once, and they attempted to rob our father."

"What happened afterward?"

"The fish ate well and there was a riot that chased us back to the boat."

Kealin scanned the distant shoreline, seeing buildings built on docks that ran all over the islands. The waves thundered against the coastline. Corson seemed to be one gigantic port, built on a foundation of wood and island rock that reached out over the ocean. It was darker here, and snowy. He looked out to see the sun just above the horizon.

"It is nearly night," Calak said.

"No," corrected Taslun, "it is only after noon. A trick of the eye in our realm. It is deep winter here, and though our realm is not too cold at all and has light, such is not the way here. When we crossed the waters, we passed into an unprotected realm. It was part of the reason why our parents did not wish us to leave. I assure you, our father would not approve of us going to this city, no matter the reason."

They guided their boat against a single dock that was open and tied the boat to a pole. A dwarf approached them, hobbling over other lines as he did.

"Elves. Great. Name and purpose here at Corson?"

Kealin spoke first. "Kealin, and with me, Alri, Calak, and Taslun. We are here to acquire a ship."

As he inscribed their names, his book glowed slightly, except for when he wrote the last one. It was then he looked up at Taslun.

"You've been here before," he said.

"I have. Long ago. Before my siblings had been born."

"I remember you. I was much younger then, and I do not feel I need to tell you to avoid what your father did."

"No."

"Good." He slammed the book shut. "If you are searching for a ship, a place called the *Spitting Crab Fish* is what you seek. It is up the road to the east, away from the docks. Beware, night is coming, and night is not a happy time in the islands."

The dwarf departed, and their path opened up. Kealin bound his cloak around him as they trudged up a snowy path onto a road capped with tall hills of snow. Most of the homes on the island seemed to have only their windows above the snowdrifts. Continuing on, there was a large multi-storied building on an isthmus of land. They went to it.

Written on a stone plank above the door were the words *Spitting Crab Fish.* A fishhook was off to the side and dark black in color. A stark contrast to the red paint all over the building. The smell in the air was like that of old fish. They heard a latch open a distance away, and a door fell down on the edge of the building before a rush of liquids came running out. It looked to be leftovers from the kitchen.

"This is it," said Taslun.

They pushed open the door and found a large dining hall with circular tables and not only a large bar running along the far edge of the wall but also multiple iron cooking pots.

The master of the building was a burly dwarf, much taller than the rest, but still small by elven standards. He looked up happily at the arrival of guests but frowned as he noticed they were elves.

"If you are looking for accommodations, I suggest you find your way back out to your boat and go to the next frigid island. There is nothing for you here, elves."

Kealin glanced around at the handful of men and dwarves seated at random across the tavern. As many of them rested with one hand on an ale and the other on the hilt of a dagger, sword, or mace at their hip, it was clear to him that elves were not a typical or welcome sight in a place like this.

"We have no issue with you, Master Dwarf. Only to be pointed toward one who can take us into the Glacial Seas." Taslun said.

There was an uproar of laughter. Around them, the assortment of dwarves, men, and others sheltering from the weather joked at the notion. Even the dwarf speaking to them was red and chuckling. He composed himself and made a motion with his hand to quiet the others.

"No issue is a good thing, elves. We do not wish for issues either. And we have some gifts from distant lands that assure such assurances."

The dwarf pointed to a statue, like a gargoyle of sorts, affixed above the bar and looking toward them with red eyes.

"A gift from the dwarves to any unwary troublemaker. I believe only one person has been killed by it. Let's not make it more than that. Now, my name is

Uris. Come and let me serve you. I will not allow a room, but I'm decent enough to offer food."

The four of them went to a nearby table and sat. The watchful eyes that before were staring them down had since gone back to their own dealings.

"This place smells," Alri said.

"Smells good," Calak laughed.

"Just keep your eyes averted from the others. We do not need to instigate anything here," Taslun warned, "I'd like to see us get through the first leg of our journey without a fight."

Kealin chuckled to himself and Taslun stomped his boot beneath the table.

"What?" Kealin asked him.

"We have lived in a realm kept safe from the outside, these people barely scrape a life from the icy North. They'd just as well stick us with a blade and use our flesh for fishing bait."

"They'd have to land that first thrust."

Calak grinned and Taslun sighed, shaking his head.

"I swear to the goddess you two."

Kealin had no intent on starting a fight but to take a purely reactive approach, in his opinion, was wrong. Even though, taking on four Urlas elves, even young elves like them, would be a rather unwise idea by any commoner of the Glacial Seas.

A FEW MOMENTS LATER, the dwarf came with both bowls and spoons, as well as a large iron pot with a stewed fish menagerie to serve them. It was warm and full of herbs.

"Be thankful for the herbs you see. Our herbs took an extra few trips before getting here. The ship that brought them is in for repairs. It seems he had a run-in with a bit of pirates, or so he claims."

From their side came a stranger with a belted sack hanging across his chest. It was a man with a short, scraggly beard that only just hung down the side of his face.

"Aye, if it wasn't pirates, it was some angry whale catchers, which are one and the same. I'm telling you, that bastard Rugag is behind it."

"And here is our bringer of spices," the dwarf said.

"The name is Vals, captain of the greatest vessel to sail the Glacial Seas."

"Greatest until the hull was ripped open and you took on water, barely limping into our docks. Aye, to be truthful, you crashed into the dock!"

"Very true, and I cannot deny I owe this man here a lot." He motioned to the dwarf.

Kealin stared this man up and down. He had a different air about him, something beyond the mere tavern rats that were clutching their ales.

"Yes, well, eat. All of you. My dealings with you, Vals, are only because of my kin who once sailed with you. By the way, you've been sleeping for so many days, I couldn't tell you, but I have it ready."

The dwarf went back behind the bar after serving the stew, and then returned with a parchment.

"Your repairs were costly. I'm assuming you do not have the money."

"Only have what you paid me for the spices."

The dwarf shrugged. "Well, perhaps you can rid our happy place of these elves. They are stinking up the place already. I gave 'em food. You can give 'em a ride on that newly repaired ship. I need to get the table clear for Rugag."

"I'd hate for that dwarf to not have a table. We both know what wondrous things he has done."

"You may not like him, Vals, but he is a dwarf and, because of this, is our friend."

"Aye, pick some better friends." He turned to Taslun and Kealin, who were closest to him. "Names?"

"Taslun."

"Kealin."

"And what about you two?" he was scanning each of them, noticing their blades and Alri's staff.

"Calak."

"Alri."

As Alri spoke, Vals seemed to become entranced.

"Dear dame, not only are you an elf but you must be one of the most beautiful I have ever seen. I've never been one for elves but you remind me of someone."

"Enough with reminiscing," said Kealin. "You have a ship and you're willing to help us?"

The man turned toward him.

Taslun leaned in to the table. "I have heard of the darkness of these waters, are you skilled enough to to

take us through the deeper regi
Seas?"

"Am I skilled enough? No, I'm
little skill who runs the gauntlet to del
even coffee to the most desolate places
little pay, mind you, but for the thrill! I ... like
no other, yes, the *Aela Sunrise.*

"I can do what is needed and of late, I work alone. Now I only have to watch out for myself. Part of the reason this Rugag doesn't like me. The only other cares I have are the animals that swim along my ship. Dwarves in this region have a long history of taking more than a fair share from the seas. I love the glacier sharks, in particular, but, too, the whales. Beautiful creatures and good friends."

"And why would a dwarf care for your love of sea life?" asked Kealin. "Why would a dwarf care for whales?"

"Meredaas be blessed, do you not know what the dwarves do to them? They take them, kill 'em for the sport of it. Rugag collects the tusks of sea lions, narwhal horns, and any item from the sea he can use to adorn or fight with. He runs his own fleet of ships patrolling the waters, killing much more than is needed for oils and food. I know people must make a life here in the ice, but he does it for fun. One day, he will get his. If I could, I would sever his head from his body like he has done to countless of my friends of the sea."

The door swung open to the building, and a man in seal pelts with horned shoulders came in. With him,

e band of dwarves, each with ice and snow on
beards, filed in.

"Very nice for you to arrive, Rugag," Uris shouted.

Rugag had a large sack with him. "More fish for you, Uris," he said in a deep tone. "Would've been better had we not been caught up with that damn Vals."

Vals recoiled down low upon the table with the others, careful to not show his face. Uris had jumped up to divert Rugag's attention away from them and for the moment it was working. Kealin realized that Uris, though a dwarf, seemed to have quite a desire to protect all of the patrons of his establishment.

"Come, I will take you where you wish to go, but we need to leave."

Rugag began to shout again. "That damn Vals took out one of my masts this time. If I see him, I'm gonna kill him. Let him taste my dwarven trident. If he wants to stop our harvesting for the life-giving food, he can join our food. It makes no difference to me. I hear men can be tasty when cooked up right with a nice batch of carrots and shrimp. Do you think you could fix that up for us, Uris?"

Uris nodded. "Indeed I could, but the spices he brings are quite nice."

Kealin looked to the others as they all stood in unison. Vals was veiled and walked ahead of them. Kealin placed his hand on his hilt and began to walk.

"Damn elves aren't making it any better," Rugag said, staring at them as they passed. "Next news will be they find us offensive for something. Go on, elf, go climb a tree. Chase your tree squirrels."

There was shared laughing among those at his table. Kealin turned, staring at them. "The only offense we take is having to listen to your raucous mouth this night."

The boisterous Rugag's smile turned to a glare. He drew his trident.

"Get out of here, elf. Head back to the woods. Your frail bodies aren't meant for the cold. You can't even hold your mead or much else for that matter. Wait, elves? I haven't seen elves up here since Valrin was running his crew out of this place. There was that shadow elf."

"The one with the white snake," one of his henchman said.

"Yes," Rugag looked to Uris, "You sure Valrin isn't here? It wouldn't be the first time you've lied!"

Uris lifted his hands as Rugag pointed his trident at him.

"Are you really threatening a man that gives you shelter from the ice?" Kealin asked. "Put it away. You know not whom you speak of regarding me and my kin."

Taslun fell back from the others to grab Kealin from behind. "What are you doing? We do not need this."

He began to pull Kealin outside when the dwarves at the table stood and began toward them in a shuffling of stools scraping the wood floor.

Kealin walked outside with Taslun. The icy wind cutting through them.

"You're the one that says we should command respect as elves of Urlas," Kealin said mockingly. His brother was less than pleased.

"Yes, but not now."

Taslun stared at Kealin who smirked, "Do you think those dwarves would not have figured out why we all just got up and left? You delay what was coming anyway. Now, they are upset. Their attacks will be sloppy."

Alri and Calak were waiting with Vals when the group of them came out of the building.

Rugag held his trident, and now others held weapons too, forming a half circle around them as they were pushed toward the water's edge. The dwarves had been careful to block the path to the docks.

Kealin looked around, seeing the names of the ships and noticing Val's ship, *Aela Sunrise*, not too far away. Its lettering was crisp against fresh paint.

"We do not wish trouble, dwarves" Alri said.

Kealin and Taslun stood beside each other. Calak was a few steps back, but all three had fallen into their stances. Their blades could be in hand in under a moment's need. There were sixteen dwarves before them. If they were skilled enough to fight, it was at least a fair fight by elven standards. A dead dwarf was not worth much but was something to smile about and to be encouraged in the lands beyond Urlas.

"We do not wish trouble ourselves," said Rugag. "But know we do not care for any at all beyond our people. I will let you live. Five elves. That is something to see."

Taslun released his grip, but Kealin kept his.

"We travel away from here and will not tarry any longer," Taslun said.

There were shared nods, and the dwarves parted the path toward the ships that had been recently repaired. Rugag's own ship was at dock not too far away, and the fact his adversary's ship was just repaired had been completely ignored by the dense dwarf.

They began toward the *Aela Sunrise* at the moment when Rugag had noticed his mistake. At some point, not only had he missed Vals but, in his haste for warm food, he had ignored the direction they walked toward.

"Elves, why do you go toward that ship?" They continued toward the ship as the dwarves hastened their pace. "Come here."

They did not listen. Vals jumped to the ship and motioned for the others to come quickly. Vals drew his sword and began cutting the mooring lines.

"I know that cursed blade anywhere!" Rugag shouted, "Vals!"

Kealin drew his blade also and began cutting lines as the others made it onto the ship. The dwarves were following just behind. As Alri and Calak jumped aboard, Vals had made it to the helm and the ship lurched backwards. The dwarves made it to the edge of the dock and, one by one, began to board until the fourth one missed and plunged into the water, starting a scene of shouting and screaming. Dwarves were not the best swimmers. Rugag did not make it on board.

"Kill them!" he shouted from the shore through cupped hands. "Bring me Vals, dead or barely breathing, but bring me Vals!"

Taslun stepped forward as a dwarf drew a chained spike. The dwarf began to spin the spike.

"It isn't personal," the dwarf growled, "but we need the captain."

"No, it isn't," Taslun replied. In a motion, he drew his blade, rushing the dwarf. He was past him before his blade had cut through his neck. Kealin and Calak were upon the other two, and in quick slashes, both fell dead. Alri looked at the last one who ran for the edge of the ship. He had thrown his fillet dagger onto the deck as he ran, but it was a poor choice for fighting. The dwarf was almost to the railing when Alri brought forth her short staff. She made an entwining motion with her staff, and the man fell flat, caught in Alri's invisible snare. She dragged him back to the center of the ship.

Taslun and Kealin placed their swords on his neck.

"Tell your master to not hinder or assail this ship in any way ever again"—they each cut the tips of their blades into his cheeks—"or we will kill him and every dwarf under him."

The dwarf said nothing, but quivered. Alri used her staff as if she was shoveling trash from the ship, and dumped the man from the deck. He hit the water with a splash, and those on the shore began a hasty rescue with small fishing boats.

Vals worked to pull up one of the sails. The ship had been fitted to allow a single man to raise and lower the sails. He moved between masts, turning cranks and tying lines. If any would have asked to help, he would have refused it. This was his ship, and he knew her well. At last, they were making headway.

"Thank you!" said Vals.

"They seem the lowest forms of soul," said Taslun. "Not even worth killing."

"His kind has slowly killed all of my crew, leaving me to be by myself. My last man died a few weeks back. He was an elf, too, a good man. But enough of that. I have had much luck through the years. I expect it to change in time. Where are we to go? The Glacial Seas are quite expansive."

Taslun looked at Kealin. "Well, as to where exactly, it has been hidden from us. But we are to look for horned beasts to guide us."

"Horned beasts?"

"Whales, or maybe as you had said, a shark of some kind," said Kealin.

"Then I know where we must go," said Vals. "It is true fortune that has found us together."

As the ship made way, leaving the island behind, Vals went around the main masts and pulled a crystal out of the deck of the ship. He placed it in a metallic altar, and an image appeared in the air around them. It was a map.

Kealin stood with his arms crossed realizing that the winds blowing over the ship seemed off compared to how they should have been. The ship was moving at great speed without the need to adjust the sails.

"You see, most dwarves help me, as you can see

with the gears to work my ship. This here was a gift of a different type. This ship is old and has been on the seas longer than myself. It is a relic in truth, from a race of seafarers beyond histories of songs I know. I doubt you have heard of them, being from the south."

Kealin looked up at the image. The contrast of glowing shapes with the backdrop of the starry night behind gave a somnolent feel to the air.

"What is this?" Taslun asked.

"It is a map, but not of parchment. It is one that shows the world as it is now."

The longer Kealin looked, the more he could see. The image was somehow above the lands. The clouds moved across the image, which even had the speckle of moonlight on the water. There were heavy clouds covering most of the map, except for where outlines of the islands were. Kealin could only imagine that this was how birds must see the lands from the clouds as they flew over.

Vals went to the map and pointed to an area to the east. "Here," he told them. "There is an island and the creatures I believe you seek. The creatures are called narwhals. Smart beasts, they are, but also prized to the types like Rugag. There are many narwhals in these waters, but some of the largest I have seen are here in this cove."

"Can they speak with us?"

"The question is whether you are able to listen, not whether they can speak. All animals can speak if you can turn your mind to hear their voices."

Vals went to the helm and turned the ship due east.

The winds cut across the bow as the sails adjusted to the change.

"Where are you four from? Vumark? Further south?"

"No," Taslun said, "We are of Urlas, I doubt you have heard of it."

Vals laughed, "No, no I haven't. But there are hidden places across these seas and even farther places. I have spent a lifetime upon all of these oceans. I've seen my fair share of sights, that I can say."

KEALIN LOOKED across the deck to see Calak standing by himself. He went to him.

"What is it, Calak? Are you well?"

"I am," he responded in a hushed tone.

"You did well earlier. It was necessary, what we did. Do you understand?"

"I know. I had always believed war would come and we would fight then. That wasn't war."

"It is the same, Brother. Someone wished to do you harm, and you stopped them. That is what matters. If we were upon the battlefield, it would be the same—you against one with the thought in your mind of your next target before you have killed the first.

"Taslun is in love with the thoughts of our people, and I do dare tell you, in some ways, his belief is wiser. I do not wish to die, so I keep honor as a second-rank thought. I will survive."

Calak nodded. "I agree with that."

"Well, for now, you remain behind Taslun and me.

I hope you will not be required to fight anymore. Watch over your sister."

"Always."

THE NIGHT PASSED UNEVENTFULLY, at first. Calak and Alri slept below deck, as did Taslun. Kealin remained awake, conversing with Vals.

"Yes, I have found the ocean provides all we need as people if only you show it the respect it deserves. I have survived storms I did not think survivable even with the blessing of Meredaas."

"I have only read of Meredaas," Kealin told him. "I understand he takes the form of a large fish."

"Yes."

Kealin looked at him, "You have seen the god?"

Vals smiled, "I have seen more than you can imagine, though I have suffered for it."

"Hard to imagine a religious need when you're running spices for a dwarf on Corson."

Vals chuckled and nodded, "I imagine that is a difficult thing to imagine. I have had many titles and purposes through my life. No different now. But it is here on this ship that I feel most at home. Even when I'm sleeping, I have dreamed frequently of the ocean. With my many days on it, I have never fallen out of love with the waters. However, I have had my misfortunes. I am constantly challenged to learn more, and I can tell you a curious wisdom is knowing that there is something new upon every rock and within every glacier. I run supplies, yes, but the adventure to have within these waters is unlike any upon the land."

Kealin looked at Val's sword. It was not elven but it was rather elegant. There was something more to Vals of the *Aelu Sunrise* but it wasn't his place to question more than he should, he thought.

A sudden change in the winds preceded Kealin noticing a sound over the waters. It was melodic and deep; the polar lights, glimmering above the waters, seemed to almost dance with the slow tones.

Vals smiled and closed his eyes. "My friends, I have not seen them in some time."

5

UPON THE AELA SUNRISE

THE OTHERS DID NOT IMMEDIATELY AWAKEN. Kealin went to the side of the ship and looked over the edge. The water was breaking over something, and as he looked closer, he noticed a strange shape emerging from below the black depths. It was a creature unlike any he had seen in all his years in Urlas.

"Embrace them. They come, for they know we seek them," Vals whispered.

Kealin continued to stare; from beneath the surface came their horns, long and silver, gleaming in the mix of starlight and moon above. Vals began a song.

"Starlight above us now we watch,
Sea-maids know what we do not,
Blessed souls amongst the ice,
Spiraled horns of magic thought."

The others were awakening. Joining Kealin, they watched as the pod began to emerge. There were at least eight narwhals following the ship as it continued sliding over the starlit waters. A ribbon of green appeared across the skies, splitting the lights already bending over the seas.

"Wura's presence," said Alri. "I have never seen the lights of the far north."

"A shame, but I am glad you see them now," Vals said. "The polar lights shine with the stars, and the glimmers above are a welcome friend most nights. If you look with a careful eye, you may even see a glimpse of the god Wura."

"Like Meredaas, I doubt he wishes to be seen by many," said Kealin.

Taslun looked to Vals. "How much longer until we reach the island?"

"Still some time. It will be midday when we get there. It is still well before dawn, but I expect you already know to not wait for the sun."

"How do you know the time, then?" asked Calak.

"The stars move in a way that I can watch for my favorite constellations. See there, my friend the seahorse."

Vals pointed upward just past one of the masts. Kealin could see the grouping of five stars and remembered from texts within the Urlas Woodlands of the creature Vals spoke of.

"I do not see it," said Taslun.

"You can't?" Alri said. "It is there. Its head and nose are the higher two stars; its body curves down the remaining three."

Taslun stared. "I see what you say, but I still do not. Perhaps stargazing is of more importance to archons than Blades."

Kealin could see it, and he went to Vals and pointed.

"So you gauge the passing of time by the position of the stars. So morning would be when?"

Vals nodded and pointed to the far horizon. "The bright star you see just coming up makes up the shell of the sea snail. Upon its full rise and nearing the setting of the sea horse, we will have morning. Though, we will not see the sun. Instead, at the very most, there will be a faint blue gold. But this time of year, even that is rare. It depends on how far North we actually go."

Kealin nodded but then decided to lie down himself. He had been up for some time now, and given the midday arrival at the island, he wished to rest.

TASLUN KICKED HIM. "LITTLE BROTHER, AWAKEN."

Kealin opened his eyes and sat up. Alri had made tea in a small kettle on a small stove of stone Vals had lit for them. A sweet aroma struck his senses.

Vals brought over a mug to him.

"The sea snail is sitting, and now the penguin arises! It is midmorning! We have made good time!"

Kealin stood and joined Calak at the side of the

ship. An island was now in view. Two massive glaciers were at either side of a sheer stone structure sitting as a lone tower on the isle.

All around them, the waters were alive with narwhals, their horns piercing out of the water and dancing in circular formations as the *Aela Sunrise* made its way to the shore.

"Yes! My friends are doing well," said Vals.

The ship came into a shallow harbor. A stone dock with an icy metal pole was the only place available to tie up, and one not normally used, except by Vals himself.

"Right, then," he said, throwing a rope over it. He exited the ship, followed by the others, and immediately they spotted a person emerging from the structure.

From afar, it appeared to be just a normal woman. If elven or human, Kealin could not decide, but as she drew closer, he knew it was neither. She was no one like he had met before.

In her eyes, he saw shifting blue. Her hair seemed to float with a soft glow upon it, and from the adornments of her body, he could make out shells of the sea.

"Valrin of the *Aela Sunrise*, it is good to see you. I understand from the seals that you took quite a blow with your ship while facing Rugag."

"Bastard pirate," Vals replied. "I gave him a scar, for sure. He had killed a few seals and took many fish. I did him some damage. But he will be back."

"Sadly, I do know," she replied. "He is as constant

as the tides of the sea. But justice comes for all in their own time."

Her eyes scanned over to Kealin, and she stared. He heard a whisper on his mind that he couldn't make out.

I do not understand.

But the woman just stared at him; a slight smile parted her lips. She turned to the others, looking them over in turn.

"Elves of the Urlas Woodlands. A rarer sight than most in the glacial waters of the North."

"You are right," said Taslun. "We come by the words of our shaman Iouir, seeking your narwhals as our guide to find you."

"Then you are incorrect, for I have no narwhal to call my own. These creatures of the sea are my friends and are completely their own. The family who brought you in has taken incredible liking to you all. I doubt you will continue in the Glacial Seas without them near. A good occurrence; that confirms you mean no ill toward them."

"We do not."

"Then what can this sea-maid offer you? I have short time on land. I must return to the depths."

The woman began to walk toward the water as Taslun rushed to speak.

"A darkness approaches Dimn. We go to help the god."

She paused. "You seek a path to the sky temple, the birthplace of winds, passed the maelstroms of protection. I cannot help you with that, for I am of the sea, of allegiance to Meredaas, sacred protector of the ocean realms. Dimn is of the winds. If darkness comes to the winds, then our world will falter. I had thought the poisons of ill were only to the south. I shall let Mercdaas know myself."

She began walking into the water, her body changing form as the small amount of clothing she wore turned to scales like those of a fish and her legs melded together, forming a fin. She went into the surf, disappearing for a moment before arising again just at the water's edge.

"A mermaid?" asked Alri. "I never believed I would have a chance to meet one."

"Now you have, child of the woods," she said to them. "You seek the Isle of Knowledge, a place to the far north of here, nigh the top of the world. I know that Valrin has a map of the old ones. I will mark it with a symbol. Do be wary of the Wight of the White Lands. That place of snow is not for the faint of spirit. A being dwells there now, and it is not one of the living such as are we."

With a turn, she went back under the water; the nearby narwhals turned and went out of the cove as the structure on the island faded from view in a thick fog. They were now alone on the shore.

Vals went to the ship and brought the map to view. The others followed. A single mark in the image of a fin appeared far north and beyond any other islands. There were dense clouds over the area.

"That water is treacherous. Storms brew. I have even heard of dragons that way. But they should not fear myself or this vessel, so that will play well to our journey."

"You do not fear this journey?" asked Kealin.

"It is an adventure, my friend. If there is risk to the sea and its creatures, and helping you four will assure the survival of my sea, then so be it. You have yourself a captain crazy enough to head to the far north! Besides, in my younger years I would have never turned away from a challenge."

The ship was underway again. Leaving the waters of the island, they turned north. With the expanse of the starry sky above, Alri and Calak worked to make a meal from the stores of the ship, with a mix of stored meat and a jar of seaweed. Calak added spices from Vals' personal supplies, and after a little bit, they had a decent meal worked up.

They each had a bowl of the concoction.

"You elves cook well. I am surprised I cannot do business with you."

"Hidden realms make that difficult," said Kealin.

"True. Most hidden realms are a bit tricky. But this is good. I am glad I took a journey with such experienced cooks. How old are all of you, anyway?"

"Older than you by a few lifetimes, and that is only our younger sister. She is two hundred."

"But she looks not much older than a young woman, no more than twenty years, by my guess."

"But she is two hundred," said Kealin. "It is the way of the elves."

Elves did not talk of age. There was no point when you were essentially immortal. It held very little value, and as such, that would be all Vals would be told.

"Well, I am forty-three in the years of men. I'm not old by any measure, but I am not young as I was when I first became a captain. Had my own adventures then," he paused and sighed, "Much has been lost in my life but now is not the time for this discussion. Perhaps, one day. I can say that I've fought that Rugag for longer than I care to admit."

"In forty-three years you have surely met an elf. We cannot be that strange to you," Alri said.

Vals paused, looking at the four of them before returning to his food.

"I have. I saw the beginning of the wars in Taria."

"Our parents went south to help Kel with the Itsu gods," Calak said.

"Then they go to a battleground that has worsened many times over. I once stood in the city of Saelmark, one of the oldest of the woodland regions there. I had many friends in those parts through the years. Still, if Kel has called the Blades of Urlas, it must be a dark time indeed. I worry about my old friends."

"You meet all of these people as a spice runner?" Taslun asked.

Kealin was thinking the same thing. Everything about Valrin or Vals as they were calling him, seemed distant. It was almost as if he was making an effort to not give them many details.

"Titles when you're a man like me, fit only as long as they must. The only one I truly claim is that of Captain. Though if you ever find yourself near the dwarven capital of Harrodarr, you might learn more of my dealings in trade and spices."

As Vals laughed, returning to the helm, Taslun looked to Kealin. Kealin was curious what his elder brother was thinking but as he raised both eyebrows and looked down at his soup, he knew. Taslun didn't believe him.

A bit later, they stood together at the front of the *Aela Sunrise*.

"He's a man of the sea," Taslun told him. "He weaves his stories to entertain the occasional guests but there is no truth to his ramblings."

"So sure of yourself with this?" Kealin asked.

Taslun glared at him, "You take issue with our own people and tradition but you want to believe that some random man has had a few passings of moons being more than a mere traveler? The race of men is weak, they do not understand life as we do. They crawl upon the ground, reproduce, and then fall to old age in just the time we perfect our tenth focus sword work under Master Rukes."

Kealin looked back to Vals then back over the open dark blue seas as his brother pulled his hood down closer to his eyes.

"Have you seen the blade at his hip? I have never seen an ornate blade such as that."

"It isn't elven," Taslun sneered.

"Perhaps it is better then," Kealin said, mainly to prod at Taslun.

It worked. His brother took a deep breath in frustration, suddenly headed to the helm. Calak and Alri watched as Taslun pointed at Vals.

"Okay, please settle something for me, Captain."

Vals raised a single eyebrow, "I am but a mere man, dear elf. I'm not sure I can settle anything for you."

Kealin snickered. It seemed to him that Vals was a bit more discerning than even Taslun expected.

Could he hear us? Maybe, he can just sense my brother's mocking tone?

Taslun drew his blade from its scabbard. The slight curved blade rippled with a fiery enchantment as he offered the hilt to Vals.

The Captain took it, looking down the edge and spinning it in his hand before offering it back.

"A fine blade. The Urlas smiths must work diligently."

"What of your blade?" Taslun asked. "It isn't elven."

Vals shook his head, "It isn't. But I hardly find it of need for an elf with a blade of his own to worry over mine."

"He just likes swords," Calak said, teasing Taslun." Apparently, when elves cross into around 750 years, that's all they think about."

Now Calak was giving Taslun a hard time. Kealin chuckled to himself.

Taslun returned his blade to his sheath and began to turn away when Vals thrust the hilt of his blade directly beside Taslun's cheek.

"Go on, elf. Study my blade."

Taslun looked back at Vals with wide eyes.

"See if it meets your standard."

Kealin approached them both as Taslun grasped the sword, spinning it about. This was clearly no mere blade and Taslun's amazement as he looked down the blade was obvious as he tried to hide his smile. He twirled the sword, a soft white glow, subtle but strong, cast a faint glow in the air around them. It had begun to snow and the blade crackled as the snowflakes melted upon its steel.

Taslun nodded to Kealin and Vals confirmed he could give it to him.

As Kealin took the blade, he could feel a strange sense in his mind. He could not see or make out what image seemed to be drifting just on the edge of his imagination, but as he looked to Vals, he had a deeper understanding of this captain.

"Those notches," Calak said, "On the hilt. There are signs of your victories? Fighting other captains?"

"Something like that, but no. I have faced many enemies, even as a young man. But that blade was made by no mere man of the south nor a dwarven forge. That is a Dwemhar blade."

"Dwemhar?!" asked Taslun. "The Dwemhar have been lost for longer than we've been alive. Since before the founding of Urlas. How would you come across their blades?"

"Spice trading," Vals said, a slight grin.

He took back his sword and placed his hand on Taslun's shoulder, "There is an advantage to the sea," he said, returning to the helm as Kealin made the observation that his ship kept sailing straight even without a hand on the wheel. "I indeed do have many stories, some for entertainment, some for veiling truths, and some that are too unbelievable for even the elves of Urlas."

THEY TRAVELED FOR SOME TIME. Many hours, in fact. As the fog rolled over the bow of the ship, the only light was the moon high above, casting a glow to the air. Vals began to look around.

He didn't say anything, but Kealin was unsettled by his erratic movements. Vals went to the helm and turned the ship to the right. He then ran to the aft of the ship and looked out. Taslun and Calak had noticed the change in direction and looked up from the reading that both had been engrossed in after finding that Vals kept a supply of books from his travels.

"Now this is an odd fact," Calak said. "There are dragonriders to the far south. This has a literal listing of different breeds. Trenk breed? Hmm, I've never heard of that. I thought most of the dragons were dead."

Taslun shrugged, "Well this one is like a book that teaches language. There are basic scripts and rather bad attempts to copy them," Taslun said, tossing the book back into the wooden crate.

Vals moved to other side of the vessel, looking back and then back to Taslun and Calak.

"A few of those are journals. Don't mind the one

with the bad letters. You can't blame the half-orc for struggling."

Alri had noticed Kealin's unsureness watching Vals.

"Orc?" Calak said. "Orcs are an evil scourge, they were defeated long ago."

"Well, if things don't work out like they need to, I can tell you that a good half-orc is just the kind of a barbaric ally you'd want to have when dealing with sea-dwarves."

Vals returned to the helm; this time, he went right hard. Kealin looked as the ship passed through an arching glacier and then again, left. The crunching of ice at the bow of the ship sounded like a piece of wood being torn. Just as before, he went to the rear of the ship and looked out.

"What is it?" asked Taslun.

"We are being followed," Vals shouted. "I had thought it just a trick of floating ice, but we have caught a tail. There are not many in these waters, so we can assume who it is."

"Rugag," said Calak. "What must we do?"

"Lose him. Though I doubt it is his flagship, and so I doubt he is aboard. They have many ships. We will need to rid ourselves of our hunters or risk further issues."

"There is no chance he is simply seeking sea life?"

"No."

The ship was making good pace across the waters. Vals turned the ship back right, crunching through the ice with the metal of his reinforced bow. Their pace began to slow. The momentum of their passage was not as great as before, and Vals had to take a path less likely to be navigable. He flipped a lock below his foot and another crystal that lay hidden fell forward.

The ship began to grind to a halt, and they were rocked to the deck, losing footing from the jolt. All except Vals.

"Shield your eyes!" he said.

Kealin did so but still peered out. Vals twisted the crystal with his foot, and the ship began to glow from two planks at the rear of the ship and then up to the front. Back and forth the light went, until the center masts glowed brightly. He twisted the crystal and covered his own eyes.

Kealin could feel a rumbling beneath the ship and then what sounded like searing meat on an open fire. The sky around the boat flashed from a massive stream of fire shooting from the mast of the ship in a blast of arcane power. The ship jolted again, and the waves smacked against the ship, and the ice holding it cracked and fell away.

A gust came upon them, and Vals was at the helm again, the ship lurching forward. Kealin uncovered his eyes and went to the side of the ship. The *Aela Sunrise* had burned a path through the ice by power unknown or unseen before by any of the elves present.

They were headed toward a massive island, or glacier; from the distance they were at, it was hard to tell. Kealin looked back, as did Vals. A ship was still coming.

Up ahead, the blackness of the isle became evident, and its towering cliff face was sheer.

"That is a massive glacier," Calak said.

Vals looked behind him and saw the deck of the following ship become alight.

"They are preparing to fire upon us. Brace yourselves!"

Kealin went to the rear of the ship as Vals began to make a turn around the dark isle. From the deck of the pursing ship, a light emerged, cast high into the sky and arching over the waters.

Vals turned and looked, shifting the ship to the left as far as his wheel would turn. The bolt turned downward. Kealin could see the iron tip as it flew over his head, just missing the center masts before splashing into the water, a chain hooked to it, whizzing in flight through the air.

"Down! Watch out for the tail!"

Kealin ducked just as the end of the chain slapped the deck, splintering the wood before ripping a chunk off the railing of the ship and following the bolt below. He looked back out to the ship, and Vals made another hard left. They passed beyond view of the ship, and the world became even darker.

He watched as the ship was veiled in a deep darkness and the wind died down. Vals had turned them into a passage in the glacier that was hidden unless you knew where it was, as he did.

He dropped two anchors and then joined Kealin at the aft of the ship.

"I had sheltered from a storm in this place before, but it was some time ago. I was going to go around the island and hope to lose them then, but I couldn't pass up this chance and this will work to lose them."

Kealin's siblings had joined them, and each watched out the opening in the cave. The ship rocked from the occasional waves, the creak reverberating off the walls of the cave, and the chill in the air was made worse by the fear of being found.

A dim glow was on the black sea and the ship of Rugag came into view. Vals pulled out a viewing scope and twisted a crystal on its top. "I can see their faces," he said. "They look, but they cannot find us. I believe we are safe." He placed the scope back into a compartment in the helm. "We will wait to be sure. Come, all of you. I know you may find this of interest."

Vals went to the edge of the ship and laid down a plank from the ship to the ice. There was a crunch as two metal spikes bit into the ice to hold it in place.

He crossed the void and went to a sheer wall. The others followed, doing as he did and careful of the edge. He began to point up to the wall when it began to glow.

Runic symbols began to appear, and an image of the islands appeared.

"Very strange," said Vals. "I was hoping to have enough light to show you this, seeing as I had lightning the night I came here before, but it seems it is not needed."

"What is this place?" asked Alri.

"It is elven," said Taslun, "but of a time long ago, perhaps even before the dwarves. It may be before the founding of the Urlas Woodlands, but I cannot be sure."

"It is an Edda of the gods. It tells how they took the form of men at a time and of the creation of the worlds and realms."

"The word 'Dimn,'" said Calak, "and here too, 'Wura.'"

"A remarkable find," said Taslun. "There seems to be lost knowledge in these icy regions."

"As I have said, the Glacial Seas hold many secrets. One could explore, I feel, for many lifetimes and not find what all it hides."

"They were not always frozen so. It is of interest, your work, Vals."

Vals laughed. "I'm but a spice runner for the islands, nothing more. You speak of times well before me, elf. But you also speak of something I know. There was a time when all of what we sail above was a grand and wondrous land, when the elves had just awakened, and the dwarves were still new in their working of stone and harvesting precious metals. Then came a great flood and what was once mountain hideaways and temples, became relics such as this, lost caves with more secrets than you could possibly imagine."

"Spice runner, right?" Taslun asked.

"Just a spice runner," Vals confirmed.

Kealin knew there was more to all of this. He was also sure that Taslun just assumed now that while Vals did have particular wisdom regarding the ancient past, that he was likely some type of treasure hunter or another raider of sacred sites.

That said, Kealin had seen nothing on his ship to indicate some kind of vast wealth or a bag of precious gems. Vals himself did not seem the type to care about such things. In some ways, he felt Vals and himself were very similar for not even in Urlas did the common elf have much more than what they needed. Besides, an Urlas sword had more value to them than any amount of riches anyway.

Pulling the plank up, they each took hold of large guiding poles kept along the side of the deck. A more traditional method of moving through ice, they stabbed them into the walls of the cave.

Vals cranked the anchors up to their sailing position. The others grimaced and with significant strength and force, helped to push the ship out as Vals steadied the wheel. He looked out over the sea as he did. There was no sight of the pursuing ship, and as they raised the sails once again, they began back the way they had come to avoid another run-in.

"Do you not worry the rest of the fleet is near?" asked Kealin.

"They likely are," Vals replied, "but we cannot wait for them to be gone. They are a constant nuisance just as I work to be to them. It's almost like an annoying understanding."

FOR A GOOD WHILE, their sailing was calm. Though they had now turned back north, Vals checked the map and noticed they were headed for the spot marked by the mermaid. The clouds above were patchy but growing thicker.

Even so, Kealin looked up, spotting the stars. He noticed the seahorse reaching a high point in the sky. As the others slept, he lay down too.

"Kealin," Vals said.

He sat up.

"Sleep but be wary. I cannot say for sure, but a foul stench is in the air. There is a sickness in the place we go to. Keep your mind clear by whatever way those in Urlas have taught you. I sense something ahead."

His eyes went back to the horizon, and he lay back down.

Does he not need sleep? I have not seen him lie down once.

His thoughts were chased away as a hum began to fill the air, and he fell asleep to the words.

"I glance upon you, darkening sea,
For all the adventures you've given me,
I am a steward of old, sailing fast,
Captain of the Aela's masts.

I wish to go where no man finds,
To aid the sea and all divines.
Help for the lost,
Risking life and heart,
Until from this life I depart."

KEALIN AWOKE a few hours later on his own. The familiar awakening smell of tea filled his nostrils, but only Vals and Taslun were awake.

"It is the elven way," his brother said. "We do not dwell too much on the shifting of powers at the immediate, but it seems this new danger is enough to cause a stir to even us here in our remote lands."

Vals left the helm, locking the wheel in place and joining both him and Kealin.

"It is just strange to me that you would take such sudden concern for Dimn. He is not one that elves consider as important as Etha."

"Yes, Etha," Kealin said. "Taslun says her name at least four times a day. You'd think she'd get tired of hearing him."

Taslun smirked, "I only say it to make up for your complete lack of acknowledgment."

Vals snickered, "Well, I can say that the gods do not need our constant prayers. I'd argue that their acknowledgment, at least, is something that none that have stood on the deck of this ship would argue isn't at least sometimes important. But in all my traveling, I had not seen the place you told me of."

Kealin had understood very little of Dimn besides the fact he was a god of the winds.

Vals sipped his tea. "A sea of maelstroms is not a friend to a boat like this."

"That is only legend," Taslun said. "I doubt it is true."

"What is only legend can be found to be true if you search long enough. At least, that is what I have found. I am interested to get to this next isle. An isle that is not on normal maps, especially."

"Kealin, did you sleep well?" Taslun asked him.

"Yes, as best I could given the rocking waves."

"Storms are brewing the further we go north," Vals announced. "The others will be awake soon enough. The swells will get quite large, I am guessing."

"Do you ever sleep?" asked Taslun, noticing Vals slurping down his tea.

"Sure. Just not when I am traveling. I am tied to this ship in more ways than is seen. A blessing, I guess you can call it. If it is at sail, then I am awake. An enchantment of sorts that the *Aela Sunrise* has. I do not tire while at sea, but when in port, I may sleep five days straight. I normally let the harbor master know wherever it is I dock. They like it when I pay ahead for anchoring before my polar-bear-like hibernation."

Vals went back to the helm just after setting down his cup with the others. The ship was in rougher waters. Taslun was staring off. He seemed to be thinking. He looked down and then over to Kealin.

"Have you thought of Mother and Father?" Taslun asked.

"Yes, I wonder of them."

"I had spoken with Vals; he saw an elven fleet in the South before he returned to Corson, but he would have been already north when our parents departed. He had asked about us as a people; I think there is more to him than he speaks, but I do not feel it is ill. It seems with your recent conversations, you have made a friend. It isn't like you."

Kealin smiled. "I guess it just took finding the right friend. The sea is a uniting force that I have respected for some time. It is rare a man would perform such a selfless act as to protect the sea. I can respect him for it."

Taslun patted his back and embraced him. "You grow wiser, Brother. I respect you for it."

Kealin pushed off his brother's affection. "Enough, I may speak against the teachings of Master Rukes, but I am no fool to what is good sense." He smiled.

CALAK AND ALRI were both up now, but they grasped ropes and wood. The seas had turned turbulent, and the ship was pitching and leaning as the swell increased.

"Hold on!" yelled Vals.

The ship rocked upward and then slammed back down. The horizon bounced as a flash of lightning illuminated the sea only long enough to see rolling black clouds above and a wave of rain overtake the ship.

"Take yourselves below deck!" he said to them.

Alri had been below a few times, and so had Calak. The cooking supplies and the tea were kept in storage there. As a wave of water struck the deck, rushing over the wood, they climbed one by one down into the bowel of the ship, the seawater pouring in above them. Kealin was the last one in and closed the wooden hatch. While it wasn't a massive place, there were several beds and a handful of old books.

"Does anyone else feel guilty leaving Vals up there?" asked Alri.

"He asked us to come down here," Calak replied, lighting one of the stored torches and walking around to light another to give some brightness to the dank surroundings.

"Yes, but what else would he do? Wait for one of us to be tossed overboard?"

"He respects us beyond what many men may even fathom," said Taslun. "Our love of trees may actually be less than his love of the sea. I have never seen such zeal in a man."

Kealin and Calak took a seat near a box as Alri and Taslun hung on to some overhanging ropes, looking up as the ship continued to quake back and forth.

Taslun closed his eyes in meditation. Kealin noticed that his brother kept jumping to look to the walls as the ship lurched and tossed so it made sense for him to try to calm himself. Alri, had taken one of the books and was using the light from her staff to try to read. Kealin spoke with Calak.

"Far from what we know, Brother?" he asked.

Calak shook his head. "Yes, but it is strange to see you not protesting our moves. I am not used to you going along with something. I'm used to the half-elf rebel Kealin."

"I'm still me. Do not worry your pure elven self." He teased.

"I've never understood that. I, too, think it is foolish to name you a half-elf and me a pure elf."

"It was decided when we were young by the Elders and only comes up when useful as a weapon against us." Kealin shook his head. "Taslun and you were deemed pure, for they sensed little of mother in you. I was more like mother, as was Alri. We may look the same, but it is the way our blood forms and the sense other elves have of it. The only true difference was what our people made it."

"I, at one time too wished to be a part of the others, but the older I became, the more I decided that it was not what made me. I would not allow some elf to tell me my standard. I rebel against Taslun because he holds it in such regard, but I do not wish you to do the same, Brother. My path is my own, and you must embrace yours. You wish to be a Blade Master as Master Rukes, and you should do it."

His brother nodded, but being younger and wishing to be as both Taslun and Kealin, he was torn.

THE TOSSING of the ship had slowed, and now Alri and Taslun walked around, looking through stacked books that thankfully had not been soaked by the flow of seawater when they climbed down.

"He has quite a collection," said Alri. "I have seen at least three books speaking of elves before any of our time."

"I too have noticed; he has traveled far for some of these. The tongue is not elvish or dwarvish, or even a language of man. I do not know some of these writings," Taslun commented. "It is odd and wondrous all the same."

The covering above opened, and Vals stuck his head down.

"Everyone well? Come on back up. The clouds are still black, but the sea is not so rough."

They made their way back up to look out over a dark sea. Patchy clouds were above, with whistling wind blowing over the bow of the ship. Vals brought the map to view, and it appeared they were just over the spot that the mermaid had directed them to.

Large glaciers riddled their path, but still the *Aela Sunrise* pushed on. Breaking through tough ice was one success; avoiding the spiked bodies of a glacier to the hull of the ship was quite a different one.

Vals made a series of quick turns, with more than one ending with the splintering of wood and casted ice erupting over the side of the ship. They could see land coming up fast.

"You elves test my ship! I like it, and so does she!"

The wide-eyed captain spun the wheel, banking the ship to the left; it slid along the water, building up against the ice. The shoreline came suddenly with a crack and a thud. The ship rocked back to the left.

"Get the plank down!" he shouted.

Taslun and Alri tossed the wooden plank down and made their way to the icy ground. The path was still slick and precarious from the water and jagged glaciers roughed up by the ship. Kealin pointed for Calak to follow, and turned to Vals.

Vals nodded. "Go on, I will keep the ship well. I will keep a torch burning on the side to direct you back in fog and snow. Do not fear, I will not abandon you here, friends."

Kealin nodded back and followed the others down.

Taslun and Alri were already a few feet from the shore. The winds tore across the lands that were barren with snow and rock as far as the night would allow them to see. Calak bundled himself in his coat as he went ahead.

Kealin checked his blade; the ice had kept its drawing from the ease he was used to. His brothers noticed what he did and followed suit, breaking the ice that held them sheathed. Alri took out her staff and blew into the tip. An orb of flames flickered alight, and she pointed it forward, a light source for their bleak journey.

There was a strange stirring in Kealin's chest. He looked up and for a moment, caught sight of something looming high about them. It's view was veiled by a thick fog as more icy winds blew over them. It was almost as if the place they were going was aware of their arrival. Their journey was about to become stranger than any of them expected.

6

BLEAKLANDS

THEY BEGAN across the open expanse, seeing little more than Alri's staff in front of them, the glowing orb pulsating as she worked to keep the spell controlled. Behind them, Kealin glanced to see the fading outline of the ship and then a burst of flame where Vals lit not one but two torches to light their way back.

The snow and wailing winds blew against them, and each walked with their elbows out and their heads down, attempting to force a path through the growing ice. None were wearing gloves, and so with tucked hands, they trudged. Alri was unknowingly lucky to be using her staff; the light that came off it gave her some warmth, but even that was chased away by the shifting winds. Kealin had never been so cold.

They walked for a good while before they saw the dead trees of a once-grand forest. Behind them, the light from the *Aela Sunrise* was all but shrouded. Kealin was surprised he could still see it. There was a structure ahead, and as best any of them could guess, it was where they should head.

Passing through the crags of frozen trees, Kealin jumped as he saw something move within the crags, swooping with the winds and passing over them multiple times.

He drew his blade. "Brothers, look to the sky."

Calak and Taslun both looked up, their own blades drawn as more of the figures swarmed above them, just over the screaming snowfall.

The creatures were opaque, with a dark fiery black center within their forms. It seemed that they could solidify and take the appearance as icy stone at will but most of them remained almost ethereal. They had no distinguishable arms or legs, only a gaping mouth and a bellowing sound that grew as they passed close, akin to a squelching cold gust, but not of the sound of wind at all. Taslun looked ahead.

"Lead us on, Alri. These creatures are staying high for now. Let's pray they stay there."

ALRI GRIPPED her staff with both hands; closing her eyes, she sought to increase her spell, and the magic flowed from her body into the staff. It glowed brighter, parting the snow, forcing it to swing around the orb of light she had created. She sighed, making a point to take a deeper breath of the frigid air as she felt the energies moving through her. Normally, she could feel the warmth from torch spells such as what she used now but all of her energy was focused in just keeping the spell bright enough to lead them. She prayed the creatures above did stay away. She wasn't sure she'd be able to defend them and keep up another spell. But, Urlas elves worked together. Archons, especially, were vulnerable depending on the situation itself. While she could use a spell to block dragon fire, she could not both block a spell and use aggressive elemental magic to attack. Her brothers might not have been ordained Blades, but she knew Kealin and Taslun could more than hold their own if needed. Calak, though, she wasn't too sure about. But her focus was wrong. She turned back to just thinking about leading them. Their path lay ahead and it was real. Her toying with thoughts of inadequacies of her siblings would do them no good.

THEY DREW CLOSER to the structure, now taking a path between stone pillars that ran like a long hall all the way to the towering building. Kealin realized that the tower was much taller than it looked from far away.

The creatures above began to swarm over them. Twice, one came just over Kealin. He turned as one landed at the far end of the path they had taken. The specters began to pass in between them, slowing them one by one and separating their combined force.

"Faster! Into the doorway ahead!" Taslun ordered them.

Alri was in a dead sprint, as was Calak. Ahead of them, a large wooden door was beginning to open with their approach.

Kealin once again turned; the creatures were amassing and following their path. He was well outside the comforting light of Alri's spell. Another two had dropped between him and the way they were going. He stopped as the others went on. He slid his foot back sideways behind him and brought his blade in front of him.

Taslun looked, spotting his brother. "Kealin!"

The creature's mouth gaped toward the ground, and it let out a shrill that caused Kealin goosebumps. He had never seen such an entity. The creature formed a hand from its body and pointed a clawed finger at him. Kealin rushed forward, striking the creature, his elven blade glowing red as he cut into it.

He did not fear what he could kill, but the creature was not weakened, only stunned for a moment.

It grasped his blade, even as the elvish energies scorched its hand. Kealin ripped his blade from it and began to follow the others. He had garnered enough attention himself, and as Taslun ran toward him, he ran away from the entities.

The two creatures blocking his path rushed toward him; he sidestepped, grasping one of the pillars, and swung himself out of their path, slashing his blade at them from behind, and each seemed to shake from his strike, ceasing movement. The other creatures simply rushed over the two he had struck and, in a gust of snow and spectral energy, pursued him.

Taslun grabbed him as they met and pulled him toward the door. The creatures drew behind them. The shrill of their moans caused Kealin's neck to tighten. Falling into the open doorway, the creatures were repulsed as a blue fire erupted from the tower, connecting to all the stone pillars, creating an enchantment.

In an upward rush, the creatures fled the area. Taslun looked at his younger siblings, and Kealin drew in breaths rapidly. He smiled. Someone, or some power, had assisted them.

"Close enough to death, little brother?"

"Not death, just a truer challenge than phantom adversaries in Urlas." Kealin laughed. "Strange creatures. I sense a fear they can project, greater than mere fear we conquer with our training as Blades."

"What were those?" asked Calak.

"Wights, or best I can guess," suggested Alri. "They haunt places of death, and this barren place is of that. I can feel necromantic energies. Archon Oaur told me of places like this. They are pilgrimage places for death mages, but at the same time, there are sources of wisdom beyond others here. The dead know much, sometimes more than what they did in life."

They turned to the doorway. A skeletal form stared back at them but did not attack.

Kealin's blade was already up. But whatever this was, seemed peaceful.

Taslun stood with his sword in hand to his side. "We mean you no harm. Did you protect us from the wights?"

It rattled its jaw, turning away from them, and began walking into the tower.

"Come on," he told the others.

Descending a series of stairwells leading from the door, Kealin felt a warmth compared to the outside world. Long-darkened torches lined the wall, with the occasional glowing stone affixed into the wall, lighting their path enough to where they were not bouncing off each other in the darkness. The doors they had passed through closed behind them though Kealin could not see who closed them and he could barely see in front of him.

There were the sounds of cracking and snapping bones around them. Other skeletons stood mindlessly by, staring. The one leading them seemed to crack his own jaw when he turned to let them know to follow.

Through twisting turns and into a large open room, they came to a large torch basin glowing with a blue fire. A walkway circled up to the top of the tower. The skeleton pointed and then stood back away from the path.

"This way," directed Taslun.

They began up. Kealin kept his blade pointed toward each skeletal form as they passed. He did not trust any of those within this place. Keeping an eye on those below, he followed the others as they snaked up the walkway.

ALRI TOOK A DEEP BREATH. The dead around her were oddly comforting. She knew she shouldn't feel as she did, not as an archon, but she could not help but to grin. Though she wasn't sure her brothers could see all of the specters in the darkness, she could. Their life forces appeared in her mind much like extensions of her own power, just unrealized. As they walked over several piles of bones, she made a twisting motion with her staff, causing several of the bones to animate for a moment before falling lifeless again. Outside of Urlas, she had an even greater desire to explore the more twisted art of necromancy.

An ominous sound began to echo around the room. A circular stone overhang seemed to vibrate with each tone of sound that filled the air.

"Is this music?" Alri questioned.

The sound became louder and the rhythm faster as they reached the top. The winds twisted through open alcoves surrounding the pillar in the center. All around them, they could see the grand expanse of white nothingness.

Taslun walked with Calak into the opening in the pillar.

"We come for wisdom," Taslun said.

KEALIN FOLLOWED with Alri and did not know what to make of the sight he saw in the wasteland of an island they had been sent to.

There was a massive organ, with keys of bone, and pipes blackened and sheer rising up from below the floor out of the top of the massive tower. A hunched figure bellowed over the keys. It continually pressed over the bones and arched its back with the swaying of the notes. It had no hands, but his arms moved over the keyboard just the same, each pressed down by power unseen. It was draped in a tattered purple cloth, and its hair was black, gray, and straggled down its back.

It did not turn but spoke.

"Elves within my place of death? I am honored you would visit, but beware my wights. Outside the tower is a place of death beyond my protection, and they are hungry for souls to devour. Elves are known to be quite a wondrous snack to them. Eternal blood is sweet and satisfying."

The floor quaked and shook as the organ wailed, almost deafening to them. In a motion, the figure turned. A bony form stared at them.

"I know you did not risk yourselves for my wondrous notes of gloomy death, the cycle of life but a short one. Even as an elf. What do you seek of Vankou, Composer of the Songs of Eternity?"

Taslun stepped forward. "We are elves of the Urlas Woodlands. Dread falls upon the gods of the North, and darkness encroaches Dimn, God of the Winds. We seek to assist him in whatever it is he faces."

"And why would I care of Dimn or Kel or Wura or the goddess Etha? Just as much, the Itsu are of not my regard either. I am of death; my songs fill the ears of those in their moments of passing.

"If I am to be as I was, I would play my symphony for each of you, but I have had enough of death for at least ten thousand years. Do you not see you are upon a wasteland of ice? It is those gods who went to war with me in a case of holy vengeance. I once had a garden upon this rock, and now I have but ice and snow and winds."

Kealin stared at this person of death; in his mind, he began to see the creature moving upon the minds of each of them. He centered his thoughts on the figure and spoke. "Dis beast is not what we think. You will not game with us, Vankou."

The others turned and looked at him. Taslun stared. "What did you say?"

What Kealin could not tell was that his voice was not as before. In his thoughts to Vankou, he had tapped into a gift at this point he could only imagine.

Kealin looked at them, confused. "Dis is not a time for games from this beast. He will tells us what we seek."

Alri stuttered. "You sp-sp-spoke as the shaman does."

Vankou furled his cape and approached them. "I sense a darkness here and upon each of you. You fear my songs, but not for yourselves. Though that is what you should fear it for should you continue your path to Dimn. The world is changing."

The creature's eyes focused on Kealin, and though he did not move his bones, Kealin heard its voice.

Your gift is awakening and is one that will serve you well, but know my song is nigh for many. I cannot say who will hear my song, but know that even the gods of the North face desolation. That being said, you spoke to death as the ethereal do. Your mind knows much, and for that, your life will be one of sorrow, for happiness comes only with lack of complete knowledge in our lands.

Vankou looked to the others as Kealin stared at him, unsure of his words. He knew of no gift but only his own luck. He knew there was something within his mind, but he did not understand any awakening, or so the creature had called it.

The creature continued in its normal speech. "You seek Dimn, and I will tell you of knowledge long forgotten. The maelstroms of legend protect the island and the portal to the ethereal land of the god. It is for this reason that you must seek out the shells of Meredaas to gain entry and calm the storms.

"I can help you with this. I know of a place to obtain them. There is a hermit that dwells on a distant shore marked by a whirlwind of ice. He waits in prayer for his time of doom, but I will not give it to him. He is like me and doomed to hover between this world and the next. He will not give his keys to Dimn freely. Now, leave this place before I make you a member of my choir. The last elves who came upon my island have not left, and beware them yourselves. Remember, while you are within the walls of the tower, I offer my protection; beyond this place, they are free to devour what is upon their grounds."

The creature turned back to his organ and began to play a solemn tone, meticulously striking the keys and arching his back as before.

"We have what we need," Kealin said to the others.

"You are right, Brother, but what of your speech?" Taslun asked.

"If I knew, I would tell you. Let us get back to the

Aela Sunrise. I have a feeling we have overstayed our time here."

Outside the windows, the wights were spinning atop the tower and howling. Taslun led them downward. Passing the large blue fire that rose as the sound of the Vankou's organ bellowed through the lower halls, they exited. The skeletons parted as the hurried party forced their way up the path leading to the doorway.

At the doorway, Taslun stopped and looked to the others. He lifted his hand to them. "Prepare yourselves, everyone. We make a run for the ship. We will not walk as we did before. The wights know of our presence, and they will try to divide us. Do not let them, and feel of no guilt to let them taste the power of the elves!" Taslun looked out and then back to his siblings. "Run!"

They all burst into a sprint, the colder gusts sweeping over them as they went down the pathway of pillars. The blue fire atop them stopped the advance of more than one wight already spotting them. The forms bounced off and upward, wailing as they did.

As they made their way onto open ground and the tundra toward the ship, the entire host of wights began to pursue them. The sounds of the organ of Vankou still sounded; a horrible foreboding struck Kealin, and he glanced behind him.

The icy teeth of a wight greeted him and in turn he swung his blade, cracking the creature's skull. Alri lifted her staff above them, and an orb of light expanded over their party. The creatures drove themselves upon it, and it began to falter as the magic electrified their bodies.

"I cannot hold them!" she shouted.

"Keep running!" said Taslun. "We will not defeat them. We must get to the ship!"

Kealin looked ahead, spotting the torches in the snow flurries on the awaiting *Aela Sunrise*. He could see Vals moving frantically aboard, but he could not tell what the man was doing.

"We are nearly there! Faster!" shouted Taslun.

It was then a wight slammed into them from the side. Calak was hit and rolled; stunned, he was not moving. The wights swarmed him.

Kealin gripped his sword, swinging over his head at the wight nearest to him. His blade passed through its body, glowing red as it did. Upon striking its black core, it turned to a white color and was shredded apart by a sudden gusting wind. He ran toward Calak, who struggled to stand.

Taslun was now engaged as another group of wights swarmed him. Kealin pulled Calak to his feet and ran forward toward his other brother, slashing and stabbing at the wights.

"Slash deep, strike their cores, Calak."

But Calak had left his blade, a mistake of inexperience. He went back to get it, ducking as the specters flew down, grasping at him. The creatures amassed and once again went for the youngest brother. Alri shouted, running forward. Her staff hummed in her hand, its tip spewing out a burst of light, fracturing the forms of many wights and destroying others. Calak made it to his sword, gripped it tightly, turning to see another wight dissolved by his sister's magic.

Kealin and Taslun were each fighting their own wights, and two more of them had swung down behind Alri. They gripped her, pulling her upward. The other opened its mouth over her head, and a fume of black began to flow over her.

"Brothers!" Calak shouted.

Kealin saw his sister in the air and leaped up, slashing the one holding her. It turned to nothingness, and Alri fell. He swooped her up as Taslun smashed the other one away, his sword glowing bright red as the wight struggled to get away.

Kealin looked down at Alri, who shook her head and blinked rapidly.

"I am fine," she said.

Alri pushed his grip from her, and he set her down. She struggled to steady herself as she stood. She lifted her staff. Her hair furled and the snow near her melted as, in a flash, a blast of flames erupted off her, spreading out in all directions. The wights surrounding them recoiled, and Taslun directed everyone toward the ship again. Kealin pushed Calak as he stumbled up the plank in the ice. Vals reached down, grabbing at him.

"I've got you. Get everyone on the ship!"

Kealin grabbed Calak's sword just as he managed to stand back up. As one of the beasts swooped down towards the ship, he spun the elven blades and struck the creature across its jaw. It shattered, raining down pieces of ice.

The wights were unable to pursue them past the border of the isle, which became obvious as the creatures were dragged backward as they flew near the water.

Though she had claimed she was fine, Alri did not appear well. Her skin was blanched and sweat poured from her body even in the stark cold of the Glacial Seas. She stumbled toward the water's edge.

Kealin tossed Calak's blade back to him. He swooped up Alri before running up the plank to board the ship. Taslun came last, taking down two more wights before jumping aboard to join the others. The wights congealed in a mass of blackness, forcing their way from their confines and drawing closer to the ship.

"All right, everyone is on board," Vals said.

He twisted a crystal on the side of the ship, and a wave of flames shot outward like before with the ice, but this time off the side of the ship. The wights were sent into a frenzy, fleeing back toward the tower.

He went to the helm, and the ship lurched away from the isle. Kealin held Alri in his arm. She was no longer awake, and he placed his ear to her chest. He did not wish his sister to be dead.

7

STRANTA-VEDI

His ear was pressed against her chest but couldn't hear anything. He began to weep but kept listening, shaking her. Then, like a sunrise following a harsh winter night, he heard a sound, a thud against his ear, and he felt chills.

Alri began to breathe and opened her eyes. He looked down at her.

"Alri."

She cracked a slight smile and then opened her eyes further before taking hold of him and pulling herself up.

Taslun knelt down, helping to steady her. "What befell you?" he asked.

"I do not know, but I am still weak."

"The wights of some lands have the power to spread a sickness," said Vals. "We must hope you do not have that."

Kealin looked to Vals and then over to Calak. He

stood, stomping over to Calak, grabbing him by his tunic.

"Do you not know to hold on to your weapon, Brother?" He pushed him against the edge of the boat. "You will not forget your blade again, will you? Must I stand beside you and assure you can draw it too, and teach you how to cut down your own enemies?"

Kealin looked into his eyes, and his younger brother stared back, breathing heavily and nodding. He then felt a hand on his own shoulder.

"Kealin. Enough."

Kealin let go of Calak and turned to Taslun. He stared at him, as did Calak.

"I, too, am annoyed," said Taslun, "but he is inexperienced. You may have made the same mistake yourself at his age."

"Doubtful. I should have two blades anyway; the way of the elves will get one of us killed soon."

He walked away from Taslun knowing the sting of his mock would anger Taslun.

"You had a chance, Kealin! You did not have to wield but one blade, as has our father and the fathers before. Take your chance if you want; perhaps you would be better to have his blade than him?"

"No. We alone are responsible for our actions. He yet has time to improve."

He shifted his eyes back around to Calak. "I do not wish any of my siblings to die, and you are more capable than you showed yourself. Keep hold of your sword, Brother, or take yourself back to Urlas."

Kealin went toward the edge of the deck as Alri now stood watching him.

Vals looked over his elven companions and then went to Taslun. "Our next path?"

Taslun looked over to Kealin and then back to Calak before acknowledging Vals. "I, once again, do not know the place but only a clue. We were told to go to an isle marked by a tornado of ice. We search for a hermit."

Vals brought up his map and stared at it.

"I believe it is here," he said, pointing at a spot further east of them. "But we go where not many sailors wish to go. It is a rumor of a place to most. The storms and tales of ice drakes make many fear those waters. I went once and had a run-in with a man of sorts, told me death would come to me if I ever returned."

"Truly?" asked Taslun.

"No." He smiled. "But even if he would have, he would not have been the first to threaten me, nor will he be the last. I do not fear death, for once I fear it, I give it power over me. Is it not true that from the time of our birth, we are dying? Time waits for none."

Vals went to the helm and wheeled the ship to an eastern path.

KEALIN THOUGHT of Val's words. It was odd to think of someone like this man, the fact that he was mortal and would die well before Kealin or anyone else of Urlas or other elves was strange. But that was the way the world worked. He looked up at the still-starry sky and wished for sun. It had been such a long time since he felt warmth on his arms. He brushed his skin of the ice that had formed on his hair. Taslun and Alri were busy making tea, and Calak stood by himself, looking off the other side of the ship. Kealin thought to go to him when Calak turned and walked toward him first.

"You are right, Kealin."

"Of what?"

"To hold on to my sword. I will not fail you or Taslun again. I almost got Alri killed. You were right. You would do well with my sword compared to me, but I will not give it to you, for I, too, am a swordsman of the Urlas Woodlands. I will rise to fight beside you and Taslun."

Taslun looked over, watching the exchange.

Kealin embraced Calak. "Very well, Brother. But know I will be beside you, and though I expect much, you are one of the few I will stand by if they falter. I cannot say that for others beyond this ship."

"But the way of the elves—" Calak paused. "You do not care for that."

Kealin smiled. "Yes, but you do. Embrace it. If you do not embrace it, you will be soulless in your zeal; blood lust alone is not enough. That is of our father's wisdom."

Taslun joined them.

"You tell our little brother of swordsmen of old, I see. You quoted one who knows more than most of our people of blade work."

"I quote what I have found to be true and makes

sense and what our father has said. But of whom you speak, he, too, was not pure elf."

"Riakar was a swordsman of old, Calak. He came from the waters of a primordial sea, defeated the demons of old that swarmed the living realm at the birth of our people. He, too, fought with two blades. Kealin is much lower in his skill than Riakar." His tone changed to that of teasing.

"Aye, from the look of these thunderclouds ahead, it will not be blades we need to fear," said Vals.

They looked up, seeing in the far distance flashes of lightning streaking across the sky. The winds were beginning to cut across the bow of the ship in random gusts.

"Does this weather ever not turn from cold and clear to freezing and stormy?" asked Calak.

Vals laughed. "When in the Glacial Seas of the North, this is good weather! Pray you are never in bad weather in these waters."

The ship tossed from side to side and, as before in the previous storm, the thoughts of the ship's hold and the safety that might be came to mind. This time, however, they did not descend, at least not all at once. There were many rocks and glaciers in these parts, and Vals used their eyes as much as they could stand to help him in avoiding them.

It went on for some time, but then Taslun took Alri down below.

"What is wrong with her?" Calak asked.

"Dizziness, but not from the rocking of the ship." Kealin said.

"I knew a great herbalist once," Vals said, "He could brew a potion that could cure most ailments or," he paused, "Cause them and make you wish for death."

"You have known many people it seems," Kealin said.

"I have. I have been fortunate to have crewmembers like you wouldn't believe."

"Spice running is a popular job here?" Calak asked.

Vals smiled, "Yes, so it would seem."

"But you have lost your crew?"

"I have lost much, elf. But do not trouble yourself with me. The sea takes us where fate has decided. We can only point ourselves in the direction we desire but we can do little to change the winds. The sails must take the wind, seize it, and use it to propel us where we wish to go. If you try to fight the wind, there is much trouble to be found in this world and beyond. Besides, calm waters only last so long and there are more storms ahead.

THOSE VERY STORMS were upon them. Kealin and Calak steadied themselves on the deck as Taslun had still not returned from taking Alri downstairs.

The ship arched upward, the horizon well below them. With great force, it fell downward, smacking the waves and throwing the two brothers to the deck.

"That was a hard one!" shouted Vals.

Kealin pulled himself back up. A glacier shifted in the waters and was running right for the ship's bow.

"Vals, to the right!"

He began pointing, and Vals nodded, rolling the wheel to direct the ship that way.

The scratching and rubbing of the ice beneath the ship was horrendous. Like cracking rocks and clashing steel. Kealin glanced at Calak, who just shook his head.

"Do not worry. This ship was made for these waters. It will take more than ice to destroy my beloved *Aela Sunrise!*"

The ship continued to toss, and Calak was thrown from one side to the next. Kealin ran along the railings and jumped to his brother as another swell struck the ship.

"Give me your hand!"

Calak reached for him, and Kealin grasped him by his gauntlet. The second wave tossed them up, throwing them onto their backs.

"No more, Brother. Head below. I will remain for now with Vals."

Calak shook his head and ran for the ladder, pulling the covering up before disappearing below.

Kealin went to the helm with Vals, who was in stance holding the wheel. The horizon bounced into view, and then the ship lurched down. They rode the back of the wave and then turned, curving up the next one.

The waves grew in size, the glaciers no longer a worry as much as the height the ship was being tossed.

"Take hold of the wheel with me, friend. My arms are tiring, and the seas are relentless!"

Kealin took hold of the spokes and worked to watch Vals as the waves passed under them. He could feel the tug of the rudder working to hold its course. The sails were still up, even with the twisting winds and slivers of ice striking them.

"We cannot risk lowering them. She will hold; we mustn't doubt her craftsmanship. If we do, we will not make it."

Vals coughed several times, gripping his chest. He was pale. The skin of his chest was darker than the rest of his body.

"Are you okay?" Kealin asked.

"Just an annoying cough, nothing more. Do not fear, it isn't plague. Just an old reminder of past events."

Vals seemed to force a smile.

The wind howled, and the ship creaked and made cracking sounds. The lightning began to flash over and over, and Kealin looked as a wave appeared on the horizon, a growing massiveness beyond any that he had seen yet.

"W-w-whoa," Vals stuttered. He turned the wheel center and tapped Kealin's right hand.

"Hold it. We have no choice. Never have I seen one so big. I had wondered if this would be needed."

He went to the mast in the center, sliding on the deck as he did, and grabbed hold of one of the crystals.

Kealin struggled to hold it straight; bracing his feet,

he gripped the wheel, but with every bit of the storm's energy working against him, he was not sure how much longer he could last.

"Vals!" he shouted.

But Vals was not coming back to him, not yet. The man twisted the crystal, and the masts became alight in gold. A sphere forming from the center of the ship encompassed the entire vessel, lifting it from the water and taking them over the edge of the wave.

The ship was flying. He was beyond amazed. He looked around and then to Vals. He loosened his grip on the wheel as Vals walked toward him.

"Very good. I did not wish to do this, but I had to."

At that time, the others came from below. Taslun looked around with his mouth open. "I heard the sea go silent and was sure my years had come to an end. What magic is this?"

"It is magic of a most important kind, for it saved us this night. But I had hoped not to use it. It makes the ship mostly inoperable for some time. Even after we return to the water, I will be able to do little more than steer. So I have only used it once, but that was a rather bored dragon, to say the least, and I got lucky it did not have the time to wait to fill its hungry belly!"

"How long will this last?" asked Kealin.

At that moment, the orb reabsorbed into the ship. They could see the night sky around them again, and in a slow descent, they went back toward the sea. The waves were still rough, but they had emerged on the lighter side of the storm.

"It varies," Vals said, "There are many secrets to

this ship and even to me, elves, but that is perhaps a story for once our task is done." He winked. "Over the years, I have learned to master many aspects of the *Aela Sunrise*, perhaps even to a point that the builders did not expect. It has never failed me, I don't expect it to now."

Kealin gave the wheel over to Vals and went to Alri, who stood holding on to Taslun. "Are you well?"

"I am well. It just seems that whenever I try to do much with my mind, weakness strikes me suddenly, and I can do nothing."

"We must learn more of this sickness. Vals, do you know more of the wights or the sickness?"

He shook his head. "I am afraid I do not. I know of them, but that is all. I also do not know how an elf will progress with it, but I understand a normal man would already be dead. The sickness is quick, or so I had read once."

Taslun went to them both. "We must hope that Dimn can help when we reach him."

Though the sea had calmed, it was not without further surprises. Though it could only be steered, fate was with them, and the ship had gotten into an undersea current. The *Aela Sunrise* went around a large glacier, and as it came to twist around a large rock, the ship continued to turn.

"Small whirlpool," Vals told them.

He did not seem too worried as he turned into it and ran alongside the center. He caught enough momentum to pass out without an issue, and the ship drifted into another current.

"It was a small one."

He laughed a bit and then began a verse.

"The twisting seas shall pull us down,
You cannot go with a frown.
Turn your ship and guide her true,
Keep on going to see her through!

Do not yet doubt the trueness spoke,
For it is known by the higher folk,
'Trust the magic, o' seafaring man,
Or embrace your bones to the eternal land.'"

HIS LAUGHING at their near-mortal peril was not amusing to Taslun, who walked with Kealin to the front of the ship. In the distance, they could see a column rising. As they drew closer, the column appeared to shift and bend. The winds began rushing over them, and the *Aela Sunrise* drifted toward the west, keeping distance from the column. It shifted again, and the clouds above moved enough for moonlight to illuminate the twisting ice that made a constant shattering sound as the waters around it leaped up into its grasp.

"There is your tornado of ice you were looking for. Our landing is nigh, my friends."

As they came once again near the shore, Alri struggled to stand, feeling weak suddenly.

"Why do you not stay here, Sister?" suggested Taslun.

"I will not. I will be fine."

She forced herself up, pushing along the deck with her fingertips. She was too weak to stand.

"Alri. Please."

Alri looked to Taslun and to Kealin, who was at her side. "I need to help."

"Stay," said Kealin. "You will be safe on the *Aela Sunrise*."

It was not by her own will but her lack of strength that she agreed. Vals went to the side of the ship and looked over.

"I can get no closer, but I feel we are close enough the ice should hold you here as the ship settles and refreezes. Let us hope that we do not need to leave quickly as last time."

"I hope not, too," said Kealin.

After embracing their sister, they each went over the side of the deck via the plank and began again across a barren icy landscape. Vals lit the torches as before, but they had no light to guide them, save the moon above. If any fortune could be noted, it would be that there was no storm, as before on the last isle.

As they crunched across the snowy field, they began to see large monolithic glowing stones. Each stood high into the air and seemed to release dust upward into the night sky.

"I have read of such stones," said Calak. "They

draw magic and offer it to the winds to be scattered around the lands. They need darkness to draw from the arcane energies. Moon pillars, I believe is what they call them."

"Then they have plenty of what they need," said Taslun.

ALRI DID NOT WISH to be here with Vals. She wanted to be with her brothers. Still, she felt sick. There was turning in her stomach and her heart would pound strangely, missing several rhythmic beats and speeding up before a pain flowed over her body and it would be hard for her to draw a breath.

She set, cross legged, attempting to draw in deep breaths.

It was not an archon's place to fret of actions beyond her own understanding. Her brothers were fine and she was no good to them in a weakened state.

As she set there with her eyes closed, she turned hearing Vals rummaging through a bag. He pulled out a kettle and began making tea using a small crystal altar to heat the water. He looked over at her.

"I'm sorry, I didn't mean to disturb your meditations."

"You didn't," she said. "I wasn't really meditating."

Vals nodded, "Well, that's what it looked like. You are an archon, right?"

"Training to be one," she corrected him, "I'm only 400 years old."

"Only."

Alri laughed, "I guess that's a bit odd for a regular man such as you."

He was mid sip of his own cup as she spoke and he seemed to laugh and choke slightly, "Yes, quite odd."

He offered her a mug of her own.

She looked down at the stark black drink and realized it wasn't tea and there was something floating on top.

It was strange yet smelled better than some of the finest teas in Urlas.

"Coffee with cinnamon," Vals said, "A favorite of my old crew."

Alri sipped it and was put off by its stout taste. It lashed her tongue and tasted grainy.

"Not a fan of coffee?" Valrin teased.

She forced a smile, "Not used to it."

Vals nodded with a grin, "Well, it helps many things."

He suddenly winced in pain, grabbing at his chest. He pulled at his tunic and backed away.

Alri set down her mug, moving to go towards him. But he lifted his hand.

"It is nothing," he told her.

Alri was experienced in healing magic and could see there was something about Val's chest that seemed off. His skin was red with splotches of blackness. It was only because he had pulled down his own tunic that she could even see it.

The Captain began to sweat and then took several quick breaths before sitting down on the stairwell that led to the helm of the ship. He noticed she was staring at him and quickly pulled up his shirt to cover his skin.

He took out a vial from his belt and took several small sips.

"I do not think a fermented liquid is best right now," Alri said to him.

Vals shook his head, "It isn't. A potion from a friend. It doesn't matter, if I'm being plain with you Alri. I am fortunate to be able just to help you again."

"Again?" Alri questioned.

Vals seemed to shudder, exhaling sharply. He stared at her for a moment before his eyes traced down to his feet.

"I mean, here. I helped you at Corson, getting you across the seas. Now, I watch you as you recover from earlier."

Alri tried to think through the different ailments that could cause Val's skin to change color.

He was staring at her as she did.

"Do not worry of me," he said.

She wouldn't be told by this man who was helping them to simply be silent.

"I am skilled in elvish medicine, perhaps I can help you?"

Vals shook his head, "My path is as it is. Your path, your siblings' path, that is what is ahead."

Alri stared at this man, feeling something within herself that has allowed her to peer deeper. It was a strange feeling, something new to her. But it was not mere attraction but a familiarity.

Vals smiled, “Have you in Urlas heard of the Dwemhar?”

Alri nodded, “They are mentioned. The founding of Urlas had much to do with our high elves assisting the Dwemhar in a great war. Though the details are a bit, convoluted.”

“The details at this point are not important, but the Dwemhar were a potent psionic race, an offshoot of them called the sea-peoples, or the Stranta-Vedi, created this ship and are the reason I am here.”

“You are Dwemhar?”

Vals shook his head with a laugh, “No, not in the way you might think at least. but I find that doesn’t matter. If I am or am not doesn’t change my future. One of my crew before now was—” he paused, “well, half. Aeveam,” he smiled, saying her name, “She would frequently read my thoughts and it felt you were doing the same for a moment. But seeing you sit cross-legged on the deck of this ship reminded me of her, of them, really. All of my old crew. They were faithful to me through many misadventures. I can’t help but to feel I let them down.”

Alri did not have Dwemhar magic or psionic skills. But she could feel that Vals was deeply troubled. It was strange, too, because he never seem to waiver before. Now, after the episode of his ailment causing him physical issues, he seemed much more vulnerable. Like a guise had fallen away and she was able to see who the Captain really was.

“Death comes for us all,” Alri said, “Though our race is gifted with life unending, a well placed blade or spell can kill us just the same. Your old crew must have cared deeply for you to give their lives in your service."

"We were a family," Vals went on. "Much more than a Captain and a conscripted crew getting paid," he paused, smiling. He looked to Alri. "I do not fear the path ahead for there are always greater adventures than we can imagine when we least expect them. I expect much and so I can only imagine the adventure to come."

8

DEMONESS

KEALIN REALIZED there was an inner peace that you could find when your entire body was as cold as his was right now. That, or this is what it felt like to nearly freeze to death. That as it was, the skies above them were so clear he was sure the field of stars had gained a thousand more twinkling lights. Calak had said nothing in some time, odd for him but given their circumstance it almost made sense.

They came across another bay after walking for some time. To their right, the sight of the tornado of ice, and its screeching howl, became more evident and pressed upon them not to walk in that direction. But it was a single torchlight that could be seen in the far distance that urged them forward. Seeing as there was no other point to guide them and they were looking for a hermit by a tornado just like the one they saw, they continued on.

Drawing closer to the light, the storm off the bay

swerved around them. Its dark clouds swirled over the hut, and the icy whirlwind spun snow toward them as they approached the house. It was a frightening sight to see, but the whirlwind held its position in an unnatural way. Clouds swirled above as if drawn to the very spot they now walked under.

The house was a stone hovel with a single window that glowed a yellow color in the dark night. From atop it, a single chimney came up made of larger circular stones, and around it grew a green grass, somehow alive in the frigid temperatures of the isle.

Taslun knocked on the door, but instead of an answer from the other side, the door opened. A figure in a gold hood stared out at them.

"Can I help you, good sirs, this frightfully cold night?"

The tornado seemed to slow and stop near the edge of the shoreline. The roar of its winds was horrendous.

"We have come to seek out your assistance in a trouble we have."

"Then you bring me trouble?" The voice became harsh. "You bastards of the earth, I cannot have you wrecking my home with your elven blood!" The voice then softened. "Come in, come out of the cold."

They followed the figure in, unsure if they were truly welcome or not. The inside of the hovel was plainly adorned. A bloody knife lay on a bare table, opposite a roaring fire that brought each of them much-needed warmth. Around the table was a white skin of some animal, and there was barely room for them as they huddled together. Kealin looked about and could see no fresh kills being prepared and was perplexed by the bright red blood on the blade. His hand was at the hilt of his sword, and he had no plans to rcmovc it.

Looking around further, there were no chairs. Only the figure's bed that it sat on, looking out at them.

"What assistance can this lonely hermit offer elves of the woods?"

Taslun knelt down at its level. "We have been sent to acquire a way to Dimn. A darkness encroaches the wind god, and we must assist him."

The figure did not move.

"We understand you have shells of a certain kind, capable of getting us through the storms that protect his land. Shells of Meredaas, God of the Sea."

The figure hummed a tune, much like the tune played by Vankou, and then stood.

"I do know of these shells. I have some. It is the ones that are pink. They do what you wish. The blue ones summon gods. I have both, as well as other shells. But can you do for me a task, a task I need assistance with?"

Before an answer was given, the figure's voice changed again.

"You need to give me a wretched rest, you flea-munching tree dwellers. How long must I remain awake in this torment of life? For three hundred, four hundred more years am I to be unable to leave, unable to do what I must to die? I am trapped by that wretched storm, in this wretched little wreck of a home, with these wretched tree dwellers!"

There was silence, and then it spoke again, softer like before.

"I am in need of assistance, as you kind elves wish to give me. I need a way out, a way to die, you see. I have a problem with that."

The figure stood and went to the table and the bloody knife. It picked up the bloody blade. Kealin's hand drew his sword partially out, ready to defend them.

"You see, when you insult the one called Vankou, you have problems. This is mine."

The figure took the blade and thrust it into the hood of his cape. A spray of blood came with each repeated strike as over and over it drove the blade into itself. But the figure did not stumble, did not fall. It stood just as before and set the blade on the table, a pool of blood forming around it.

The figure then reached to its cape, pushing back the veil. Kealin turned his eyes for a moment, for the sight was a hideous one. Where the figure's face should have been was a scarred mass of blood and tissue, the recent stabs scarring over between two eyes that by some power still could look out. Straggled gray hair hung down across the face, if one could call it a face.

"You will help me die, and I will give you the shells in payment."

The three brothers stood staring and not sure what to make of the arrangement given to them.

"How can you die if that did not kill you? We have but elven blades," said Calak.

"My death is a simple one," it told them. "This island has a place beneath the ground, a place where all can be explained. There is a demon there, placed by that one who plays the organ. It keeps death from me. If you can defeat the demon, I will give you the shells. It will not take much, for she can be deceived, if one can convince her that she is not being deceived.

"So the demon is a female? A human, an elf, a dwarf?"

"Just a demon," it replied. "Trapped from another realm into ours by a power beyond myself or you."

"Where is this place?" asked Kealin.

"Beneath us."

The figure pointed down and then went to its bed, pushing it away, revealing a door in the floor of the hovel. The figure took a key and unlocked a large silver lock. The door opened with a clank on the floor.

"Down there you will find her. My temptation was always to try to win my death, but I could not. I could not do it. You must betray her to destroy her. So is what I have learned. Perhaps you three can." The figure jerked toward them, grabbing Taslun.

"Or perhaps you will die instead and be devoured by the hellish creature of fire!"

Kealin drew his blade and stabbed the figure.

It did nothing but look downward. A flow of blood ran down the elven blade.

"If only, good sir, that was enough."

The figure walked backward off the blade and

backed up against the fire. "Please, go on and free me from my burden. My mind has been divided for some time in the madness of this place."

Taslun looked at the figure. "How can we know this is not some trap and that you will do what you say?"

"You do not, but what choice do you have if you wish to reach your goal? I seek death myself. What good does betraying you do for me?"

Taslun seemed convinced to Kealin, but Calak looked less than happy of their situation. Still, he pushed Taslun out of the way to go to the stairwell first himself. Kealin followed after him, and Taslun was the last.

As Kealin made it down to the lower level, he made out a grand beach. The waves came in off a blue shore, and across white sand scurried a crab into the surf. The sun was bright.

They walked together, each looking up at the sun and then across the expanse. Kealin looked around. "This is not real. What we are seeing is not right."

"I know," said Taslun. "It is the demon."

"She," corrected Calak. "But how will we find her here?"

Kealin turned and looked behind him. He drew his blade. A woman stood there. Her hair was long and dark; strands of it fell between her breasts. He could see her hips, but she wore a silver raiment across her waist that fell just above her knees. She walked toward them, a smile across her face.

He could see her eyes, scanning each of them. In

his mind, he heard wails, but he centered his thoughts, staring at her. She seemed to be more than she appeared, but he could not see it, for it was shadowy and her image remained front in his mind.

"What are three of the most powerful race in the lands doing in my domain?" she asked. "What pleasures do you seek?"

"No pleasures," said Taslun. "We seek nothing."

The demon was not to be so easily tricked. "Taslun of the Urlas Woodlands, you cannot avoid conversation with such short words."

Calak stepped forward; he drew his sword and began toward her.

"Calak, the younger brother. You draw your blade so well, but dear Alri never stood a chance against the wights, and even now she is ill. How poor of you."

Calak stopped. "How do you—?"

"Your thoughts are mine, dear elf. Once more, what do you seek?" She looked to Kealin.

The wails returned, and her eyes began to burn in his mind. He lifted his head, looking down. He dropped his sword.

"I need not this blade," he said.

He then felt her gaze leave him. She now walked toward Taslun.

"What can I do for you?" She brushed his cheek with her hand.

"You can do nothing. I am not tricked by this."

Kealin looked to him but noticed he had begun to sweat.

"This is no trick, and you can remain here with

me. No need to return to the bitter cold and the faceless man."

Taslun went to draw his blade, but her hand was upon his, and he began to waver even in his stance against her. Calak went to go beside her.

"I will throw you from this mount, demon!" he shouted. He went to her, but she raised her hand, and he paused, staring down into the sand.

He seemed afraid; his eyes widened, and he struggled to stand.

"What is it?" asked Kealin.

"A cliff, Brother. Do you not see it?"

He looked but saw nothing but the sand.

She reached into the sand and drew out a black stone. "Why not you taste the fruits of this land, Taslun? Just one taste."

Taslun looked down and smiled. "I am hungry, and it looks delicious."

Kealin looked to his brothers, Calak still worried he was to fall and now his elder brother who thought a stone to look like food.

"What is wrong? Do you not see this beach and that is a stone? Taslun, do not be fooled."

But Taslun was fooled.

"Brother, this is a berry, not a stone. Perhaps you should allow her to feed you."

Kealin turned to Calak, pushing him from his spot. He fell forward and screamed, striking the ground as Kealin knew he would. But he stood up, coughing not on sand, as Kealin saw, but black dirt.

"It was not a cliff," said Calak. "Where are we?

What is this dark place?" He lifted his sword. "Taslun, it is a beast. I can see her now!"

Kealin looked around. This beach was not real, and that he knew. They had each seen what they loved. Calak, the mountains, himself, the ocean, but what of Taslun? How could he dissuade this mirage from his brother?

"Where are we, Taslun?" he shouted.

"We are in a place of wondrous glory, that an Urlas Blade would love, but this lovely woman wants to treat those of battle to a taste of her berries. Just a moment, little brother."

She was now near his lips with the black stone. It swirled with a black fire within, and Kealin stared into her from the side.

Do not.

The demon turned and looked to him.

You have power beyond what I could seek. My master must have known this. Why would he send you here? I will kill your brother; you cannot dissuade him.

Kealin looked to Taslun. His mouth was open, and she was teasing him with the berry. Calak had gained a fearful sight and a true one when he tested his mirage, or rather, was helped to test it.

Kealin turned. The ocean rushing up, he stepped into the water, and it faded to a black dust that spread out across the dark room lit by only torches that surrounded a great circle. He turned to see not a woman but a beast of white skin and tall black horns protruding from not only atop her head but the sides. Her clawed hand held the stone at Taslun's head, and his mouth was open.

He believes he is in a place of "wondrous glory, that an Urlas Woodlands Blade would love," Kealin thought to himself.

The demon interrupted his thought. *You know not what you think. Do not try it.*

But he would. His brother thought he was upon the field of battle; a battle maiden was to offer him a treat he would well deserve with his skill, but what if the enemy was not dead?

Kealin ran for his blade. Grasping it, he shouted, "Elf of Urlas, I am your enemy! Face me!"

His brother's gaze turned, and his blade was drawn.

"No!" the demon growled.

Taslun came upon him, his blade up, and Kealin parried, throwing his brother to the side. He side-stepped and ran upon him.

Taslun turned and looked at Kealin.

"I do not fear you, foul thing!"

The mirage had not faded, and his brother still sought to fight him. He braced his blade against the slashing sword meant for him and thought of how he might change the mirage so as to throw out his brother. He stepped forward, striking twice to throw Taslun back. It was then he thought and shouted, "Calak, your blade! Throw it to me!"

Calak did so, and Kealin caught it. In a fury, he swung at his brother, swinging his blades as he did, striking high and low at his brother's parries. With the clanging of elven blades, he saw Taslun's gaze change, and now he no longer fought. He recoiled and began breathing fast.

"What trick is this, Kealin? Why do you fight me? I was upon the war grounds, facing a—"

It seemed Taslun had been drawn out of his mirage as well.

The demon stepped forward. She set her gaze upon Kealin, and his forehead felt warm. The wails began again, and he looked back at her.

I know not my power, but this is my stand. I told you I needed no blade. I can destroy you.

The demon broke her stare, and a tear formed in her eye. I cannot believe I fell for such a trick. I have been deceived by my own master. You solved the riddle of the mirages with little more than a simple distraction. My master would not have done this for no reason. I have tormented the faceless man for so long. Why now would he do this? I am betrayed to this fate and have been beaten by little more than you. It is over. I will fade, and he will die. Beware fate.

It was then the demon burst into a white fire. A wail bellowed through the cavern, and Kealin looked upon her form as she turned to dust and collapsed.

"Dis is de end for you," he said out loud.

Taslun stared at him. "You did it again."

"What?" he asked.

"Your voice, like the shaman. What happened?"

"I still don't know, but I could hear her thoughts. She said that her master betrayed her, but he had a reason. Her master was Vankou. He was whom I first did it with. She also said to 'beware fate.'"

"Force it from your mind, Brother," Calak said.

Kealin handed Calak back his sword. "Thank you for this."

Taslun embraced him. "Thank you for stopping me from falling to its tricks. Those two blades are useful. But I do not know what to think of this power of yours. It is not elven; at least, not something I know of."

Calak laughed. "That is speaking of wisdom beyond, for our elder brother knows much."

"I do not know either, but it is of no concern now. Let us deliver the news to the man above. He will be pleased to know what has happened."

They went back to the stairwell and climbed up. They found the man lying on the ground, his bleeding face uncovered and his body partially in the fire and beginning to smoke as his hood and cape started to burn. The blade from the table was in his neck, and a pool of blood covered the floor. On the table was a note and a small sack. Kealin picked up both, opening the note.

BROTHERS, I knew you could and you have. I am done with her wail; I know it is time. Do well with these gifts, for I did not.

HE OPENED up the sack and found several tiny shells of differing colors. "We have them," said Kealin.

"And it seems the faceless man has what he wished," said Taslun.

"Let us hurry back to Alri," Calak told them.

They exited the hovel as the body of the figure began to burn and the hovel itself caught fire. Within the glow of the burning structure, they stood, looking out at the bay and the tornado of ice. The funnel began to falter and then vanish into the clouds, a deep gust blowing upon them now.

Taslun looked to them and began forward, Kealin and Calak following.

9

CAPTAIN'S FURY

ALRI WONDERED OF HER BROTHERS. It had been some time since they had left. Vals was still shaking periodically but he made a point to get up, going to the helm, and simply staring off over the seas.

She returned to her spot from before, working to focus her energies to fend off the dizziness flowing over her.

She needed to be her best. She did not know what lay ahead but she had to be ready.

Closing her eyes, she took a deep breath. She could feel energy from beneath her, rising through her spine and towards her head. Strangely, she felt a greater power beneath her. She felt connected to the ship she sat upon, to the seas that wrapped its grip around the hull of the *Aela Sunrise*.

As her heart beat in her chest, she could see the crystals at the back of the ship and realized they shared properties with the very crystal in her staff.

There was more to be learned, more to be discovered on this ship. But she felt a sudden shift in emotion. A feeling like she was too late. There was a pungent smell in the air. It was something far off but drawing closer.

"Alri," Vals said from the helm. "I want you to hide."

She looked up, seeing eight ships approaching from beyond. High above them, ribbons of green and red rippled across the dark sky. Alri glanced down at the approaching vessels on a direct course for them.

"Vals, are those Rugag's ships?"

He coughed again, this time spitting blood over the helm and falling to his knees. She ran to him but staggered as she did. She was still far too weak. But she crawled to him, still. Reaching the helm, she put her hand on his shoulder. He shook his head as he pushed her assistance away.

"Hamra-Su," he said to himself.

"What?"

"It was a power, a word that used to work. I think my body is too far-" he paused. He stood up, his right hand seemed to cramp and he looked to her as he rubbed it. "Keep yourself well, protect yourself. I will do what I can. The Stranta-Vedi will not fail again."

He drew his curved blade, white fire engorging it not too unlike her brothers' ruinite blades.

"One last time," he said.

But he wasn't saying this to her. He bowed his head slightly. "She still waits for me, in a place beyond this one."

Alri had no idea who or what Vals spoke of. The dwarves were closing in. There were far too many for the two of them to face.

Vals sheathed his sword.

"Meredaas, be with us this day. I call upon you, send your warriors. Do not let us face this enemy alone."

He grabbed hold of the wheel of the *Aela Sunrise*, pulling himself up but quivering.

"Though I sail into dark waters, the lights of Wura shine above me and the deck of my ship. Etha gazes in favor, her light upon cresting waves of ice and rolling seas. Kel stands beside me with burning blade ready… just like before." Vals stood tall, taking a deep breath, "Comfort is upon my heart and I lift my eyes to gaze into the light of my final ascension, my place promised by the one that has never left my mind. Though, still, I leave behind those who have stood by the Stormborn, I sail towards greater seas."

The ship lurched forward. Vals moved several levers at the helm and the ship hummed. Suddenly, across the deck of the ship, tiny crystals appeared spinning with an almost melodic sound. The ship was nothing at all like it was before. Alri felt energy rushing beneath her feet into the larger crystals along the railings.

"The winds of Dimn bring me comfort for now all has come to pass and not one has stopped what was coming and none will."

The dwarven vessels split off. Four going to one

side and four to the other. Alri gazed out beyond these ships to see others in the darkness.

"I do not fear the shadows of death and the maw of unknowing, for I am Stranta-Vedi, Valrin, Storm-born of Travaa. No monster upon this world will cause me to stumble. Take care, elf of Urlas," Vals shouted. "I have had no choice but to speak in riddles but one day, maybe, you and your kin will understand who I was, who I am, and will remember how I embraced destiny."

Alri lifted her staff as she gripped the center mast. They were moving directly into a path with the other ships. Massive bolts flew across the deck of the *Aela Sunrise* plunging into the depths beside them but draping heaving chains over them.

Vals wheeled left, the entire ship rocking to one side as a dazzling blast of energy erupted from the larger crystals engulfing one of the dwarven ships in bright blue fire.

The dwarven fleet pushed in, two more vessels went up in flames. Vals wheeled them back in a circle, sending a concentrated blast of fire from the top of the center mast. Several blasts of arcane fire flew across the deck.

Alri was breathing fast. She took a deep breath, centering her focus and lifting her staff.

Focus, fracture, fade.

Just like in Urlas, she summoned a great ward, pushing it larger than normal and moving to shield the Captain.

Now, blood ran down his legs and the blackness she saw on his chest before covered most of his lower arms and up to his neck.

Another barrage of arcane fire struck the ward and she held it aloft.

Two more dwarven vessels exploded as the *Aela Sunrise* cut through the water and into the wreckage. Dwarves wailed and screamed, many of them trying to cling on to debris and others thumping against the hull of the ship as Vals circled around again.

"I will not leave your brothers," he told her. "But I'm going towards shore. You, hide. I have called for assistance from Meredaas. I must wait for that but I cannot risk you."

There seemed to be more ships now, six more dwarven vessels moved on a direct path towards them. The darkness of the skies fled as the burning vessels upon the Glacial Seas gave off a warm red and orange glow.

Another series of blasts and a barrage of arrow fire rained upon the deck. Alri's ward fractured.

She attempted to reabsorb the energy, focusing as the twists of magic collapsed into her.

The dwarves rammed them, throwing the ship into a spin. Two ships ran along side them and a third boxed them in.

"Valrin! You're games are finished! Where's the crew?" A dwarf Captain shouted.

Vals shifted a lever at the helm, the ship lurched backward. He moved another and all of the crystals along the railings surged with energy, sending out crackling blasts that splintered the decks of all the ships around him.

He wheeled right, moving to break towards open water. The dwarves moved to intercept, several vessels moving in behind him and more forming a blockade ahead.

Alri was sweating. She was not well. But she lifted her staff, focusing her energies into the tip. She sent splintering ice in focused blasts upon one of the vessels killing several dwarves around the helm of one of the ships.

But she needed to destroy the ships. She reached out with her hands, lifting them up to the sky.

"Etha's Fire, come down this night!"

This was an advanced spell, one she had done only once in training.

It required considerable energy and concentration, but if she could do it she could clear the blockade.

As the *Aela Sunrise* cut through the water, she felt her hair began to blow around her. She could see the light of Etha, a bright white light in her mind's eye looking upon her.

"Goddess, you must protect us. I ask for favor, bring down your fire. Destroy these ships."

But the light faded from her mind. She attempted to keep her focus but her energy, all that she could muster, faded with the failure of the last spell. She fell to her knees. As the *Aela Sunrise* struck the blockade, the crystals of the ship flashed and then went dark.

Dwarves jumped upon the deck. She looked up at their salt and ice encrusted faces. The dwarves moved in with cruel spears and swords, running past her and up to Vals.

"HAKEN-RAK!" Vals screamed.

A blast of lightning shot back their boarders, sending dwarves flying off the deck in a bumbling mass of searing flesh.

More dwarves came, two of them grabbing Alri and forcing her to her back. She tried to bring her staff up but they stomped her arm. She reached for her belt, her own short Urlas dagger tucked away in her waist.

She drew it, jabbing it into the leg of one of the dwarves.

A dwarf kicked her in her jaw. She tasted blood. She looked up at the night sky, seeing the pudgy, grotesque dwarf hovering above her with his companions as Vals flew into view, his white saber cutting into the dwarves. He moved through a shower of blood as he spun about, white fire blazing off his blade.

Alri reached for her staff as the *Aela Sunrise* was struck again. More dwarven ships had joined the fight. Alri was shaking. Vals pulled her towards the helm.

"Stay here, do not follow me. Act as if you are dead. Meredaas is coming. Just a little longer."

He smiled at her, stroking her hair. She focused on him, taking deep breaths. She then realized how inexperienced she was. She tried to focus realizing that the Captain was calm.

Blood was running from his nose. Black, scaly skin now covered his left hand.

"Do not worry of me, these are the ordained steps I must take. All will be as it should be."

He turned from her, running for one of the nearest dwarven vessels.

"Valrin! You will not escape our grasp!" a harsh voice screamed. It was Rugag. But Alri couldn't see him. She sat up. Vals was mid-jump, his sword above his head.

"Haken-Rak," he said, though softer than the time before.

A curling blast of lightning flew from his blade and shattered the deck of the ship he jumped upon. He engaged the dwarves, spinning and hacking. He did not fight like a Blade of Urlas, but with every stab and slash, he split open dwarves at every turn. Dwarves were now using the *Aela Sunrise* like a bridge, moving in on Vals in increasing numbers. But the Captain of the *Aela Sunrise* was no mere man like her and her brothers thought. He was Stranta-Vedi and though she did not know that term, his battle prowess was almost unmatched this day as much as any other day.

Alri heard a shattering crack, she thought at first Vals had been struck, but she saw a dwarf staggering away holding his face. Vals had punched him so hard he had broken most of his teeth. Still, the captain fought on.

. . .

She tried to stand. She had to help him. With each attack he was now stumbling though he had struck down over two dozen dwarves, still, more dwarves came. Alri pushed herself up, only to draw attention of two dwarves who were on the outside of the fighting.

"Grab that one!" Rugag shouted from above. She saw him. He was standing on a ship just behind the *Aela Sunrise.*

"She may know where the others are."

The two dwarves moved in on her. She lunged, striking one with her staff. She knew better than to try to use magic but perhaps, she could defend herself long enough for Val's plan to come to fruition. She blocked a spear thrust, parrying it aside as she pushed in, punching one of the two dwarves in the face. She was about to follow through with her staff when she was swept from beneath and taken down. She screamed, punching and kicking but the dwarves had grabbed her by the legs and arms, forcing her against the deck. A third dwarf stood above her. He stomped her chest.

The crushing force of his boot now pushed into her throat making it almost impossible to breathe. Her arms were bound. Her legs were bound.

Then suddenly, blasts of energy incapacitated the dwarves holding her before the spinning white saber of the captain came flying into view, striking the dwarf standing upon her.

She grabbed at her throat, struggling to breathe as she rolled over. She saw Vals, still on the dwarven vessel, on his knees. With a pile of dead and dying dwarves around him. His hands were outstretched and the golden orb was drawing up around the *Aela Sunrise.* He was sealing her in.

But the dwarves moved with haste, grabbing her, and then jumping from the *Aela Sunrise* as the ship was sealed in its golden orb.

They threw her beside Vals

He was on his knees but even as she tried to stand beside him, he placed his hand over her and held his other hand up to the encircling dwarves.

Alri couldn't do anything. What energy she had was gone. Vals hand was shaking. He had not been struck by any weapons that Alri could see but whatever sickness was upon him, had made it difficult for him to do anything beyond what he did now.

"Valrin of Travaa, Captain of the *Aela Sunrise*, finally bested." A gruff voice said.

It was Rugag. The massive dwarf was laughing as he came into view holding a large club.

"But you were always just a dumb boy to me," Rugag said. "Where's the rest of the crew? Who is this elf? Did your old friends leave you?"

Vals said nothing.

"Bind them," Rugag ordered. "The others were just elves. We will find the rest of his real crew but we should leave this place," the dwarf looked out at the waters around them, "He will have called those damn whales. Signal one vessel to remain for those elves. Kill them all or take them as prisoners. Either way, have them meet us near our typical rendezvous point south of here. That's it. Prepare to sail." He growled.

Without the tornado spinning a rain of ice upon them, the blustery winds of the night were not as bad as they had perceived before. They made their way with haste but not as quickly as the isle before where the imminent threat of attack was on their backs.

Ahead, Kealin could see the torches of the *Aela Sunrise*. He looked up and noticed the constellations and that it was early morning now. The passage of time was quick within the lair of the demon.

He thought of the happenings before, his ability to speak to the demon and his sense of her attempting to look within his mind. He did not know how, but his ability to sense and decipher the unknown was growing. Where before it was a second of foresight allowing him to parry a blade or sidestep a thrust from his opponent on the arena floor, it had become more, and a power that both Vankou and his demon servant perhaps feared.

Drawing closer to the place where they had left the ship, they started smelling a salty burning smell. It was not the torches of the *Aela Sunrise*. A golden glow was in the air, shrouded in fog rolling over the shore. Taslun was thinking what Kealin feared; the *Aela Sunrise's* enchanted shield was up. At least it would provide safety in the event of an attack, but as they came closer, they saw no one on the deck.

"Where are they?" Calak asked.

Kealin and Taslun were silent. Looking at each

other, they then went to opposite ends of the ship, searching at the water and then back up at the ship.

"Vals! Alri!" Kealin shouted. But there was no answer.

Charred and broken pieces of wood rolled in with the tide.

10

LOST

"They must've been attacked," said Taslun. "Check for tracks leading away from the ship. Perhaps he and Alri fled."

Kealin ran along the edge of the shore, away from the wreckage. He scanned the ground, looking for displaced snow or the imprint, at least, of something out of place. The ground was untouched. Not a single rock had been turned, nor ice broken in random pools that he was careful to not slip on. He stopped, scanning the dark horizon of the open expanse of the isle.

Alri. Where are you?

He turned to the water, and he saw what they had not before. A ship was beyond the *Aela Sunrise*, and a smaller boat was in the water, approaching his brothers. Upon the deck, stout men were busy loading into another boat. It was dwarves. Some of the same from the tavern back where they had run into Rugag and his crew. His brothers were not looking toward where the dwarves were coming from. The wind was howling over the water and they were likely hiding their faces from the icy cold.

He moved along the edge of the water himself. "Taslun! Calak!" he shouted. But the wind was not in his favor, and his voice did not carry to them.

The dwarves were upon them, and though Taslun drew his blade, he lowered it as Calak was taken to the ground at spear point. His elder brother dropped his blade and lifted his hands in surrender. Calak was pulled up and forced toward his brother as the other group of dwarves landed closer to Kealin and began to spread out in a half-circle.

He couldn't hear what was being said but needed to get closer. He looked behind him. An old pathway carved out by a long frozen-over river ran further down and would provide him some form of cover in the darkness. But taking this approach, he would still be seen. He felt he had no choice. It was then he heard the water break to his right. He glanced over.

It was a narwhal.

Hello, friend.

The narwhal seemed to turn to him. He heard melody and an echo in his mind. A word appeared, and he spoke it as he heard it in his mind.

Tulasiro?

"Is that your name?"

The narwhal blew air from its blow hole.

He smiled. There seemed to be a careful friendship developing between them. "Do you know where Alri and Vals are?"

The narwhal moved in the water, swimming outward to the open sea and then back to the shore.

"If they are gone, we cannot go that way yet. We must get the ship, and my brothers are in danger."

The narwhal turned to him, rolling his horn along the shore and blowing air.

"Will you help me?"

Kealin heard sounds in his mind as before, and felt calmness upon himself.

It was then a voice shouted across the winds. "Come on! A beast is on the shore."

They had spotted the narwhal, known now to Kealin as Tulasiro.

The dwarves closest to them, and most of those who had come in the second boat and not right by his brothers, were now coming his way. He lay down in the snow. Drawing his blade, he held it close. In the bleak darkness, he would look like little more than a dark patch.

The dwarves went to the water's edge, but Tulasiro had already left.

"Look around here. You know it will come back up. Stupid creature," the one growled to the others.

There were five in total. They each looked to the waters and not to where their own actual danger lay in waiting, at least, to Kealin's plan.

The one on the furthest edge would be the easiest to slay, but was not his first target. He would take the one in the front with a single stab in the open spot in his rusty armor that he had failed to maintain. Strange for a crafter of metals as were dwarves, but he had never seen dwarves like these. The second strike would come to whichever dwarf turned next to him, and then the next would be whoever was still standing. The last, who would have likely frozen in some form of shock, he would take as a tool for bargaining.

The dwarves looked at one another.

"Likely not even a whale. Why would one come into shore like this? Stupid creatures. Perhaps if the group of them wouldn't have run into that harbor, we would've never even have found them."

"You know how Rugag is, though, always thinking of that Vals. This ship was taken with ease beyond what we could've guessed. All of this time and we take it so simply! We got him and that little elven woman. I can't wait to get off this rock and to her."

The dwarf began a bellowing laugh as he thrust his hips.

"Patience, Luraa," the one on the edge said. "We need to find that other elf. Two are not enough. There is a third. We know it, and so do those two elves. I had thought them Urlas Blades, but they gave up without a fight. Weak Blades are more how I see them!"

The one speaking did not draw another breath as Kealin's blade slashed his neck and squirted a warm rush of fluids, casting a fog in the air.

The half-elf cracked the dwarf closest to him in the head, knocking him into the water, as he slashed the remaining dwarves across their chests in one arching spin. One of the two fell, and the other backed away in shock. His plan was working. He knew these bastards were weak. The winds worked to his advantage, for as another dwarf cried out, his sounds were muted by the gusts and his head was taken off.

Looking around, the last dwarf trembled, holding the spot with his open hand that Kealin had slashed. He backed up to the edge of the water and dropped his weapon.

Kealin grabbed him by the throat. He was heavy, but Kealin lifted him up, staring at him. He had a desire to kill him if he did not wish to use him as he did. His pulse thudded in his hands; he could feel his heart pounding in his chest. But that was not the way of an Urlas Blade, and it was not what he needed to do at this time.

He lowered him to the ground and kept him in his grasp by gripping his armor. He squirmed as Kealin walked with him, approaching the group surrounding Taslun and Calak.

The other dwarves did not notice Kealin right away, but as he emerged from the darkness, they saw him, cursing and running forward before the half-elf lifted his quarry for the rest to see.

One of the dwarves slapped Taslun and then turned toward Kealin.

"Well, elf, it seems you are here. Your friend here had told me you were dead." He motioned to Taslun.

Kealin smiled. "Perhaps he meant you, if you do not answer my questions."

The dwarf laughed. "You threaten us? We outnumber you."

"So you do. But his friends did not seem to be able

to do much against me." Kealin placed his blade against the neck of his prisoner.

The dwarf looked around with widened eyes. "He killed the others in cold blood, sir."

Kealin's grip turned tighter.

"You mean to tell me that an Urlas Blade murdered my men? Do you not have a code, Blade? Your enemy cannot have their back turned when you face them. A fair duel, you call it."

Kealin pressed his blade against the edge of the dwarf's neck. He screamed as it pierced the first layer of his skin, blood running down the blade.

Taslun looked on and looked to Calak. He was looking down at his blade that the dwarves had removed and tossed only a few feet from them.

"The Blades of the Urlas Woodlands do have such a code. I do not, for I am not a Blade," Kealin shouted. "Where is the elf taken from the *Aela Sunrise*? And tell me of Vals. Where are they?"

There was silence in the group of dwarves, and two of them slowly inched to his far left, almost out of sight. The other two, closest to his brothers, had walked toward his right. He looked to Taslun, who made eye motions to his sword lying in the snow.

"You will not murder him, elf. You are too pure for such an act as a dwarf might do."

Kealin tightened the grip on his blade. "You force my hand, dwarf, for I will learn what I want, in any way I must."

He pulled the blade through his quarry's neck,

slicing his vessels and cutting through his tissues. The dwarf gargled and fell to the ground.

"What have you done?" the dwarf shouted.

The others around him began to back up as Kealin stretched out his blade. The dwarves, who before had been stalwart and confident, looked to their boat. Taslun and Calak went for their blades, and they were not hindered.

The dwarves turned and ran for their boat, the lead dwarf pushing one of his companions into Kealin's path as the remaining ones fled.

From the waters near where the boat floated, the narwhal Tulasiro came from the depths, shattering the vessel and throwing debris onto the shore.

The dwarves turned again, and their leader pushed them toward the elves. Calak and Taslun struck at their aggressors, as Kealin moved into the last one. He pointed his blade at his neck as Tulasiro came from behind, resting its horn against the dwarf's back.

"I . . . I . . . don't know what you want."

"Name where they have been taken!" Kealin yelled, his blade against the dwarf's neck.

"Rugag took them. He went south. I can take you!"

"Can you take us?" asked Calak.

"Yes! Yes! I will gladly take you. They headed back to town, an isle like before. They will not be too far from here."

The dwarf smiled, but Kealin did not return it. Taslun placed his hand on his shoulder. "It is not the way of our people, Kealin. Do not kill him."

Kealin had no plan to.

He stepped back from the dwarf, lowering his blade, but before the dwarf could move a step, he buried the blade into his leg. The dwarf screamed and gripped his knee.

"Kealin!" Taslun said.

"They took our sister, and he was a part of it. Tell me you would not do the same. Do you wish to take him with us? I do not."

Kealin walked away toward the *Aela Sunrise* as Calak and Taslun looked at one another, speechless.

The shield around the *Aela Sunrise* was set and could not be passed by Kealin's knowledge. He tapped his sword on it and found it was not a riddle they could easily solve. He turned; Tulasiro had disappeared into the depths. He looked to the others. The dwarf was still wailing in pain.

"We have a ship, but it is that wretched dwarven one," he told them. "I know not the magic the *Aela Sunrise* is protected by."

"Nor do I," Taslun said. "We can use their ship. The other rowboat is over there."

The dwarf had become silent, and with their backs turned, they did not see his wobbling approach. In a last attempt of fight, the dwarf drew a knife, bleeding profusely from his leg as he did, running toward Kealin. Calak turned, seeing his approach, and slashed the dwarf down before driving the blade into the man's chest.

Kealin jerked around and looked to Calak with a nod. He then glanced up at Taslun. "Dwarves. At least in the Glacial Seas, they cannot be trusted," Calak said.

Taslun seemed thankful the threat had been dealt with, but the beliefs of the Blades still stuck in his mind.

Calak and Kealin went to the rowboat and steadied it. They boarded and rowed toward the ship. None of them really knew how to sail, and as they came closer, they noticed the battle scars left on it by the *Aela Sunrise*. Its sails had been burned to mere cinders. It seemed otherwise intact, though there was a lot of wood floating in the water. Kealin wondered how many ships Vals had taken down before he was captured. He was never one for the gods, but at this moment, he prayed that the goddess Etha was watching over Vals and Alri.

ALRI WAS ALONE below the deck of Rugag's flagship. The ship itself was massive, larger than the other vessels by at least double. It's ornate, dark green wood had golden fixtures from the upper deck down to the lowest deck. She had seen dozens of dwarves, many in the best of armor compared to many of the dwarves they had seen before. She was surprised Rugag had not led the attack against the *Aela Sunrise*. That said, Rugag did not seem the type of dwarf to lead in such a way. Besides that, Alri saw how Vals had used his ship to devastate many of the vessels that attacked them — she was sure Rugag knew how capable Vals' ship was and didn't want to risk his own vessel.

She hadn't seen Vals since she had been locked in her dark and damp cell. There were other cells but no other prisoners around her save for one that was strapped to a table in the center of the room. She wasn't sure he was even alive. His skin was blanched and there was a horrid smell, unlike anything she had ever smelt. But, studying the room in the bleak darkness with only a handful of swinging lanterns suspended up from the rafters she knew there was more to this place than she could see.

Alri rolled her archon crystal between her fingers. She never thought it would come to this, she never believed she would actually be contemplating death. In all her visions of potential futures, this was not one of them.

Kealin and Taslun will find me.

A door opened in the darkness and the man tied down on the table jerked his head up.

"Oh, lovely." A voice said.

Alri hadn't heard this voice.

The man on the table began to tremble.

A figure walked in, holding a single curved bone in his right hand as he hobbled towards Alri. He seemed to be injured, at least, at first glance. But as he came closer, she realized it was not an injury at all but that the man had a crab claw as a foot. He glared at her.

"An elf, good. Those are tasty. Those are… rare. I am your future, you will be my past. There is much our captain desires and," he looked her up and down, "I do not think you can provide all he wishes."

He continued to stare as Rugag's ship pitched from one side to the other.

The man before her was still staring. He wore a dark coat decorated with large pieces of bones. Around his neck there was a necklace of some shriveled flesh. Not cured meat or other edible, but of some bodily organ. It was wrapped in green twine and seemed to move at random on its own.

"Do not look at the heart of my one true love!" he slammed his hand on the cage.

"The best part of her was what I took from her. Quite a snack, if taken in small bites." He began to stroke the heart. "I was betrayed, elf. Do you know what that feels like? No, you do not. But I will give you the same treatment in time, I think. The removal of such an organ is a type of magic that only I can do. They call me a monster, Rugag's Demon. But that is ludicrous!" He laughed, "Demons cannot be owned! I am a monster though. A lovely and horrid monster. My victims call me The Cold Master. For you," he tapped the cell again, "I am The Cold Master."

He made his way over to the table, now ignoring Alri.

The prisoner began to tremble as The Cold Master began to run his curved bone dagger up and down his arms.

"Have you decided to reveal the place you put Rugag's payment or shall I remove more parts of you? I think we're down to only two more toes."

The man reached out into the darkness to his side. Alri could hear him weeping.

"No, no. Both of them fell horrible sick and..." he sighed, as he began to laugh, "They slipped into The Cold Master's embrace."

"No! Please! You told me you'd heal them if I told you where we put the bones."

The Cold Master slashed his knife down the man's side, splitting open the tissue as the man screamed.

"Now, now. I told you I'd look after them. When I saw they were sick, I did just that. I found their issues. The one, your brother, he had a hole in his skull. I tried to seal the wound with hot iron but it seems that was not the appropriate treatment. But he did stop screaming. Oh, but your love, she cried your name, moaning like a whore. We assumed she was suffering from possession and I had my Master tie her to the front of his ship. It was a horrid storm we passed through but, after that, she was quiet and cold." He laughed, "Quite cold! So, I brought her in here and laid her beside your brother. So, do not fear, they are here with you and are healed of what they complained of."

"You're a damn monster!" the man screamed.

The Cold Master turned to Alri, "You see? No one remembers my name!"

He turned back to the man, making several more slashes in his flesh.

"Coins, dear sir, coins. Rugag wishes to know this. Perhaps, he will kill you quickly if you just... name... the place!"

Alri sunk back down in her cell. She clutched her crystal still. She knew she could cast one spell but that was not enough to help her here.

Etha, help. I do not know my path, I do not-

The blood curdling scream of the man being tortured only a few paces from her tore her from her prayer.

The man began to buck about, coughing and spewing blood.

The Cold Master sighed.

"Not again. Rugag will be most displeased with me. I guess I will wait a bit and then get to work on the next one."

As The Cold Master walked out of the ship's brig, Alri watched as the man convulsed on the table. As a witness to his last movements as he still drew breath, Alri bowed her head. His convulsions slowed and life fled his body in the cold, dark void of the Glacial Seas.

KEALIN NOTICED there were countless dead dwarves in the waters around them. They had not been struck by magic but by the gnashing tooth bite of a swung sword.

Taslun pointed out, "A courageous man, Vals. He fought well to hold this ground, it seems."

The dwarven ship was easily boarded, being lower to the water and with the surf not as torrential as before. They made their way onto it and began to look around.

"Check what stores you can find. We must hope there are sails somewhere," Taslun said.

"Do you know how to sail, Brother?" Kealin questioned.

"I have not thought of how yet."

They each took turns looking through a large collection of nets and spears, more than a few bottles of wine, and dry goods. The dwarves were well stocked, but they could not find any spare sails.

Kealin walked along the rails, looking into the waters. Two massive ropes went out from the decks and followed around two large cogs. He guessed the anchors were below. Tulasiro broke the water, and as he stared into the waves, other narwhals appeared, their horns gleaming in the starlight.

What is it?

The narwhals all threw themselves forward, diving down into the depths. Taslun and Calak came beside Kealin.

"What do the narwhals want with us?" Calak asked.

"Tulasiro," said Kealin.

"Who?"

"One of the narwhals. Its name is Tulasiro. It was the one who destroyed the boat, trapping the dwarves. I do not know what it and its brethren do, but—"

The ship began to lurch with the waves, and a moment later, the narwhals had appeared just below the surface. The ship began to move forward into the sea. The ropes hanging off the sides slipped forward, splintering the rails, and the elves steadied their feet as the ship dropped downward and then leveled out, a burst of frigid water coming over the rails of the vessel. Kealin went to the front of the ship.

The two lines that had been tied to the anchors now were straight out, and the flippers of the narwhals flapped as the ship was pulled forward.

"They must know," said Kealin. "Tulasiro spoke to me before; I believe they know where Vals and Alri are."

"As strange as your words are, we must hope that they do," Taslun stated.

It was some time they traveled before Taslun came to Kealin. Calak was eating a strange fruit he had found in storage, and Taslun had brought Kealin bread to share with him.

"You must keep your strength up, little brother."

Kealin glanced down at him and then back to the sea ahead, his eyes scanning the horizon for signs of Alri and Vals. "I do not need that," he told him.

Taslun stood, eating his own bread, but it was more than a snack he wanted with Kealin. "That dwarf, back on the shore, I wanted to talk to you about your actions."

Kealin glared at him. "Our sister has been taken. I will not let some scheming dwarf dishonor us in such a way by withholding what he knows."

"I know you do not have the respect for our people as I think you should, but you must embrace good conscience."

"My conscience is well, Brother. I know why I do what I do. I will strike someone from behind if it means saving any of you. Besides, he got what he deserved from Calak."

Taslun sighed. "Our brother is on the fence, and he could be as his people or resist like his brother."

"Then I hope you keep him near you, Taslun, for I would hate for him to also feel your judgment."

He went silent, but Kealin continued. "I may have resisted the ways of the Blades, but I listened to the Blade Master, learned what I could, and have increased my skills so that you may see that, if nothing else is true, I am worthy to stand beside you. I am not of pure elven blood; our people made sure to tell me that from a young age. I was not given pardon as you were."

"Brother, I only pray we use wisdom in all of our decisions."

"I do," he replied. "The wisdom imparted to me by our teacher."

The polar lights were above them, a greenish ribbon across the sky, turning red and purple as swift winds blew the clouds, showing the moon once again. The speed of the narwhals was magnificent, and Kealin was sure they were moving faster than they had aboard the *Aela Sunrise*, except, of course, when they had floated for a time above the sea itself. Alri was counting on them. Vals was counting on them. They could not fail. That Kealin knew for certain.

11

THE COLD MASTER

ALRI DID NOT SLEEP. She did not move. She could stop staring at the body upon the table and for the longest time she simply watched blood drip from one of his flaccid arms, creating a pool and small river beneath the body. She clutched her archon stone, hidden in such a simple necklace, the dwarves didn't remove it when they had checked her for weapons.

But her greatest tool, her staff, was gone. Unlike her brothers, the teachings of Master Oaur at Nidea Archon didn't cover much that didn't involve a staff and magic. A weakness in her training.

She heard his voice even now. *An archon must never be captured. Our knowledge is sacred and it would be better for our lives to be forfeit than to have it fall into the hands of our enemies.*

She sighed, *This is it? Am I just to die.*

The thought of such an act was not one she feared but it seemed so futile, so weak. These dwarves may have captured her but what could they do with her knowledge?

She rubbed her archon stone, her lifeline.

One spell. A blast of fire could break this lock. I could get out. But then… to where?

Being on a ship in the middle of the Glacial Seas made escape a very difficult goal. She didn't even know where Vals was at this point. Was there another holding area? Was he dead?

The clamor of screaming filled the hold as her answer became evident.

The Cold Master's laugh echoed through the room.

Several dwarves cleared off the table where the Cold Master's previous victim had been resting. His body fell onto the ground before the dwarves kicked it out of the way.

Then, Vals flew into the room, striking the table and rolling off the other side.

"Pick him up, pick him up!" The Cold Master shouted.

Vals was alive. His face was swollen and he had cuts and scrapes all over his body. His coat was ripped and tattered, his tunic, also torn. As he lay in the blood of the previous victim, his eyes didn't stare at Alri at first.

"Bring him to the table," The Cold Master ordered.

Vals sighed, trying to push himself up. It was then, he caught sight of Alri.

"No." He said.

As the dwarves grabbed him, the Captain drew a small knife from his boot and stuck one of them in the neck.

The dwarf gasped, falling backwards as Vals pulled himself up to the other dwarf, jabbing him in the soft spot of his upper leg. The second dwarf screamed.

Vals went for Alri when the Cold Master snapped his hand with a before unseen whip. Vals dropped his knife. He turned as the whip struck him across the face. He fell to the ground.

As the one dwarf lay dead and the second one began to convulse, the Cold Master growled.

"Stupid dwarves, can't even properly check a sea rat for knives."

He picked Vals up by his hair, throwing him onto the table.

Vals tried to sit up when the Cold Master slammed his right knee with his clawed arm. It cracked and Vals screamed.

"Think about trying something else," The Cold Master told him. "First, you disrespect our captain by trying to stick him with a spear head and then you hid another knife in your boot and stuck poor Bydon in the throat? Do you know how far me and that dwarf go back?"

The Cold Master looked over to Alri and then began to laugh.

"Not far at all. I hate these bastards! Stick a few more!" He backed away from Vals, "Well, get up! Get to your sticking, sea rat! Oh," he covered his face with his hand, "You seemed to have injured your knee!"

He slammed his claw on to Vals' shattered knee.

"Damn, I can't seem to fix it!"

Vals screamed again.

Two more dwarves came in, stopping just short of the table as they saw the bodies of the two dead dwarves on the ground.

"He had another knife. You worthless frogs can't even search a man. How in the dead gods do you even reproduce with your own kind if you can't even find a damn dagger!"

The two dwarves stood there, motionless.

"Get over here and tie this man down! We need to know what he knows!"

The two dwarves hurried to the Cold Master's side, tying Vals down. Alri watched helplessly from the cell. The knife Vals had snuck in lay just outside her cell but it was outside her reach.

"Now, Rugag only wanted to know where the others are. Not the elves, as you keep playing stupid about your crew! Where is the shadow elf? Where is the Dwemhar woman?!"

"I told you…" Vals grimaced, "They are dead."

"They aren't dead!" The Cold Master shouted, "We saw you not one moon ago, we saw the elf, the woman, and even the little white sea serpent! They weren't dead."

Vals spit, looking back behind him as he tried to move his arms.

"I could say the same about old Bydon but he's dead now."

"Get out! Get out!" The Cold Master shouted,

sending the two dwarven assistants scurrying away like two starved mice. He placed Vals' head in the grip of his crab-like hand, squeezing it.

"I tire of asking the same question. I know very well the deeds of Valrin of Travaa and his cursed crew! No mere prisoner with a knife could have landed a hit on any of your crew. You forget, Rugag was present at the time of the great calamity. He is one of the few who know the truth of what transpired in the Glacial Seas, yet, you will lay here bleeding and deny that the rest of your crew even lives? What, did they choke on a fish bone!?"

Vals gasped. The Cold Master squeezed his throat, using his other hand, he grasped a small hammer and struck him in the upper leg.

Vals tried to scream but simply shook uncontrollably, his voice muffled by the lack of air he could draw in while being choked.

Alri could hear Vals trying to speak.

"Oka- Oka-" Vals coughed, "Okay."

The Cold Master released his grip.

"Then tell me where. Tell me the place. Perhaps, he will let you live, let you all rot in a cold dungeon for if you do not, I will much enjoy slicing up every single piece of you."

"They-" Vals coughed again. "The shadow elf-"

"Yes! Speak it!"

"A man, he was in my crew. He had a way with language. Not the shadow elf. Another." Vals gasped, "He would have wanted me to tell you this. The shadow elf, he's at your home. Given your hand, it might not be a pleasant thought, but— the shadow elf — he is with your fucking mother!"

The Cold Master screamed, ripping Vals from the loose binds that held him and throwing him across the room.

He charged towards Alri, unlocking the gate and grabbing her by her hair.

She tried to cast a spell with her archon stone but he threw her across the room. She slammed into the opposite wall. Pain shot through her back and side as she tried to push herself up. The Cold Master forced a cold metal device on her neck.

A sickness plunged into Alri's stomach as she felt him tighten the device to her. She couldn't tell what it was but she tried to stay on her feet as the Cold Master swept her towards Vals who was just sitting up against the wall on the opposite side.

"You seem to favor this elf? Do you know this device?"

Vals shook his head.

"One pull of this chain, and she loses her head. This lovely blade will slice right through the beautiful skin and delicate vessels of this young flower." He still held Alri with his clawed hand around her arm. The device dug into her neck. She glanced down and could see a single, angled blade with some type of trigger mechanism that was connected to a chain that the Cold Master held in his other hand.

"We do not need this one to find the others. Elves are trash, not worthy of the chow to keep them alive. I've already been ordered to kill her but not before I have a bit of fun. I get to remove her organs while she is alive. I've been working on some potions to prolong her life… perhaps you'd like to make it fast, just tell me, allow her to die? Torture her slowly?"

"No."

"No?" he questioned back, "Then tell me where they are. It is a simple question. A simple answer."

Vals slipped his good leg forward, standing up as he grimaced, shaking as he steadied himself against the wall.

"They are all dead. Just as me, just as those that came before me. I cannot live beyond this night. Do you not see the affliction upon my chest? No deal, no chance for any of us. But let her go."

"You are right, no chance."

Alri felt the shift in the Cold Master's stance. She tried to reach for her archon stone but in one motion, the Cold Master pulled at the chain.

Vals was upon her before she could even gasp. His eyes widened, as warm blood began to pool around Alri's neck.

Vals stared at her, letting out a blood curdling scream. Alri glanced down as best she could, the blade was dug into the Captain's bones. He stared directly at her, weeping as The Cold Master shoved them both away from him.

"You can't even let her die peacefully!"

The Cold Master kicked both of them in the legs and stormed out of the room.

They lay there, Vals arms locked at her neck, warm

blood still pouring out of his wounds as he began to breathe faster.

The two dwarves from before returned, removing the device on her neck and dragging them both into the cell.

"Get up here, now!" The Cold Master screamed.

"He is pissed," one of the dwarves said to the other.

They slammed the cell door close, tripping over one another to try to hurry to their summoning.

Alri felt her own neck, the ache from the device was small compared to the gaping wounds on Val's arms.

She tore at her own clothing, making tourniquets. She tied both of them on his upper arms and slowed the bleeding. She grasped her archon stone, preparing an incantation in her mind.

"What— are- you— doing?" he asked, taking many breaths between each word.

"I can heal you, I can fix this."

Vals shook his head, "Survive, escape this. My body is broken and you cannot heal my greater affliction. Meredaas will not fail to hear my prayer, The Sea God will bring his followers. Your brothers- they will come. I feel it."

"No one is here, Vals. No one can find us."

He smiled, "You know little of the sea, elf. But I can hear them. I hear their songs. The whales, -narwhals. They are coming. You, you have to act."

Alri looked around the cell. She then saw the knife

Vals had used just outside the cell door. Then, by some bit of fate, she realized the cell door was not locked.

"Vals, we can both get out of here."

"I wonder if she remembers?"

Alri wasn't sure what he was talking about.

"She?"

"She. My love. Aeveam used to tell me she could sometimes hear her voice."

Alri had no idea what Vals was talking about. He had said the name Aeveam before but it seemed he was talking about someone else.

"I can feel her, she is close," Vals said. "She comes to take me."

Vals was pale, he was not breathing as fast as before but his eyes were no longer looking around as before. He simply stared ahead.

Alri felt the ship lurch to one side and the sound of the anchors falling from the sides. They had stopped.

She began looking around, trying to sort out what she should do.

I wonder if we are at some port?

If that was true, then she could maybe actually escape. But she couldn't just leave Vals. They needed something. She needed her brothers… but they weren't here and Vals was obviously hallucinating now.

She grasped her archon stone and then looked out of the cell again.

She could get help. But not in a way that an archon would. No, not at all. She looked to the body of the one she had witnessed die when she was first placed in this cell and for the first time in her life, she knew exactly what she would do. It had to work.

As Vals lay barely breathing, she set within the cell with her legs crossed, clutching her stone. This would take her a while but she was confident she could do it.

She closed her eyes, feeling the wood of the ship around her and seeing the life forces of mice scurry about. She could feel life beyond this room and for a moment, saw a glimpse of the outside. It didn't seem like they were in a port but she regained focus, seeing the dead but still warm body kicked cruelly into the corner of the room. She saw the fire deep within, the life force she sought to increase with the flows of necromantic magic building within her.

This was not an elven power, this was something of her other lineage, that lineage which even now in the darkness she found herself in she knew was not just some simple race of the lowly blood of men. But at this moment, her focus became clear, she would awaken the one that had fallen and he would aid them.

"What are you doing?" a voice said, shattering her concentration.

She opened her eyes not in fear but in power, the wisps of purple energy still flowing just above her face as the cross Cold Master stared at her.

"You are an evil one. You have been like that for some time. What curse do you try? What darkness dwells within you? You are a wretch of an elf, weak, broken. I will not taint my tools with your blood. I will sell you to the market, make some gold off your flesh!"

The winds shifted in the room and a cold screech

echoed around them. The cold master turned as Alri's necromantic creation jumped upon him.

She pushed herself to her feet, watching as the summoning bit into the Cold Master's neck and head. He fell backwards, over his treacherous table and began screaming louder and louder. Alri pushed open the cell door, brandishing the knife as the Cold Master snapped his claw. He cracked into the summoned undead just as Alri leaped upon him, thrusting the knife into his throat, over and over.

He screamed, blood gurgling in his open neck wounds as Alri then plunged the knife into his eyes before turning to see a boot just before it struck her in the face.

"Stupid elf," Rugag shouted.

She pushed herself away, trying to back away from the pirate captain. She managed to put her back against the cell door before he moved towards her.

The Cold Master was dead. Her undead summoning was dead.

But Rugag remained calm. He walked around Alri, holding another neck blade just like the one that was on her own neck before.

"Valrin nears death," he said, looking into the cell. "I will not bloody my own blade with his cursed blood." He pulled Vals up. The captain moaned as he put the blade on to his neck.

"He suffers from more than what we did to him. A pity. I would have liked him to suffer more by my own hand."

Alri gripped the bars of the cell, pushing herself up as several other dwarves came from above deck.

"I am not a monster, elf. I only sought revenge. This man has terrorized my kind, destroyed our home, even. You have no idea."

"You just want his crew," Alri said, "But he told us even before you captured us, they are dead! Just let us go, let him die at peace. Put us on any island or port you choose. I have no debt to you like he did and he draws near death."

Rugag smiled, grabbing Alri by the arm. "You think your kind has no debt against dwarves? You think I will just let you go? Elves are a scourge. Every elf I have ever met has been nothing to me but unyielding terror."

Rugag struck her in the chest with his fist.

She gasped, trying to catch her breath as her face struck the floor. She felt his boot upon the center of her back.

"You will suffer, elf. Be sure of that. There will be no swift death for you."

"Captain!" a voice shouted, "Captain! To deck! Our brothers join us with their quarry!"

12

SILENCING

In the distance, they could see blots on the horizon. At first, it looked to be more glaciers. A bit ago, they passed four large ones that had caused Kealin's attention to perk and then fall.

This was different. Four small glints of light were visible, and it seemed, at least from afar, they were the ships that they were looking for.

Kealin looked down into the water as one of the narwhals broke off from those towing and made eye contact with him.

He nodded after hearing its message, and looked to his brothers.

"The ships are ahead. Dey will lead us in. We are expecting other creatures to help. Vals is liked among those of the sea."

Kealin noticed his speech had changed for a moment, but thought nothing further of it. His blades were ready.

For the sake of those bastard sea-dwelling burrowers, Alri better be untouched.

Taslun and Calak stood beside him as the broken dwarven vessel gained upon the ships. The fact that it was a dwarven vessel worked to their advantage, for the large catapults on the four ships remained unlit and undrawn even as they ran along the stern of the ship on the far east side of the column.

As they looked along the enemy ship, they ducked down, hiding behind the wreckage of the railings as other dwarves began to look on. Two ships over, there appeared to be a ship of grander design. It had bright green railings. It was the flagship of Rugag. The lost vessel of their fleet arriving, even with burned sails, was a very peculiar occurrence.

"We go together. Clear the decks one by one," said Taslun.

"Agreed," Kealin said. "If you spot Alri or Vals, stay with them. If we see Rugag, kill him. We move ship to ship all the way to the flagship."

Taslun looked at Kealin but said nothing of killing Rugag. "Together, Brothers."

The ships were next to each other, and it was clear the narwhals had left the ropes. Those aboard the dwarven vessel shouted to one another, talking of the burned sails and the lack of a crew. The elven brothers knelt with their blades. As dwarves began to board the ship, Kealin led the attack, jumping from one ship to the next.

He landed with little more than a thud. His eyes scanned the deck, and he squinted, looking for either his sister or Vals. His brothers landed next to him, and it was then the dwarves of the ship noticed they had been boarded.

Calak and Taslun went right, sliding into a stance with swords behind them. The dwarves charged them; one had a net, while another two had spears, and the remainder, coming from a galley at the aft of the ship, came with what weapons they could find. They were cut down one after another.

Kealin worked the opposite way, cutting down two dwarves near the deck-mounted crossbow. Shouts filled the air from the other ships as dwarves laid down planks to cross from one ship to the next. Kealin leaped onto the nearest one, slashing each dwarf who came between him and wherever it was Alri and Vals were. One by one, taking down the dwarves and spraying blood across the ice-encrusted deck, he began to feel frustrated. This ship, too, was lacking whom he searched for.

Calak and Taslun turned the wheel of the furthest ship, and it crushed into the one next to it, starting a chain reaction of colliding and splintered wood. They joined Kealin on the second vessel they had taken.

"Wake, Rugag!" someone shouted.

Kealin looked, spotting a trio of men running from the third ship, which he guessed was, in fact, the flag ship, into a locked room adorned with the jaws of sharks.

The dwarf at the helm turned the third ship away from the second ship as the fourth ship on the outside moved to protect it; its crossbow was readied and aimed at the second ship that the brothers had now managed to clear of breathing dwarves.

The crossbow fired. Its bolt tore across the deck. Its tail slapped just over Kealin, close enough for him to hear the buzz of its chain across his ears.

The fourth ship was moving along the front of the second ship, now even further from the green-railed flagship of the dwarves that tried to move away from them.

From the depths of the sea, an explosion of ice and water came as Tulasiro broke the surface with its brethren, the pod of narwhals smashing into the side of the crossbow-firing ship. Tulasiro crushed the mechanisms of the crossbow, rolling off the side and back into the depths.

All across the ship, more narwhals struck the dwarves. The wooden deck splintered with their weight, and the dwarves fought back, sticking more than just one of the large white whales with spears and hacking at them with axes. The fourth dwarven vessel was destroyed.

The flagship of Rugag now moved alongside of them. Without their other ships, they would have to fight. The dwarves were much more prepared and now they were garbed in armor.

Taslun went to the crossbow and fired into the center mast of the ship. With a crack, the bolt slapped across the deck and took down many of the dwarves. Rugag appeared and shouted, climbing to the helm of his ship and twisting a crystal of similar design as the one on the *Aela Sunrise.*

The air began to sizzle, and a stream of fire shot across the bow of the ship from the flagship, catching the other two vessels on fire.

The dwarves boarded the ship, and the slicing and clanging of metals filled the air as the dwarves proved better opponents now that the surprise of the attack had worn off.

Kealin spun his blades, facing now two dwarves who pointed at him and proudly charged Their mistake. He parried each of their rusty spears down, thrusting back up with the edges of his blades and slashing through the vessels of their necks as he continued forward.

The ship under attack by narwhals had been reduced to a sinking mess, its occupants, both drowning in the frigid waters and being skewered by the horns of the narwhals, wailed into the night sky. Other creatures had come now, too, and enacted a long-awaited revenge on their hunters. The ocean was angry, and the waters were very much alive.

The dwarves were losing their hold on the elves, and Rugag knew it. He disappeared into a hidden recess under the helm with two of his dwarves, and returned dragging Alri and Vals.

Kealin shouted to alert his brothers. "Alri!"

Taslun and Calak looked, suddenly feeling a renewed vigor for battle.

Like some type of sudden blessing for Rugag, more

dwarves swarmed the deck of the flagship and crossed over to attack the elves.

Each elf had at least four assailants at any moment, and as one would fall from the glowing red blade of an elf, another would take its place. The deck of the ship had become a slippery mess of bloody ice and sea foam.

Calak had broken through his attackers and leaped to the flagship; Rugag pushed the two dwarves near him, and he was engaged. The younger brother worked to slice his way to his sister. Alri was awake and could see what was happening. She looked to Rugag, and though she had been beaten more than once, she could see through her swollen eye enough to make out his knee. She kicked him, and a crack followed, the dwarf grasping at his leg.

She scurried up, weak but on her feet. Taslun and Kealin defeated the last of their attackers and made it to the ship. Calak cut down the remaining two dwarves and approached Rugag.

Taslun and Kealin went to Alri.

"You came. You didn't leave me."

"We would never, Alri," Taslun said.

"She is not who you should worry of now," Rugag announced.

Rugag forced Vals to his knees. A circular collar of some design was now on his neck, and the dwarf held a tight grip on the chain that would trigger the device. That said, the dwarf was trembling. Kealin looked it up and down and did not know what device he held. His eyes met Vals', whose own gaze was not even upon any of them standing upon the ship. The Captain seemed barely conscious.

"There," Rugag said. "Quietness. I am under no belief that I will survive this. I wished to have the *Aela Sunrise,* but it is out of reach due to this man's devices. I, at least, had him, and a nice elf for a bonus, but I did not know the sea would react as such. These beasts, good for oil and bones, not to mention the narwhals and their lovely horns, a good profit, but that is no more. My ships are sinking, and even now, what I had built is burning."

The fires of broken oil lanterns had engulfed the dwarven vessels. Flames had begun to catch even the flagship and were beyond extinguishing.

"But he will die first."

Kealin noticed Rugag about to jerk the chain of the neck blade. He lunged forward, bringing both of his blades beside Vals' neck and just blocking the blade of the device from closing down on his soft flesh. Taslun slashed Rugag across his chest, dropping the dwarf on to the deck of the ship then jumping to grab the device on Vals' neck, dropping his sword as he did.

"Get it off! Get it off him!" Kealin shouted.

He was holding the neck blade from closing down on Val's neck, grimacing as he forced the mouth of the device open, keeping it from clamping down.

"Calak! The other side!" Taslun said.

Vals fell to his knees, he was bleeding from both of his butchered arms. His skin was paler than Kealin had ever seen on a living person and black scales covered most of his face.

Calak had managed to break off one of the levers on the jaws.

"That one!" he said, as Taslun did the same on the opposite side.

Kealin kept his ruinite blades steady, the fire from them burning Vals' face on either side but as his brothers broke the device further, he pulled the device apart with a loud crack.

Vals collapsed.

Kealin and Alri both cradled him. Blood still trickled from his arms. He stared out at the sky.

"Bandages." Calak said.

Alri tightened the tourniquets on his arms.

"What did that bastard do to him!" Kealin shouted.

"The neck blade, I had one. Vals used his own arms to protect me."

Taslun knelt down beside them.

"You saved my sister, Captain. I must do what I can to save you." He looked around, "Calak! We need to find a smaller boat. Check the other side, something. This ship is sinking."

As Taslun and Calak began frantically sorting out their escape, Kealin continued to hold Vals.

"I was already saved," he whispered.

The fire crackled from the burning ship as seawater began to overtake it.

"Take care of them." Vals said, "They wait for—" he paused, looking at Kealin. "They may not understand."

"Who?"

Vals smiled, his body becoming looser, as he laid back against Kealin's chest.

"I see her," he said at last. He glanced over to Alri, "She was waiting for me. She is here."

With that, the Captain of the *Aela Sunrise* took his final breath.

RUGAG LAUGHED, "Not soon enough. I have defeated him after so many years. I have broken him and it is too bad I didn't get the rest of them."

Kealin and Alri both scowled at Rugag. Taslun's blade had split open his chest and part of his neck. Blood ran down his body as he struggled to breathe.

The dwarf looked out at the sea, seeing the many narwhals around them. His armor was broken, his chest split open by Taslun's blade but the dwarf still lived.

Kealin took one of his blades in hand as Alri still held Vals

"And now I die," Rugag said, "but not before I say this: your world, my world, will end. Darkness approaches the Glacial Seas. All you four do is for nothing but to prolong suffering in your own hearts. Even your path now takes you closer. This was all meant to happen like this. Valrin was just a step. I am happy to know your ends come. May you sickening elves go the same way as Valrin, but much slower and more horrendously."

Kealin grabbed Rugag by the neck, feeling the dwarf's pulse quicken as he held him by the throat. He squeezed him, feeling the cartilage crack and his vital vessels squirm in the half-elf's hand. Rugag choked, slapping at Kealin's hand.

"You're not worthy of the death you meant for my sister and for the Captain."

He stuck his blade in Rugag's stomach, twisting it, and slowly pulling it back out. The dwarf quivered and then gasped. It was the most satisfying but yet most empty kill he had felt. He pushed the dwarf away, sending him falling backwards. Vals was dead, and there was nothing that could be done for him. But his killer lay dead beside him.

Taslun looked at him, but he had no protest to this killing.

"What did he mean?" asked Calak. "What darkness? How does he know of our intents or fate?"

"Put it from mind, Brother," Kealin said, "as you told me before. As it stands, we still go to serve Dimn."

"Hurry, Brothers. We are still not safe," Taslun said.

The ship was sinking around them, and there was not a nearby boat seaworthy enough to hold them.

Kealin looked to the waters where Tulasiro had been. As the sea rippled with the ships burning and cracking into the icy water, the elves ran to the highest point of the ship not engulfed by flames.

"What do we do?" asked Calak.

The narwhal pod came around the edge of the sinking ship and slowed. Kealin saw that Tulasiro was closest.

Do you wish me upon you, Tulasiro?

He heard the sound of the narwhal's song, and he smiled, leaping from the wrecked ship to the body of the narwhal. He caught hold around the form of its head. Its skin felt strange against his, and though he was not in the water completely, he was very cold. The others followed suit, jumping onto the narwhals as the ship began to disappear into the void of the ocean.

"I cannot believe what has happened," Alri said. "All of this, I don't know what we are to do."

Taslun looked back at the ship. "Have faith, Sister. Be happy we were able to save you."

Kealin looked back to see each of his siblings. He felt a strange hate for what had transpired, but at the same time, he was thankful. A stirring was within him. Vals had wished him to take care of the narwhals. For once, he felt purposed to do something beyond himself, but he did not know what to make of it. Vals was a good man, and in that, he found respect, a feeling he did not have for many. He thought of Rugag's words, as well, unsure of what to believe of them.

The pod of narwhals made their way away from the wreckage with a careful pace. It was difficult for them to keep the elves above the surface of the water while also propelling themselves forward.

Kealin did not know where they were being taken, only that his hands were aching from the cold water. He did not know how long he himself could hang on, much less Alri, who was not in great health to begin with.

He looked up at the sky. He could just see the constellation of a sea snail, but he had not been watching the time as of late. Tiredness filled his body, or was it the numbness in his fingertips spreading to his arm and causing it to be painful to take any amount of breath into his chest?

Vision clouding, he made out the polar lights bright above him. The water seemed to be moving faster, pushing them along. A strange current.

Meredaas. Master, Tulasiro said to him.

Your master, I thank him. We all do.

Tulasiro moved more quickly and broke through ice. Kealin pulled his arms up as much as he could muster to prevent the ice from scratching him. He turned to glance behind, and it seemed that Alri had fallen asleep. At least, he hoped it was that. Her condition of the wights was a mystery to him, and her true health was unknown.

He looked up to see the shore ahead. It was a cliff-faced island, and the beach itself was inside a rocky grotto lit with glowing flowers. It reminded him of some of the groves near Lake Eldmer back in the Urlas Woodlands, but it had been some time since he was able to look upon them himself.

The yellow, orange, and red flowers sparkling upward were dotted with fairies fluttering from bloom to bloom.

He felt himself rolled onto the shore, and then the thuds as his siblings were placed the same way by the narwhals. As the pod of narwhals left, the fairies floated over them, and he felt himself growing more tired and falling to sleep.

He looked around, seeing still the polar lights but

then rocks and a blackness to their left. It was a cave. Within the dark, he saw two blue eyes looking back at him. He wished to sit up but could not. He fell asleep, unable to stay awake any longer, but very much not alone.

13

ICE DRAKE

Kealin opened his eyes. The sky was unchanged to his just wakening self. The winds were calm, and though he was very cold, his body felt restored. Aches from the past few days had been healed.

He sat up, seeing that Calak was up and walking around their stony surroundings. Taslun was some distance away, walking near the edge of the water, standing ankle-deep on a pebble beach. Alri, too, had just awoken. Taslun noticed her first and went to her.

"Alri, how do you feel?"

She smiled. "Better. Though I still feel the sickness within me, I feel as if I have been healed to some degree."

The fairies from before flew high above them. Kealin could see better now that they were in a large cave. He looked to his left and the darkness. He remembered the eyes from before but looked around, finding no sight of them.

"Kealin!" said Calak. "We are in some cavern, but we cannot find a way out. It seems we must wait for the narwhals. That is, if they come back. Did they say anything to you?"

Taslun turned to look at him also. It seemed the general belief was that he might know something, given his gift.

"I do not know. I just barely remember being placed here."

"Well, we took the time to search, and there is no way we can find. We had thought to climb out near the entrance and make our way up, but the stones are too slippery and we have nothing that will give us grip."

Kealin stood and walked toward the darkness of the back of the cave.

"We checked as far as we could. It is no good," Taslun told him.

What his brother had said was true. The edge of the cave dropped into a blackness with no discernible end that he could make out. For a time, they appeared trapped.

Kealin went back to Alri, who was still sitting on the ground.

He came behind her and embraced her, holding her tightly in his arms.

"I was worried, for a moment, that you had been lost."

"I, too, had worried of that. I had never been as happy to have heard a shouting clamor as I did as you three attacked the distant ship. Even from my cell, I knew it was you. I knew you would come for us, though Vals—he tried so hard. He wasn't just some sailing man. They overwhelmed us at the *Aela Sunrise.*"

Taslun and Calak, looking up and down the edge of a tidal pool in the cave, looked up as she began to speak.

"What did actually happen?" Kealin asked.

"It was sometime after you three left. At first, it was fine. He talked about his old crew. He made coffee and then… and then he saw them. He was like nothing I had ever seen. The ship suddenly changed before my eyes, it had what looked like tiny crystals all along the railings. He took down so many of the ships before we were overwhelmed. He then took the fight to them," she paused, "I don't know how many he struck down. They tried to take me and he tried to seal me in. But they got to me. They then tortured him. They threatened to kill me and he stopped them. I don't know if his crew is truly dead. The way Rugag talked, the way he seemed to all but say they weren't. But, he protected me. Vals seemed to welcome death."

Kealin looked over to his brothers. Though they were listening, whatever they had seen in the tidal pool had led them further. It was clear they had found something. Taslun drew his sword and attempted to chip off pieces of the wall.

"I wasn't strong enough," Alri continued, " Rugag was angry. Angry for no reason I could understand. He hated Vals." she wept. "I don't know anything else. I knew the world outside of Urlas was bad, but I didn't realize it was like this. It is even worse that I lost my staff. I am powerless."

Kealin kissed her forehead. "Do not worry of it, Sister. Vals was a good man, he died protecting you, protecting us… I only wish I had been there sooner. Perhaps, he would still be alive."

Kealin remained strong for his sister but within, he felt a deep grief for the man he had only just met. He felt a connection to Vals not too unlike the feeling he had felt when meditating. Even still, since they had left Urlas, he felt a stirring within him almost as if a suppressed energy had returned to him and was just outside his grasp. Vals seemed to be a part of that and his loss stirred a greater sadness deep within him.

"I think I have found something," Calak said.

Kealin looked over, standing up as his brother pointed.

"This is no cave. I do not know what it was for sure, but these writings are like those in the cave Vals had showed us. There is brickwork beneath the rock here."

"I wish that it helped us in some way," Taslun said. "This cave may be no more than the one before. If it is a ruin, the rocks are no help to us in finding our way out."

They spent a considerable amount of time exploring the cave or ruin, depending on which brother was asked and at which particular point of debate they came to. Alri too helped. Though thankful to the narwhals to have been brought here, they believed they were abandoned.

There were no supplies, no sources of food except for the sea, which was almost pointless given there were no tools for fishing. Kealin at last resolved to stare into the blackness of the cave. He had seen something there the night they arrived. In time, he sat down, convinced that what he saw would return. The narwhals had picked this place for a reason.

It was many hours later when his siblings had gone to sleep, cold and hungry. He stared into the blackness. There was something more. He had heard a scratching sound below him, and now it was only a matter of waiting.

Kealin drew his blade and looked down further into the depths. The red glow of his sword permeated the shadows. It was then the cave quaked and he heard sliding in the ice. From below, what appeared to be two burning sapphires shined toward him.

"Elves of Urlas Woodlands, I had heard you were upon the Glacial Seas. The narwhals are holy beasts, and they brought you to my domain. Why?"

Kealin looked back to his siblings and noticed no one had awoken. "Come up to me," he said downward. "Let me know to whom I, Kealin, speak."

There was silence for a moment that was split by sudden scratching and a rush of cold air blew over Kealin. The others behind were stirred awake. Kealin looked on as, from the depths, a massive face appeared. Its eyes burned with blue fire, their light shining down a scaly snout, and an icy breath blew over Kealin as a mouth full of teeth opened.

"Seen enough of me, elf? They do not have

dragons in your woods, I suppose, which is not a surprise to me. This is my home you have intruded."

Now surrounded by his siblings, Kealin sheathed his sword. "We seek to go to Dimn, but the dwarf known as Rugag caused us to be taken well off course. We had been upon the *Aela Sunrise* with Valrin, but his ship is of no use to us now, and he has fallen."

"I do see, but why would the narwhals bring you here? I suppose my fairies healed your wounds?"

"Yes," said Alri. "We are thankful."

"A thankful elf, that is something hard to find. One of you speaks from within."

"What?"

"One of you can speak from the mind. I sense it. Who is it?"

Kealin closed his eyes. *Me.*

"I had thought it you. I watched you four this day; you seemed to have uncovered a secret within this old harbor, but you could not find the way out."

"There is just stone. There is no way that could be found. Or I assure you," Taslun said, pushing past Kealin, "we would have found it."

The dragon moved his head in close to them and snapped his teeth toward Taslun. "Your brother is whom I respect. You are an elf, pure as can be, by your assurance of what you do not know. Do you not know that we dragons have less than the lowest amount of respect for you elves? Do not speak with me as an inferior or even an equal. I speak to him, for I care much for him and the division he has begun in these seas.

"The one seeking death has been given it by

Vankou. The Lord of Death is gaining power again, and yet you tell me you go to Dimn when it is clear you are in service to Vankou?"

"We are in no such service," said Kealin.

"But yet you defeated the demon on the lonely isle?"

"We did that for the shells of Meredaas."

The dragon turned his eye to them and blinked.

"Go toward the corner of the cave. I shall reveal to you what you missed, but do not feel bad. It is by my will alone you can leave. Otherwise, you would've become my snack."

The dragon dropped into the darkness, and a gust of wind and a splash followed.

Taslun turned to Kealin when the water further out at sea exploded, the dragon emerging some distance off and taking to the sky.

They ran toward the edge of the cave and looked up as the massive creature landed some place above them. There were scratches and rumblings above, and then, in a distant corner, the sky became visible as the quaking dropped rocks rolling all around them.

"Come on," said Taslun.

The four of them proceeded toward the opening and emerged on a large icy platform. The ice drake was on all fours, looming above them. Taller than many masts of the ships they had been on and capable of eating each of them at once with less than a single bite from its jaws, it lowered itself down on the ground, looking over each of them.

The rest of the island was built around a large

central mountain. Though icy and dark, the mountain smoked and a red glow pierced the night sky like a lone beacon on the sea.

Nestled in its shadow were what appeared buildings, but rock covered most parts of them. Even the platform they were standing on had markings and signs of craftsmanship. Kealin noticed large harbors overrun with rubble of rocks that had come down from the mountain and went into the water.

"You four elves are the first in some time to be upon this ground. A seafaring race was destroyed many millennia ago here. Their legacy is now covered in stone. I have been here for some time, protecting it from eyes needing to see it. There is much to be found here to the right person, but that may not be why you are here? You seek Dimn. Why are you drawn to him?"

"He is in danger," Taslun said. "A darkness approaches his holy place."

"And you have seen this?" the dragon said. "Be wary of vision, for it can be clouded with simple words spoken beneath the breath."

"Not us," said Kealin. "Our shaman within the Urlas Woodlands. There was darkness already upon the gods of the North. Our parents went to assist them, but we, too, sought the shaman, learning of this darkness upon Dimn."

"If your parents needed your assistance, why did they not take you?"

"We are too young," said Calak.

"Young? Do you speak to a dragon like myself of

age? Age does not matter in the way the world spins. Perhaps you are not ready for such a task, but then, you have traveled far and became sick." The dragon looked to Alri. "The wights of Vankou's isle have infected you."

"They had," Alri stated, "but I feel better after the sleep I had here."

"A temporary healing. Though, I know a way to relieve your symptoms. It must be why the narwhals brought you here, as opposed to an inhabited isle. It is all making sense to this old dragon.

"But I still do not see why I should help those such as yourselves. Dimn is not one to waste time with rumors, but I will say I have spoken to him of late, and he is worried much of his brothers further south and rumors of dealings in those lands. Perhaps he, in his wisdom, has become careless. The Heart of the Winds may be at risk, and if that is so, we have greater worry than Dimn himself."

Taslun stepped forward. "That is why we are here. We are to assist Dimn and protect our people."

"But you know not what approaches. How will you help when you do not know how?"

"It doesn't matter," said Kealin. "We go to his assistance, no matter what he faces."

"And you, Kealin, you are most susceptible to lies. Your mind has power beyond simplicity of sword. You hold not your own creed as a Blade, yet you seek a holy one to protect. Guard your own mind, for you have released the one to death that was forbidden it. There is something else at work beyond what you know. But of that, I will watch for myself. Yes, Dimn is in danger. I am master of the skies of the Glacial Seas, and those of the Itsu do approach Dimn.

"Know, that I cannot harm them. Their ethereal bodies are not affected by dragon ice, and I do not care of the affairs of gods, only that of the world itself. Your blades are elven; your bodies carry the lifeblood of the earth. Be happy by my words that you can harm them."

"Is Dimn not a god?" asked Calak. "Can he not destroy them?"

"That is blasphemy in the eyes of a god, dear elf, but yes, he can. Only, he will not be able to stop them all. There is more. A being is within these Itsu. I cannot see it beyond a growing dark magic, but you four may be able to learn more. I do not know."

"We need a way to the place of the maelstroms," said Taslun. "We thank you for your assistance, but we must get to Dimn."

"I can provide a way, and I will do so. But it is your sister who needs assistance first. Go into the place beneath the mountain. Retrieve an amulet kept upon the altar in the center chamber. It is large, but you will be able to carry it with ease. Bring it to me, and I will heal this ailment. Think of it as payment for deeds beyond these today."

Taslun nodded. "It will be done."

The dragon growled and then took to the sky, its wings blowing snow and ice from the platform they stood upon.

"You agreed quickly," Kealin said.

"I didn't feel we had much a choice in the decision," Taslun said. "Why ask questions that we do not want an answer to?"

"Oh, you mean something like 'what is in this place we go to?'" Calak said. "At least it is not wights like before."

Alri shook her head. "I hope not, and I hope nothing of ill is here at all. I have no staff to assist you three."

From the platform, they followed a literally frozen road. Walking along areas not sheer with ice and made up of more rock, their way was precarious. Aside from falling, sharp rocks and tiny crevices large enough to break an ankle but not actually swallow you up ravaged their way. Passing to a lower portion of the path, they looked to either side of them. Kealin noticed wrecked ships preserved beneath the icy waters. Even with the many years under the surface, they had held up well. Their design reminded him of the *Aela Sunrise.*

He wondered of them. Between the caves where Vals had hidden them and now this place watched over by an ice drake, he knew not of what race these people were. The annals of his people had said nothing of a Glacial-Sea-dwelling culture, but perhaps it was not knowledge the elves embraced or agreed with.

Their path began upward. Three grand stairwells reached up toward the volcanic mountain, but instead of steady footing, they found their path even more difficult, as broken stairwells mauled with the sheer stone and ice forced them into a sluggish ascent.

Kealin drew his blade and smashed ice from a

foothold. He leaped up and, in the same motion, drove his blade into the stone. He reached down for Alri.

"Come, I will push you up."

Alri followed, and he tossed her upward. She slid but found her footing as the others did, as Kealin did, working slowly to go upward. They were only another few paces from the top, but it was here where the damage dealt was the most severe.

As they made their way up, it was in deep scratches in the earth they found footing, but this was new damage in terms of the ruins. Kealin was the first up, and after helping the others, he looked around.

The rocks near a center door had been smashed. The door itself was recessed in and was ajar but frozen. Its blue paint was emblazoned with golden tridents and the effigy of a whale. Large scratches were made into the rocks going up the volcano, and cracks ran up toward the summit.

"Do you think it the dragon's doing?" asked Calak.

"Well, he would not fit in the door. Perhaps that is why he sent us," Alri replied to him. "We can fit. But I do wonder if we should."

"We don't have a choice," said Kealin. "Aside from the continuation of our quest, he can heal you."

Taslun lifted his blade and looked around the edge of the door. Kealin did the same as he stepped on the opposite side. Alri looked down at the ground. Kealin looked at her. She was scared.

Do not worry, Sister.

She looked up at him and smiled, but with a raised

eyebrow, unsure of what she heard. He had gained more knowledge of his skill, and still he did not understand how. Since his time with Vankou, somehow he used it more. He smiled back. It was good he did not need to speak; he knew his tongue would change as it had before.

"Keep a keen eye, Brothers," Taslun commanded. "Alri, if there is trouble, stay near me."

Kealin entered first, with Taslun just behind. The world within the mountain was crystalline. The entire interior had been frozen. Beneath them, the lava of the mountain flowed but did not melt the ice. They walked in a cavern of corpses. Though it was difficult to make out, it was clear the race of seafarers that the dragon spoke of were not all destroyed by a cataclysmic eruption but had suffered a freezing from within. From the shapes of the ice, it seemed it had come from the door inward. Considering the fire beneath them, it was not any normal ice.

"I do not know where it is we should search," said Taslun. "The dragon had said it was in a center chamber."

"It is large, too, but able to be carried with ease," Calak quoted with a hint of sarcasm in his tone. "Let's just continue further in until we cannot go any further."

It was a good plan to Kealin. There was a stillness in the air that brought a colder chill to his skin. His blade glowed red as always, but he found himself wishing it gave off heat.

Alri shuddered. "It is very cold," she said.

"Do you feel well enough?" Kealin asked, stopping with her as Calak and Taslun went ahead.

"I feel more than a chill. I am dizzy. But I will manage." She forced a smile.

He took off his cloak and placed it around her.

"Alri, Kealin, come quick!" said Calak.

The two of them caught up with their brothers, finding they had made it into a large room more cavernous than the previous ones. There were more iced figures here. In their hands were what seemed like staves, pointed upward.

Kealin stared up. It appeared the stone covering was not like that of the rest of the mountain.

"I believe this room was open to the sky at some time," said Taslun. "Perhaps these were casters, providing a shield from an attack."

"So they were frozen as ice came upon them?" asked Calak. "That does not make much sense."

"It does when there is an ice drake outside wishing for us to retrieve something for him."

"That which I believe we have found," Kealin said, pointing.

In the center of the room was a large chest covered in stone. It was cracked down the center. A large white bone of some kind was stuck in it; the end of the bone sticking up into the air had been hacked away, or so it appeared.

They began removing stones, and as pieces were placed aside, a silver chain could be made out. Kealin looked to the strange bone in the one stone. He questioned what it was but could not explain it. He went back to work.

It took some time and many breaks, but at last they came to a final stone on the far end. It was a capstone, heavy, and even with many hands, unable to be removed.

They began to use their blades to chip away at it. One by one, the elven brothers worked their way, and the stone began to crumble into itself. Cracks formed with each strike, and with a shout, Calak delivered a strong blow, and the stone shattered. A black stone, the amulet, had now been unearthed once again.

"I look at this massive chain and do not believe our dragon acquaintance has told us the truth. How can it not weigh a ton?" Calak said.

He was right, or so Kealin thought. The chain itself was nearly as long as the *Aela Sunrise*. The amulet was easily the size of a boulder.

"I cannot guess what we have been lied to about, but he would have not sent us had he not assumed we could do it," Taslun said. "Let's lift it up and take it out. This cold is wretched, and I much prefer the winds outside."

They each took position at places along the chain. Kealin wrapped his hands around it and braced his back by tightening his stomach. He took a deep breath.

"On a count of two," Taslun said. "One, two."

Kealin lifted but found not at all the weight he was expecting. The amulet indeed was light and came upward without much muscle at all. Had he lifted it any harder, it likely would have flown upward out of his hands.

"Seems the dragon was right," said Calak.

They exited the room as they had come in. Though now holding a massive chain, they wormed their way between statues and walked with haste toward the still-cold but warmer world outside.

It was only a few paces from the doors when a gust came upon them from behind. At first they each ignored it; instead, their assumptions and excuses convinced them to not worry. But upon a second gust, Kealin looked behind, and a deep haze came upon them. A great light began to shine, and they dropped the amulet.

A voice came upon the air. "Do not take what we took to hinder them. We cannot assist again. You will awaken more than the one of music can as of now. Do not, we beg you. We will not harm you if you leave it, but flee this place now or face damnation."

The haze was upon them, almost as if choking them. It smelled horrid, and Kealin coughed.

"Go!" shouted Taslun.

Their view was obstructed, but they knew the gateway was just ahead. Kealin began to sprint, though it was not until they passed the void and returned to the outside that they could all see again. They knew not to stop. The gusts came upon them again, and the ground trembled. Kealin glanced behind them as he did; the others did too, and it seemed the haze had followed them.

They looked up, searching for the dragon, but

could not see it. It hadn't returned as of now. They continued running toward the platform above the cave. There was no other path.

The ground rumbled more, and there was a shrill sound behind them.

A crack formed in their path, and they stumbled, sliding to a stop as they looked behind. The fogs were converging together. From the top of the volcano, a dark smoke rose and a fiery blast rocketed into the air, arching downward and striking the fog. Lava spewed onto the ground around them and further split the earth they stood upon.

The fog began to glow red and black. Stones from the ruins flew toward the combining mass, and two white eyes stared at them.

Kealin scanned for another way forward. He saw one, but he was not sure if his brother had the same idea.

Taslun had already let go of the chain and drew his blade. He turned to them. "Go, do what you must to get the amulet to the platform. Continue on to Dimn. I will stop this beast."

"Yes, Brother!" Calak shouted. He, too, had seen the path Kealin saw, and began toward it, the amulet dragging behind them as Kealin and Alri now fell to the back part of the chain. They ascended upward and further up the frozen ground to the platform.

Kealin looked back to Taslun. His blade shimmered a bright red as he took a dueling stance with the creature, now brandishing a golden trident emblazoned with flames. In a few paces, Taslun walked to the side before charging in true Urlas Blade form.

His brother faced a being at least four times his size in height, but it made no difference, for in a great leap, he struck high, and the creature was pushed back. It stumbled before stabbing toward the flying elf. Taslun evaded, twisting and parrying the blade as he used the momentum to toss him back toward the ground.

Kealin stumbled, not watching his footing, as they began a last ascent up toward the platform. His legs ached, as did his throat. The cold now bothered him, after the frigid air of the cavern and then the burning fumes as they left. Reaching the platform, he dropped the chain. He drew his sword and then pointed to Calak. "Stay with Alri."

Looking up to the sky, he saw no dragon, and his brother was sacrificing himself for the act the dragon had commanded. It was not like the dragon was waiting outside to help them. They were alone, and Kealin had to act.

Taslun was locked in parry, blade versus the spikes of the creature's trident. It roared, the ravenous sound cutting through the cold as Taslun gripped his hilt tighter, his arms being forced out of his protective form as the creature began to glow brighter. A white opening appeared just below its eyes, and it spoke.

"You had a chance to leave it. I will stop you and return what we took from the one of songs."

The white opening closed, and the creature began to shrill again. Taslun began to falter. But it was then he perceived another approaching. He looked beyond the creature and spotted Kealin mid-jump, his blades angled downward, landing atop the creature with a rock-cracking downward thrust.

The creature recoiled, swiping Taslun away and throwing Kealin off of itself. Kealin rolled across the ground and stopped just short of the sea water in one of the harbors.

He shook himself; he had hit his ribs quite hard and coughed as he went back toward the beast. His brother was again engaged with it, and his swipes were becoming sloppy, doing little more than deterring the trident.

Kealin ran forward again. The creature turned this time and slashed the prongs toward him. He ducked and rolled, making it inside the creature's attack range and slashing upward. His swords couldn't break its skin. The creature stomped at him, and vibrations sent him wheeling backward again.

It turned to Taslun now, raising the trident before smashing its boulder-like feet again, knocking the elder brother to the ground. It held its trident back, rearing for a final strike, when the air around it turned frosty and a blast of ice struck from above.

The dragon roared upon the ruins, and its form struck the creature, sending it into the opposite harbor in a roll of ice and flames, its stony form fragmenting and falling downward.

"Go to the others!" the dragon commanded.

Kealin went for Taslun and pulled him to his feet.

"Good work, Brother!"

They both began a careful flight to the others atop

the platform. They went as quick as their feet would carry them, careful to not slip as the ground thundered behind them. Within a short time, they were with Alri and Calak. They turned to see the battling titans.

The creature had come again from the sea, its trident in hand. The very volcano seemed to be quaking beyond control as it struck at the dragon who took to the air, clawing the creature as it did. The dragon would then circle high, out of the reach of the fiery trident, before opening its mouth and casting a sheet of ice upon the creature.

Multiple attacks engulfed the creature, and each time, it recoiled, breaking from the purposed icy prison. It eventually ended up before the door of the volcano. The mountain quaked again, and lava flowed from the top; the flow of melted stones came upon the creature, and it began to grow in size.

The dragon flew over them, and they ducked. An icy fog fell upon them as the dragon arched up high before diving toward the creature. Magics swirled from the mountain and around the center of the creature's head. A single beam of light burst forward from a glowing crystal that emerged from the head of the creature. The beam itself nearly hitting the dragon in the neck.. But any hope it had to defeat the dragon fled as a blast of white and blue struck it, causing its form to be pushed against the stone. The dragon pummeled the mountain, and there was a final shrill sound. The dragon was upon the mountain for a moment and then flapped backward, landing near the ruins of the harbors.

The creature did not move, even as lava still poured upon its form. What life source or enrichment it was to be given from the fires was no more. The dragon had defeated it.

It took to the air again and landed upon the platform. Looking down on them and the amulet, it stuck its head through the chain and cocked its body; the chain rolled over the dragon's head and came to rest down its neck.

"I thank you four for your deeds. I see now why your journey brought you here, but merely not for my own terms to be met. I must do something for you." The dragon went back toward the harbor and dove down into the sea. In a few moments, it returned clutching several long objects that looked almost like strange logs. It dropped them into the harbor.

The elves made their way back to the water, and the dragon waited for them by the waterside. Kealin watched in the ruined harbor as the waters stirred. The narwhals had returned. One horn broke the water first, and Kealin knew at once that it was Tulasiro.

In the water, too, were four boats. They looked like they were made of black stone.

"These are boats of the race who built this place upon the rocks. They will do well to traverse the maelstroms, and know that the narwhals will be of great aid to you. They know the way to Dimn and will take you there."

"And our sister's healing?"

The dragon looked down upon them and then turned its head.

"That is of Dimn's healing power. I did have the way, as I said. This is my part of our agreement. Get to Dimn and do not wait."

Kealin did not care for the dragon's deceit. It knew well they expected immediate healing. "Why do you lie to us, dragon?"

"I did not lie in full. You will get your healing. Tell me who else was to direct you to Dimn without fail? There is not a soul. You will learn these icy realms are more than they seem. They are a desolate place of many imprisoned and tortured souls. You have assisted a greatness here, elves of the Urlas Woodlands. Your part may soon be over, but at least know the narwhals will take you the rest of the way."

The dragon looked up to the sky and stretched out its wings. With a few flaps, it took to the air. Kealin stared at its feet, learning now what the bone had been inside the mountain. The dragon had a large claw from its right foot missing; a cruel stub remained. He did not know what they had done today, but indeed, more than they were told. The dragon needed them to retrieve the necklace, but Kealin sensed there was more to this plot. Like before, they had been used for another's purpose.

As the dragon disappeared into the night sky, the flow of the volcano had lessened, as what power had driven it to quake had dissipated, and it returned to the way it was when they first saw it. The lava flow had cooled and was hardening as the Glacial Sea winds began to blow hard upon the island.

"Look," Alri said.

Three fairies were floating over her, twisting up and down her arms and legs before encompassing her entire body.

They heal her one last time, but we must get you to Dimn. Evil is coming; we must go quickly, Tulasiro said to Kealin.

"We must go with de narwhals. Dey will take us to the true healing you needs."

Taslun nodded. "I will not understand your new gift, Brother, but I think I am happy you have it."

14

THE MAELSTROM

WITH THE RUMBLES of the volcanic island beneath his feet, Kealin worked with the others to pull the ships to the shore. The vessels felt as if made of stone, but floated with ease. He climbed in and, after a short search, was not able to find paddles.

"How are we supposed to use these?" Calak asked.

Kealin look into the boat but found it mostly bare. He noticed a single latch built into the side. It was a crystal of design, like those of the *Aela Sunrise*. He pulled it, and from the front end of the boat, he heard a splash. A moment later, Tulasiro came to it, and he saw the horn of the narwhal make a dive below the boat. He steadied himself into a seat.

Friend, am I to ride as you pull?

The boat lurched forward, and he laughed. "This way. Move the crystals inside the boat!" As he said this, he forced himself to watch the way he said it. The desire to slur his speech nearly overtook his ability to enunciate his words. To him, it was obnoxious. But whatever 'gift' he had, was serving them well.

The others got in their boats and did the same, and each had a narwhal come to them. Kealin smiled, water lapping over the edge as Tulasiro pulled him faster away from the island. They circled and awaited the others to join them. The remaining narwhals seemed to come to each of the ones guiding the boats, and then departed. The four narwhals pulling them circled once and then headed east. The polar lights were above, shining down upon them and reaching to the far south in twisting waves.

Calak laughed. "Perhaps Wura also guides us to the realm of his brother Dimn?"

Kealin looked up, the sky rushing above them as they raced across the open sea pulled by the narwhals. He took a deep breath of the air and felt a warmness within himself. He was at peace upon the seas.

The narwhals began to swim faster, and the winds coming over them became beyond strong. He tucked down into the lowest portion of the boat. He now could only see the sky, but it seemed the best way to ride as they sped on. His siblings did the same.

He felt for the shells in his pocket. How they would play into their exact finding of Dimn or reaching Dimn, he did not know. He could feel the rush of water against the bow of the boat and felt the rhythmic flapping of the narwhal's fin beneath. With peace setting in and his body beckoning further rest, he closed his eyes.

. . .

He awoke to a cold splash of water. He blinked, clearing his vision, but then gripped the sides of the boat as he stared down, his feet against the opposite end of the boat. The sea was in front of him, not the sky like before. He was pulled upward as his belly sunk in.

Tulasiro!

But the narwhal did not respond; its form became visible for a moment as it jerked out of the towering water, slapping the boat the opposite direction before surging on, pulling him up the crest of a wave. The sea had turned turbulent. He pulled himself up as the boat prepared to dive again. He looked behind and noticed the other three boats trailed behind with his siblings in similarly precarious positions.

Alri was clinging to the back end, and Taslun hung from the front, his feet dangling back. Calak was somewhere in between, sliding one side to the other as his boat became airborne before crashing back into the sea.

Lightning flashed above in repeated dazzling white. There was no rain, only waves and rocks, many rocks. At times, it seemed either the ground had appeared below, the sea swallowed up in the waves around it, or there were indeed that many crags from below poking up. Slurries of ice splashed into the boat like tiny boulders on his legs.

Bracing himself, his fingers ached. The icy splinters attacking his joints and numbing his fingertips made every bit of movement difficult. He felt weightless again, and he prepared for the slam on the water as before. Kealin had no doubts as to why many had not dared go this way before.

The winds became horrendous, howling over the water as the towering waves of the sea became calm and stilled.

Kealin sat up and felt himself barely able to look over the edge of the boat. He was still shaking from his harsh awakening.

A towering column of fog shot up from the sea, interlacing a large rocky island with crafted stonework and sea-weathered stones. He looked up as far as he could, but the night sky was blotted out further by dark clouds. He could not see very much.

The winds shifted again, and a horn called out, or so it seemed. The mountain moaned, and a twisting blast of ice and winds tore out of the fog toward the edge of the horizon.

Is this it? Is this the mouth of the winds?

The wind died down as before, and the waves began again. The narwhals began pulling them faster; they were gaining speed as they went toward the island.

"Are we here at last?" shouted Calak.

"This looks like an old place, that I can see," replied Taslun.

"We have been to many old places. How do we know?" asked Alri.

Kealin turned and looked forward. He then shouted, "There is swirling ahead, and it is maelstroms we have sought beneath the palace of the wind god. Brothers, Sister: we have arrived, but I do not know how good this happening is."

He looked forward, and the winds cut over him again, sliding the boat across the edge of the water. Tulasiro twisted its path, and it was clear what was happening to them. The horizon began to fade from view as they cut down into the sea, drawn into the twisting slope of a turbulent whirlpool.

Kealin braced himself against the boat. He did not know what it was they were supposed to do, for deep in the darkness there was no light, no guide, no arcane sign, just blackness and the icy reminder that the intent of this maelstrom was destruction.

He held shells in his pocket, but he still wondered at their purpose. He reached in, fumbling them between his fingers. It was then Tulasiro dove down into the wall of the maelstrom. He held his breath, feeling himself tugged under the water. Kealin opened his eyes for a moment. Through the darkness of the water, he was able to see the body of the great whirlpool. Tulasiro ripped them to the right, and he closed his eyes. He was out of the water suddenly, and he looked to see the narwhal had pulled them over the center of the maelstrom.

He looked down into the mouth of the beast of the sea. Beneath him were the skeletons of ships long lost seeking this place of holiness. There were many bolts of lightning, and in a flash, he spotted his siblings spinning around, their narwhals still holding to the edge.

Tulasiro had brought them to the other side and swung its tail to increase their speed again.

Shell.

The narwhal spoke to him, but he did not know what it meant. He felt the shells. There were many colors: orange, pink, blue, among others. He remembered the hooded man and his letter but couldn't remember the exact colors and their meanings. He took a blue one. The narwhal again dove and then ripped them across the mouth of the maelstrom. He tossed it into the swirling waves. In a few moments, a radiant light shined from beneath. The cyclones dropped from above them and became water spouts.

Not that one.

He braced as they slammed against the opposite side. He looked again. He had the orange one. They returned to their path; he was pulled again into the water for a moment and then across the chasm they went. He threw the shell into the waves, and an orange flash shot flames into the air, nearly striking Kealin himself. The sky above them shined with a bright flame as the clouds became as flames above them.

Wrong.

He looked to his siblings. They were farther down the maelstrom. So far down that he had difficulty seeing them, and if not for the light above from the last shell, he would not know if they still were with him. The maelstrom churned, and Tulasiro struggled to keep a good path. The waters above had begun to be sucked into the center; the maelstrom was about to close upon them. He placed his fingers on another shell. Thinking to himself, he went to his mind. He imagined the maelstrom as he felt the shell. He saw the maelstrom collapse. He moved his finger to the next, the maelstrom swarmed with glaciers. He then grabbed another.

This one was different. He saw light shooting toward the sky. The maelstrom faded, and there was bright light. He pulled the shell out. It was pink.

Tulasiro pulled them from the maelstrom, swam hard, and burst through the watery grip again. Kealin looked over the edge and tossed the shell. Wind caught him, and he was dumped from the boat. He struck the water and gasped as the frigid grip embraced his body. He looked but he was beyond the reach of the narwhal. The shell struck the surf, and a blinding light followed. He felt himself go weightless, and then an icy feeling struck him that was colder than the water he found himself in. His eyes went dark, and then he opened his eyes to see glowing blue rocks above his head as his body was pulled down a waterway of some kind. It was only a moment later, and he felt his feet fly downward, and his face headed toward a pool. He pushed his hands out to break the impact, and he was underwater.

He looked up, kicking as he did and pulling himself to the surface. He glanced around. He was alone. There was a lone shore ahead. He swam to it and went to his feet as quickly as he could manage.

Kealin looked around. It was an underground cavern. He was alone, and where his siblings were now, he did not know. His eyes scanned the rocks around him. The unnatural blue glow was something he had not seen in the Urlas Woodlands. Runic etchings ran along the walls and were in an obscure dialect of elvish that he did not know.

The shoreline was sandy and had no vegetation. He began along it, searching for nothing more than a way out. Walking along a bare wall, there was no loose stone or hidden door that he could find.

This was no accidental cave, but he could find no way out, and the way he had come in was not only out of reach but flowed with water beyond anything he could fight to climb back out of. He wondered if he was at the bottom of the maelstrom or some other kind of trickery. In all of his wonderings, he did not know what "out" was or where he had ended up.

Making his way to the opposite side of the room, he found a monolithic stone with runic inscriptions like the wall, but now glowing as he approached.

It was then the entire room became bathed in light as the runes covering the walls were now glowing. The stone burst into red flames. The pool he had landed in bubbled, and from the surface emerged a figure.

Kealin drew his sword, but it became heavy. His grip was forced open, and his sword dropped to the ground. He knelt to pick it up, but could not lift it.

The figure had turned to that of a woman made of water. Her hair was a darker hue of black, but her form was a constant renewal from the pool she stood in.

"Kealin Half-Elf of the Urlas Woodlands, you have come far to end up within my cave."

He pulled at his blade again.

She shook her head. "You do not need that here, but soon you may wish you had your second blade."

He stood and pointed.

"How do you know of me?"

"I am of the sea, dear Kealin, the maelstrom beneath the palace of Dimn. I know much of those who draw near me."

"If you knew it was me, you knew the purpose of my siblings and me. Where are they? What have you done?"

"They are where they are supposed to be. I am but a maelstrom of the Glacial Seas and am tied to protecting the way to our lord, Dimn. You appeased me as needed, though."

She reached behind her head and revealed, in a strain of her watery hair, the pink shell.

"Then why, if I appeased you as you wished, was I brought here?"

"Kealin Half-Elf, I brought you to this place so that I may look upon you. There is much within these waters that has transpired, but the Glacial Seas have been at relative peace for some time. Your events, your gift of the mind, and the deaths of those you love is that which was foretold."

"Deaths of those I love? Where are my siblings?" Kealin shook his fist at her. "If you harmed them . . ."

"They are where they should be. The maelstrom

does not lie, but there is fear in your steps. Death is awakened and released. Its demon was destroyed, its beast released. Those of the seafaring race whom you've seen whispers of and visited the ruins of their city worked with great difficulty to do what you have undone.

"In truth, without your presence with them, your siblings would already be dead. You have kept them safe, but it was your sole quest to come here. I am afraid that fate has determined your path, and though it is here with the holy Dimn, I fear you do not realize what has been done. The glory of the Stranta-Vedi continues on, you embrace what comes. As did the Stormborn, as do we all."

"Stop speaking in your riddles. What has been done? I did not awaken death. The Stormborn? You mean Vals or… Valrin. He was killed by Rugag! Explain to me your words! How can you awaken a state of existence?"

She did not answer.

Kealin pointed his sword at her, "I want to go to my siblings."

The woman spun about the pool, the tides increasing within the room. She paused as the watery chasm that he had come from before began to flow faster.

"I have warned you, and it is not as a maelstrom of death but as a force of the sea. The narwhals will not listen or help just anyone, and so, with you also having the shells of Meredaas, I knew there was more to you. But I am just a maelstrom, and you a half-elf. Perhaps I say too much out of turn. I never quite know when to stop turning, you see?"

Kealin was more confused, but the words he heard drove him to a near-madness. A maelstrom, of all forces of nature, had personified itself as a woman of water to speak with him.

"Kealin, doom is upon your heart. Guard yourself well, for there is life beyond the breaths you take here, and the sea will be your only comfort in those times. This place was made some time ago; I was happy to speak with a soul after so long. It is tiring dragging so many to death within my mouth."

The figure smiled and began to flow from its form into the room. The water was now at Kealin's knees. He picked up his sword and ran around the room, looking for a way out again. The waters were flowing in faster than ever.

In a few moments, he was floating, the water rising more. He shook his head, unsure of what to do next but still swimming, and then, the water pushed his head against the ceiling of the room. He gasped, breathing heavily and pushing himself against the rocks. The water crept up his face, covering his eyes, his nose, and then coldness consumed him.

He felt a tug to his feet and was powerless. His body was dragged with force, twisting and turning away from the room. There was a great current in the water, and then he felt himself leave the sea. His eyes saw only light and then a blinding flash. He felt himself fall to a hard surface, and he could breathe.

. . .

Kealin felt numbness all over. He was no longer cold. His skin was warmed from above, but still he could not see.

"Kealin."

He heard the voice but found it difficult to respond. He thought the words in his mind but could not lift his head.

"Alri, help me!" he heard.

He felt hands grip him, and he was rolled over. He blinked several times, but his eyes were blinded by the light above.

"He is alive!" A voice said, "Kealin, can you hear me?"

He nodded and blinked; his vision was getting better. He looked ahead, seeing Taslun and Calak. Alri supported him from behind.

"When you were lost to the water, we thought you were done, dear brother. I am relieved to see you well."

Kealin looked around. The ground was gray and like fog on the sea. It was daylight here. The sun shone brightly above them. Around him, it seemed the ground went out as far as he could see.

"What is this place?"

"We made it, Brother. We made it to Dimn."

"Well, we made it to his palace grounds. We have not been here more than a few moments before you arrived," Calak told him. "I noticed you tossing the shells and how they changed the maelstrom. I guess you picked the right one?"

"Yes."

Taslun gripped him under his arm. "Can you stand?"

Kealin nodded and stood, though his knees were shaky. He steadied himself and then felt for his sword.

"What happened?" asked Alri.

"I do not know. I fell into the maelstrom and ended up in a cave."

"A cave?"

He then realized what the woman of the maelstrom had told him. The dread upon the air suddenly felt heavy upon him. He looked at each of his siblings, and they stared back.

"What is it?" asked Taslun.

Kealin thought to tell them in full what had transpired, but they were words he wished to validate by speaking again. "A woman was there. She claimed to be the maelstrom itself. She was curious of one who wielded the shells of Meredaas."

"Why you get to speak to all of the females of these seas, I will never understand," said Calak.

Taslun laughed. "You forget about the truth that while one was a mermaid, the other two were creatures of another type: a demon and a force of nature. Not exactly material for one to love."

"You cannot say that, older brother," Alri said. "Do you remember the elf who fell in love with a tree and spent the greater part of a thousand years waiting for it to speak to him?"

"Yes, but he died from starvation."

Alri winked. "Yes, that is what happened. But that proves love knows no boundary."

"Aye, food!" said Calak. "We have not eaten in some time."

Taslun shook his head. "Good brother, you never stop eating."

Kealin smiled at his siblings. The sun made them all livelier than they had been the entire journey.

"Let's go this way," he said to them.

A stone path was visible, still shrouded with the fog, but walkable. To their right, there was green grass, but it was still and there was a constant shroud of fog. This was a bizarre place. Up ahead, they could see a structure.

They began up the path that rose higher off the landing with each step they took. Coming closer, Kealin could see columns that surrounded a square stone building. Atop each of the columns, there appeared to be miniature tornadoes twisting upon their set platforms.

There was a set of four steps that went toward an entryway with open doors. Kealin paused on the first step and turned, waiting for his siblings to join him. The land around them was clouds. At the level he awoke, it was not obvious, but now above it all, he could tell.

As Taslun at last reached the stairwell, Kealin noticed he took a knee. He turned back to see a robed man looking at them. He bowed in turn.

"Elves of the Urlas Woodlands, you have traversed much to come here. I am Dimn, Northern God of the Winds."

Dimn was not what they expected. Not that they

knew for sure what to expect, but he was a man not much different from them. Kealin heard his brother stand and looked over at him.

"I am Taslun. This here is Kealin, Calak, and Alri. We have traveled with news of greatest importance."

Dimn nodded. "I will hear your news, but I invite you into my home first. I have prepared food for you. We will speak of this news then. I am quite curious of you four. Not just anyone can find their way here."

Kealin stood with the others and followed Dimn inside.

The interior of the palace was a series of columns sparkling with what appeared to be actual stars within each of them. The floors were polished and sheer and reflected the glimmers from the pillars.

Dimn took them around a large pool of water and to a corridor to the right.

"The eastern corridor is this way. I have a place here for you four. I have made it to be comfortable for you. It has been some time since pilgrims have come to my place."

"Maelstroms do not help," said Calak.

Taslun glared at him.

"Do not judge your brother so harshly," said Dimn. "Calak tries much to appease you, Taslun."

Taslun looked away and up to Dimn. Kealin turned to Taslun and raised his eyebrow.

"My knowledge should not surprise any of you. The winds carry much through my temple. I hear names, whispers hushed but caught in passing. I feel the blow of northern snow and the burn of the far southern sands. With all of that come words and stories of many times more than even a god cares to hear.

"But of the elves of the Urlas Woodlands, I keep an ear out of special regard. Your people are within a protected realm. It is that which surprised even the gods. I doubt you could have news beyond what I know already. Had I not heard you were approaching, I would've departed for my own business in the south, but for now, I take time for you."

The room they were taken into was made of glass. As Kealin walked in, he jumped at first, looking down, for he saw the open sky both above and below as he passed the entryway. Dimn walked well ahead of them and walked around a large table that appeared as if it was a massive bird's wing made of silver. Beneath it, and connecting it to the floor of the room, were tiny tornadoes spinning in place just as the ones outside the temple did.

On the table was every form of fruit and vegetable known. In the center was a large portion of meat.

"I do not eat," said Dimn. "I know of your love for nature, so I assumed what you might like. A sea kraken was of olden age, and it came time for his death. I knew of this and spoke with Meredaas; the creature was well to be sacrificed for your consumption."

Calak did not seem to mind. He sat down ahead of the rest and began to fill a bowl with many items, including the sea kraken meat. Though Alri and Taslun joined him, they were not nearly as enthusiastic.

Kealin sat beside them but did not touch the sea

kraken. In truth, he was not hungry. Vals had only just been murdered in his mind, and the words of the maelstrom haunted him.

Dimn remained in the room with them, and as they each finished, he served them drinks in silver chalices.

Dimn was strange. Kealin had expected a much different entity, not a man. But there was no doubting the power he held. After pouring the drinks, they needed a stir. He pointed toward the liquids and swirled his fingers. Winds filled the room and stirred the drinks before he handed them out.

"Wine of the clouds and the headwinds of the west. Berries like these are hard to come by but do grow within the grove to the west of my palace."

Kealin sipped the wine; at least it was sweet and like that of a blueberry, but lighter. He set the cup down as Taslun began to speak.

"Dimn, the shaman of the Urlas Woodlands told us of darkness approaching this place. The Itsu approach."

Kealin expected a look of surprise from Dimn, something beyond the stare he gave to Taslun. He turned from them and looked out over the skies. "My brother Kel is dealing with the Itsu in the South. I am headed there to deal with what is at hand in those lands. The time would come when those of the Urlas Woodlands would come to me; I knew of it as long as I knew of the Prophecy of the Glacial Seas. There are workings now in motion.

"I had heard the Blades and archons made their

way south to assist in the war, but then I learned of you four, and then I found the stench of death upon the air, and power had been reawakened. Old and foul energies flow outward. The song of Vankou is playing on the winds. The ice drake returns to its master."

"So it is true?" asked Kealin. "There was something to our journey beyond what we sought here with you. Our steps to reach you were not what we thought."

"If you mean that you inadvertently opened up a way for an evil long held in these lands to terrorize these seas, then, yes. You could not have known, but the way of an easy path to the shells of Meredaas should have been a clue to you. Though Vankou knew of other sources for these shells, he sent you to his demon instead. One of you speaks with the ethereal knowledge of the old race. Who is it?"

Kealin nodded.

"Then you are who was sensed by the Lord of Death. I knew not many of you were left. The steps you took were for Vankou, but you are here. I take your warning but do not feel it valid."

"Are you talking about his power that he developed?" Alri questioned. "It is like our shaman in our village. Their voices sound the same when he is using the power. We have all been confused but thankful for it."

"To do what you have done, Kealin, takes a mind of extreme power. I am surprised you still use the blade at your hip if you have access to such knowledge," said Dimn. "Who is this shaman?"

"An old man, not elven. He goes by the name Iouir and is older than most elves we know. He has lived within our realm for as long as I know," said Taslun.

Dimn opened his eyes wider. "A Dwemhar, then, one of the last, no doubt. Is it he who sent those of your people south to assist Kel and the elves there?"

"Yes."

Dimn turned away from them. "I may have misjudged you, then, my friends. I know much of your shaman, and he is a wise man and a devout follower of myself. He would have not sent you this way without knowing of the danger you, Kealin, possess."

"What I possess?" Kealin asked. "I did not ask for any gift. I am of elf and human blood, none else."

"A false statement," Dimn corrected. "You are of elf and Dwemhar blood. As are all of you, only that your brothers are more attuned to the elven attributes and you to the Dwemhar. Your sister is like you; however, her training may have tuned her energies away from the Dwemhar powers. I cannot know for sure."

"You are saying our mother is of this Dwemhar race?" asked Taslun. "How can we not know this?"

"Indeed, but do not let it surprise you that you do not know. Such descendants are very rare and become rarer. There are some who live to the south, but even they do not speak of it. The Dwemhar were greater than the other races in many ways, but of most importance was the power of their minds. The ability to manipulate the world around them, not like casting magic, but literal control over others' thoughts and actions, was a power that did not make others comfortable.

"Even Shaman Iouir is not full-blooded, though. Unless my own mind has been deceived. The Dwemhar resided in many places of the ocean, including these very seas around you, but the race fell into ruin. Many Dwemhar were lost in one of the first cataclysms, a massive flood that created these seas. At that point, the Stranta-Vedi, the seafaring Dwemhar, rose to prominence, but they were but a small spark in the fire that was the Dwemhar race. The race is nothing as it once was. I do wonder how many went into hiding."

"Stranta-Vedi?" Kealin questioned. "The maelstrom mentioned that name and the Stormborn."

"Vals mentioned the Stranta-Vedi," Alri said. "But he also acted as if he wasn't sure about the sea-race, like he didn't know who they were."

"Because he was Stranta-Vedi," Dimn said. "I am sure he could not just openly tell you all of his part in the world. He was the Stormborn, one meant to guide the future Dwemhar to reawaken what was lost. But his fate was tied to yours, his own life force restored to give him time but his body cursed to not last beyond it. In truth, it was not that long ago that he and the crew of the *Aela Sunrise* stood against great evil in these seas. I do wonder if any will ever know the extent that Valrin's actions had in altering the world. Perhaps, one day, those that are curious of his deeds will seek out those that know more of him. He is not unknown to the races of the world. The gods weep at his fall but not even Etha could have stopped his mortal death again."

There was a silence among them.

Dimn smiled, "But of all of you, your shaman must have seen it worth the risk, even with what has happened because of you four journeying here. He sent you four, too, a particular number to us gods.

"There is much happening in the world, but if the Itsu are coming to this place, they must seek something, and I think I know what it is. The Heart of the Winds must not be halted, or the world would become a nightmare of uncontrollable seasons, the balance of life would alter, and all would die. At least, those not of the gods. But still, I question the coming of Itsu. I had thought they were banned to their realm." He paused for a moment. "Come with me, all of you."

The wind god beckoned them to follow him back into the main chamber, walking them deeper into the temple. In a center portion, beyond a crystal column, was a large swirling vortex they could look within.

"This here is the source of the winds of the world, the clouds, fog, rains. Long have I guarded this place. If this place is defiled by the Itsu, I do not know what may come."

"How can we help you, Dimn?" asked Taslun. "How can the elves of the Urlas Woodlands serve Dimn?"

"First, you can be helped by me, more than you can help me." Dimn looked to Alri. "You are unwell. Your soul has been bitten by a wight of Vankou; I feel though you seem well now, that its blackness is upon you."

"The ice drake said you could heal her," said Kealin.

"I do know the way, and I offer the advice to you freely, but one task remains. Alri can heal herself from within with a renewal spell. I know the words, but it is a staff you need, for it must be cast by the one who is afflicted. I can direct you to a staff, seeing as you do not have one."

"I did," said Alri, "but it was lost amid unfortunate events in the last few days."

"Many unfortunate events have happened as of late." Dimn began to walk away. "Follow me, elves."

He took them away from the Heart of the Winds, passing a large chamber opening up from the left.

Kealin noticed a crystal-walled case off the main path. It was between two large torch basins and, as was the theme of the temple, had tornadoes circling atop pillars beside it. Within the case was silver armor; it was sectioned and had from the arms what appeared to be wings hanging from it.

"What is that?" he asked.

Dimn stopped and turned. "It is wind armor of particular power to myself in the defense of this place, though it is not of just a god's use. I guard this place in the form that you see so that I may use it, if needed. My normal form is well, large, but the portal into this place is better defended with that armor. It allows me to go between the realm gates of the clouds and the maelstrom at will. But its use is not worth going beyond this place, for its power is tied to the mountain. My other form suffices when I leave."

Kealin noticed a large sword, as well as a curved spear, was crossed behind the suit.

"How would any assail this place?" asked Calak.

Dimn smiled. "The Itsu are crafty and places not as secure; at least, not with the way the world has come to. Others such as foolish dwarves, or men, or in some times long ago, elves, tried, but they drowned in my maelstrom's fury." He smiled. "This way."

They followed him as he wished, turning down a long corridor that made it appear they were soaring through the sky like birds. To either side, an open walkway was blown by clouds and torrential winds, but from within the hall, they could neither feel nor hear the sounds, only see the wisps of gray clouds twisting around the chamber. At the far end of the hall, a stairwell circled downward.

"Go down," he told them. "You will find the old worship places for pilgrims. It is beyond there, behind two sealed doors, that you will find the staff you seek. You receive a great object, Alri. Long ago, you would've needed much more in wisdom and power to claim one of my staves." He handed her a rolled parchment from his robes.

"Within are the words you will need to heal yourself. A scarce spell, also not typically given so easily."

Alri bowed to Dimn. "Thank you for helping me."

"The gods of the North are not of malevolent intent, but hurry back up and we will talk further of what troubles are imminent. If you four have come to help, you will assist me with the Itsu, if that is what approaches."

Alri headed down first, followed by Taslun, who rushed ahead of her.

"You still have no weapon, little sister, and we do not know what evil may lie ahead."

15

DEMONS AT THE GATE

THEY PROCEEDED down the curved stairwell for what seemed a longer time than was necessary. It was very dark, but after several steps, the passage straightened out. They could now see the way ahead. Their path was lit every few feet by faint red glowing stones, not much light at all, but it was just enough to see the steps.

Ahead, they could hear a whistling wind, but it was not clear where it came from. They came to an area where two green torches provided plenty of light. A doorway was there, with a veil hanging down. On the veil, a silver inlay of the four points of direction and a maelstrom. Alri put her hand out and walked first, disappearing beyond the veil. The others quickly followed.

Kealin found himself in a moonlit walkway. He looked to his left and could see the sea rippling in the distance and the dark skies of night. He looked behind him and noticed that where the veil had been was now solid stone. He pushed on it with no budge from the surface.

"Where are we?" asked Calak.

Alri walked ahead of them, and Kealin ran up beside her. The stone hallway ended abruptly at a wall and turned left. Kealin touched her shoulder and then drew his blade, moving up ahead of her.

It was a temple of some kind, with rows of pews in a square room with a high arching ceiling. Windows surrounded them, and snow and ice had built up on the outside. He moved through the center of the pews; a large doorway was at the end, and he went to it, attempting to open it. He pushed. Nothing.

Taslun stayed with Alri, who walked to another hallway around a center altar that mirrored the hallway they had come from.

With Calak's help, they both pushed on the doorway. It cracked and then creaked open with a gust of wind and snow. There was a landing just outside, and as the doors were forced open, Kealin and Calak walked outside. A ruined stairwell that led downward was broken apart halfway from a stone dock, but it was a great distance to that point. The sea tore upward at them. They were on the base of the mountain in the temple, and it was clear why few had come to visit Dimn, at least, in their normal realm.

"The veil must have been like the maelstrom, a split in the realms," said Kealin.

"Well, it is cold," said Calak. "And I do much prefer the realm of Dimn." Calak smiled. "Come on, Kealin."

Kealin took hold of the doors but found they had already begun to freeze in the snow. He managed to free one, but even with his brother's help, they couldn't get the second.

Calak shook his head. "Leave it. It's not like someone will be coming up those steps anytime soon. But it is a bit draftier in here now."

They walked toward the other hallway where Alri and Taslun had gone, and found that they had progressed through a large door and were now at a second door. This one was stone with a silver runic inscription. Alri was reading it to herself.

"Did you enjoy making it the temperature of the Glacial Sea in here, little brothers?"

"It is a view to see, at least." Calak laughed.

"What does this say, Alri?"

By this time, she had knelt down and was reading the last of the inscriptions. "It was a decree, by the Saints of Dimn. Most fell in battle against some beast seeking its way into the mountain to reach the god. The last few made an inscription, remembering their struggle. It reads, as best I can translate:

To those who remain in the days that follow, know that we did what our god would have us do. To join in revelry of death against the Ice Demon of the Glacial Seas, we do recount our fall to the last patrons of Dimn. The stairwell is no more, and we have shut the doors. While they are sealed, this place is protected from the beasts. We have no food, but it is in Dimn we are strong.

I will be the last of the Saints to draw breath in these hallowed walls, the sanctuary once kept warm by the prayers of the patrons of Dimn. It is beyond this wall I will seal myself away, awaiting the end, for my brothers and sisters have all become ill. The magic protecting our doorway has been made no more. I will go beyond the wall, my last act of sacrifice to Dimn. He has betrayed us to this fate."

"It seems the Saint was stalwart and then despaired," Taslun said. "So this is the second door Dimn spoke of?"

"I assume. I will attempt to open it as before."

Alri placed her hand on the door, and it began to glow; she spoke a word to herself, and the door cracked. Stepping back, Taslun stepped in front of her with his sword out.

The room was dark. A single form could be seen against the far wall and, as torchlight from the hall would provide, it was clear the Saint was true to his runes.

Sitting upon a stone bench, a recessed room of prayer had become a grave. The robed figure still clutched a staff in its hand, and there was nothing else to be found.

"Then that is the staff," said Kealin.

Alri stepped forward; placing her hand on the staff, she pulled it from the decomposed grip of its last owner. The bones of the hand cracked as she pulled it free. At once, the staff became alive with a radiant light, and she smiled.

"It is good to have a staff again," she said. Alri unrolled the parchment Dimn had given her and murmured the words to herself.

"Well, heal yourself, dear sister," said Calak.

ALRI WISHED her brothers knew exactly how difficult it was to move from offensive and defensive spells to healing ones. By default, healing spells took more energy than even a static ward under barrage or a concentrated blast of elemental energy. Still, casting on one's self had its own issues. She would have to balance both the rejuvenated bliss of a rapid heal while keeping the arcane acuity to a level where she could actually heal herself. Alri held the staff just over her head, a mist fell over her eyes and down to her shoulders. She closed her eyes, focusing on the energy flowing from her staff into the top of her head. She exhaled, allowing the energy to roll down her body, moving down her chest and into her lower stomach and legs. It was here, she felt the darkness within her, the sickness. The healing energy, like rain upon her body, was splitting around this one particular spot of her energy centers.

She grimaced, allowing the energy to bounce back up within her, focusing and surrounding the sickness. Her right hand trembled as she envisioned the blackness evaporating. She was never the greatest at regular healing but even so, it had worked. She felt a release within and the sickness fled. She looked up to Kealin and then to the others.

"I am well now," she said. "The words worked."

The parchment she was still holding turned to dust.

"THEN WE HAVE DONE what we came to do," Kealin said.

Taslun knelt down to the corpse. He placed his hand above the skeleton. "In death, you are honored, last of the Saints of Dimn. May your stand be remembered."

"To die to protect a place is strange to me," said Calak. "To defend your people, yes, but a god and his temple?"

"We honor him regardless, Calak. To die in a stand against odds beyond yourself is a glory beyond understanding, unless your sword is next to the one who does it. Such is that of the Blades of the Urlas Woodlands."

A roar shook the room they stood in, and pebbles fell from the ceiling. Kealin looked to Taslun, and they both filed to the end of the hallway, glancing into the temple hall.

Another roar rumbled through, and a blast of white shattered the windows on one side of the hall.

"Back to the other hallway," Taslun commanded.

"That door is sealed," said Kealin.

"There is some way out," said Taslun, "and it is not out the door to the seas! Alri, your staff. I am sure of it; it will open the way back to Dimn."

They both peeked around the doorway again. It looked clear for the moment. They looked at one another and ran. A blast of ice shot through the open door, spraying the back wall of the hall and turning it to ice. Another roar followed. Kealin and Taslun had made it to the second hallway.

They peeked around as Calak and Alri did the same.

The doors swung open, and a plume of snowy dust flew in. Eyes stared in. It was the ice dragon from before.

"Vankou wishes his will upon you, elves. I thank you for my freedom, and I am happy to realize you made it through the maelstrom. But now, you will freeze."

It opened its mouth, cracking the foundations of the hall, causing the front half to shatter and fall to the sea. With a blue blast summoning around its mouth, Alri rushed forward, her staff out; she summoned a blast of wind, knocking the dragon's mouth back. Calak ran behind her for the hallway, and as the dragon recoiled and spewed its icy breath, she summoned a shield of fire that turned the breath to water. A deluge bounced off the halls around them as Kealin and the others scrambled to get as close to the wall as they could. The dragon's blast had been thwarted, and as the dragon took to the sky, she joined the others in the hall.

She placed her staff at the wall, and the way began to materialize before them.

There came a strange laughing growl. Kealin looked back to the double doors leading outside. A form appeared, hunched and made of bone. It was very small, perhaps only coming to his waist in height.

Following it were many others just like it, tiny skeletons, at least to that of the elves' standards. They held spears and ran for them.

The brothers ran to meet them, slashing and cracking at their bony forms, turning them to no more than piles of bones. Kealin took a glance at the now-gaping opening in the hall. Alri had opened the path. He then looked out one of the windows to the sea. It seemed the dragon had made an icy bridge from the sea to the hall, and a steady flow of the skeletal warriors were upon them.

Backing into the hallway, they slashed and parried those they faced with ease, but their numbers inundated the hallway.

"This way, come on."

Alri had opened the doorway, and they fled one by one. Crossing the dark void again, they watched, but they were not followed. They had escaped the attack upon them.

Taslun checked each of them, but they had escaped without injury. "Good. Let us go to Dimn."

"Will they not follow?" asked Calak. "They must have magic like us."

"They cannot pass into this realm," said Alri. "Those are unholy creations, made in the living realm beneath us but as long as the god holds dominion here, we are safe."

They made their way back up the stairwell and were happy for once, to be warm again.

Following the way Dimn had taken them, they

returned to the Heart of the Winds to find Dimn reading a book.

"We found the staff, although it was a less than happy occasion for us. The ice dragon we dealt with before has attacked, as well as skeletal creatures."

"We are safe from them here. They cannot cross into this realm, but they are of Vankou and more of what you four have unintentionally awakened. Can I see the staff?"

Alri came forward, showing the staff to Dimn, who took it in his hand.

"My Saints fought well."

"This is from the last one. His body was in the chamber."

"I knew it so," said Dimn. "Their prayers did not fall upon closed ears, but there is much in the ways of gods that our patrons do not understand."

"Is that our fate?" asked Kealin. "Do you not fight yourself? Could you have gone to them or, if not, brought them here to protect them?"

"The sickness that your sister was affected with had already taken them. Vankou was there. If I would have gone, there was danger for myself and all the realms. As I said, I must protect the winds. That is my intent and purpose. That drake below is full of ice, but nothing else. He was bound to his master, though he did not wish it. He could not help but complete his task. His amulet has been returned to him. It took many lives to take it the first time. He was sent to watch that path, I am sure. But it is of our other path we must speak now. You four are here to aid me, and I shall use you. It is quite simple. Protect this place. Even if I am unable to stem the tide, you must not let them here."

"We understand," said Taslun.

"Can you be killed?" asked Alri.

It was a fair question, in Kealin's opinion. Taslun seemed baffled that Alri would ask such a thing.

"Not by any force of your world, no, but the Itsu are of my world, and, yes, though it would take much, I could be. Your fate is your own, dear elves, but if you will stand with me, I accept it. I want to show you something that may come of need."

He turned to a pillar that stood just the height of the rail of the Heart of the Winds. Placing his hand over the flat surface, a crystal appeared.

"This is to be used as the final move. If I fall and if you cannot hold them back, twisting this will lock down this temple. You will not have escape, but they will not be able to get in."

"And what would happen if we hop into this place here? Seems like an escape worth using," said Calak, looking into the swirling winds.

"I do not recommend it," said Dimn. "You would be gambling with fate beyond what I think you should."

Kealin looked over the edge and to Calak. "Keep your blade up, if it comes to that. We will not need that option." Calak smiled, as did Taslun. Blades had an unwritten rule of death before retreat, and it was well followed.

Dimn walked toward the doors of the temple and,

leading them to the steps, stood looking up. The sun was nearly down, and the expanse of skies continued up above them. In the clouds below them, the edges of the polar lights stretched out like snakes in the grasses of clouds.

"This place has been my domain for as long as the skies were above the world below. It was in that time that the Heart of the Winds was first threatened, in the age when elves were but infants crying within the trees beside the lakes. It has remained almost unchanged since then. I added the way into the mountain for my followers, but that was a long time ago. The Saints of Dimn were once plentiful in the Glacial Seas."

"What is it that this Vankou wants?"

"To leave his island. Indeed, call it foolish for a god to not know, but his purpose is now lost to me. He has power beyond most, that of death itself. His music is the last a person hears prior to his demise. Kel banished him to that island."

"Is he a god?" asked Kealin.

"He is not in the form as I am a god. He is magic; he is an entity of the grave, dwelling within the realms. A dangerous place that can be both a prison and redemption."

"Can he cross into this realm?"

"He could, but only by way of the maelstrom, and he may try, but I do not fear him. It is the Itsu, the gods of the South, who grow in power. Kel has used much of my wind, accenting his own powers in the battle against them."

"Our parents are there," said Alri. "They went to assist Kel with haste."

Dimn looked to her. "I do wish I knew more of their purpose. While you four were below, I reached out to my brothers, and there was not a response. A shadow is upon the northern shore of the lands, as well as further south toward the deserts. Much evil is growing, and this is but one single front in what will become a larger war."

"What do the Itsu want with this place?" asked Kealin. "What is there to rule over if the world is thrown into its own destruction?"

"It is not rule over the people they want; it is to destroy us gods. I cannot hope to tell you of a simple answer to the war between us gods, but know that besides destruction, the Itsu seek every weapon of war they can wield to defeat us. Kel's answer has been destruction of much, but I feel that, in time, will prove undoing. The strife of the south is poisoning the land."

"Other than your armor, do you have a weapon here they would seek?" asked Taslun.

Dimn nodded. "A weapon is any item that you use to harm others. A person's hands can comfort or choke. It is in the way you use them, correct? The power creating the gusts of the world is here. But if they do not seek to destroy this place, possibly, it is for but one other item."

He turned back into the temple and took them to the farthest reach of the hall. Past the Heart of the Winds and down a long open-air corridor, they came to a large black stone that towered above them.

Dimn rubbed his hands along the surface, and it split open; a crack of light shot upward as high as they could see.

A single white chest set on a shelf within a small chamber was now visible. Dimn turned a lock, and it opened. He lifted the lid and reached in. Pulling something out, he cupped it in his hands.

"Behold a power of the gods."

He opened his hands, which held a small orb. It was white and seemed to swirl in its center.

"Like enchantments that are placed upon staves of magic, the Heart of the Winds must be watched and fed. The power within these orbs comes from the very life force of the skies. If used as intended, there is no harm, but if a staff or wand was to be made with this, a person could have control over winds, fog, and the force that entails. This may be the point of such an approach by the Itsu, but we know nothing for sure."

Taslun approached, and Dimn offered him the orb. Taslun took it and then placed it back into the chest.

"They will not take them," he told him.

They each felt a rumble beneath their feet. Dimn looked out toward the entrance of the temple.

"The maelstrom is active. Someone is below."

They began a hasty walk toward the front of the temple. Though Kealin and the others were headed toward the gateway, Dimn turned and went to a wall. He moved his hands across it, and an image of the swirling seas appeared. The angry maelstrom was in full view. From the view they could see, Kealin could make out the arms twisting beneath the water, creating the whirlpool. Massive ships swirled in a circle.

"Why do they try?" asked Taslun. "Do they not know they will be destroyed?"

Another ship approached the maelstrom; this one fought to not go in. It turned hard; from its bow came flaming bolts, like streaks of red flying away, aimed at something veiled in clouds.

A blast of ice followed, and the flapping of the dragon's massive wings became visible.

"Vaugar," said Dimn.

"Vaugar?" asked Taslun.

"The ice drake's name is Vaugar. He is chasing ships into the maelstrom. He must have flown south, grabbed the vessels, and brought them here."

"Why?"

"I do not know."

The dragon swooped down. They could see the masts of the ship splinter, and the ship lurched backward. The maelstrom was filling with debris. The dragon hovered atop it and looked down within. A light blue surrounded its body. It let out a blast of white, and ice began to fill the mouth of the maelstrom. The arms of the maelstroms were caught in the ice. A shroud of blackness approached from the side. As the waters of the maelstrom slowed almost to a frozen halt, the blackness went into the maelstrom. A fire overtook the ice, first red, but then green, turning to a shade of gray, and then black.

"What does she do?" asked Kealin.

Dimn stared but did not speak.

The swirling fire began to reach upward in the image. Dimn walked toward the gateway and looked out.

"You can only get in with a shell, correct?" asked Calak.

"That is the way it is made."

"Was that black shroud the Itsu?"

"No," said Dimn, "but I will deal with it."

Dimn turned from them, moving with haste to the hallway where the wind armor was. They heard the sounds of metal clanking, and then Dimn emerged again. His armor was silver, and the wings were outstretched. His helmet had two large spikes, and down his back was a furling cape. In his hand was his spear, and down his back was his sword.

"I will return," he told them.

He ran outside and then leaped; his wings caught air, and he took to the sky before diving down into the clouds.

They ran back to where they could see the maelstrom, to see a golden light strike the heart of the maelstrom. Vaugar flew around helplessly, appearing to be trying to reach Dimn, who had passed beyond the ice drake's ability to harm him.

Watching the spinning black fire with no knowledge of what was going on within caused an uneasiness to befall the siblings.

Taslun paced between the gateway and the wall, while Alri and Calak just stared at the image. Kealin held his hand on his blade. He leaned against one wall of the temple and stared across the clouds below.

He had never thought he would be upon such a place as this in all his imaginings of his own life. A place such as this was not one that could be imagined. A literal temple within the clouds, high above the lands. Even to an elf, such a place was mystical.

The ground rumbled again, and Taslun went to the wall. "I cannot see anything. The image is gone."

Kealin drew his blade. "Prepare, Dimn may not have been able to stop this force." Calak and Alri both came beside him.

The clouds below the temple began to swirl, mixing with darker ones below and creating a funnel, sucking the winds from the temple inside. Small cracks began to fracture the ground.

Taslun drew his blade and stepped in front of Kealin. The force of the wind grew sharply, forcing them to lean back to keep their balance.

"We hold this ground. We do not falter, elves of Urlas."

A blast of ice came from beneath the clouds, spiraling upward into the sky, and the winds stilled.

"The dragon," said Alri.

"But it cannot come into this realm," said Calak.

"Little brother, not every belief is certain," said Taslun.

The head of Vaugar emerged from the clouds, the amulet they had retrieved glowing orange from the dragon's neck. It turned toward them, spewing a stream of ice.

Alri jumped to point at once. Her staff out, a fiery shield came up again, decimating the attack. The dragon flapped its wings, struggling to force itself up and out of the portal.

Kealin ran forward. He went to the edge of the path and just to where the clouds swirled. The dragon looked at him.

"What do you do, Kealin? Do you now know that Dimn's power fails?"

He ignored the dragon and attempted to step toward him. The dragon roared, and he stumbled back, nearly tripping backward and off the path itself. Taslun grabbed him just as he fell backward.

"We cannot leave the holy realm, Kealin."

The dragon snapped its jaws. "You were meant to assist us, Kealin. You can speak with my lord as none before. You must embrace your gift and see the error in your ways."

Kealin looked to the dragon, staring Vaugar in his eyes. He looked as deep as he could, trying to feel the dragon's persona, his emotions at the moment. He felt rage and pride; a coldness was in Vaugar's chest.

"Dis is not de time for fake words, dragon!"

He struggled to speak, annoyed by his own words. This was not useful to him in the least.

The dragon cocked his head and laughed. His wings still flapped as his clawed legs slowly breached the cloud line of the sacred realm. Vaugar took in a deep breath, arching his neck.

"Come, Brother!" said Taslun.

Kealin ran with Taslun just as the icy breath struck the ground and traced behind them as they fled toward the temple.

Alri pointed her staff and closed her eyes, speaking to herself.

Her staff burned with white flames, and a blast of air struck the dragon, flipping its head back and causing the dragon to struggle to raise its head again.

"Into the temple," shouted Taslun. "We must wait for it to come closer. If we can get its head toward the doorway, we may have a chance."

Alri stood in the opening as Kealin and the others lined up along the wall surrounding the opening. The idea of facing a dragon that had defeated the seafaring people in a mountain set up just like this temple was not comforting to him.

Alri's staff let fly another blast, this one aimed not at his head, but his body. Vaugar looked down and let out a shrill roar.

"That was not my strike that caused that wail," said Alri.

They peered around the corner to see the dragon sucked downward, its claws scraping and scratching to hold its place, as something dragged it back beneath the cloud layer.

Dimn emerged from the clouds, his form visible for a moment, before aiming his spear downward and plummeting back through the clouds.

They all filed outside. The clouds had stopped swirling but remained blackened. Kealin scanned the cloud line. He was tethered between the two thoughts. Either Dimn would come back up victorious, or he would be turned to a glacier by the ice drake and they would run back into the temple.

The clouds seemed to be shifting, and then, in a shining gleam, appeared Dimn. He landed on the road just below them, his wings flapping water from the feathers.

"I have thrown down the dragon, but I do not know if it will remain there," he said. "Come into the temple; time is short, and there is much that must be done."

He walked past them, and they followed.

Dimn moved with an annoyance, taking off his armor and placing it near the wall. He went to the Heart of the Winds and leaned over it. No one spoke, but instead they lined up, ready to serve him as needed. Kealin still had his sword out; unlike his brothers, he felt there was no reason to sheath it.

"Elves, it seems I may have been wrong about our situation. I do not blame you four, but you were betrayed to this fate. I am happy you have come, but it is in the path you took that Vankou gained an upper hand. He has said for ages he cared little of us gods, but the Itsu have made him care. I believe now that all gods of the North are in danger."

"Is Vankou now against you personally? Is he not held below the realm?" asked Calak.

"I cannot be sure. The dragon was able to breach the realm, but only while the maelstrom was silent. It seems the amulet it wields has power beyond what I knew, and Vankou does not seem to want it back, as of now."

"What is it that the amulet does?"

"It allows Vankou to go beyond the realms, but

only in a way as to speak with us gods. It was given to him some time ago, but when those of the seafaring people went against him, they stole it in an attempt to further rob him of power. Then the gods bound him to the island, but there is too much confusion in the workings of the enemy.

"I do not know when Vaugar became his pet, but it seems Vankou wished to use the ice drake against you four and to pacify this temple."

"Does he seek the orbs?" asked Kealin.

"I do not think so. Vankou was attempting to slay the maelstrom itself, or at least, to quiet the storm. I dispelled him. But I sensed something else. The Itsu have grown in strength. Before I sent him away, Vankou mentioned their coming. They may have discovered a way to ascend to this realm from that of their own, using the normal realm as a bridge through Vankou's working.

"Perhaps Vankou had his own intent, too. I do believe he hoped to overwhelm the temple originally, but he fears the Dwemhar blood, so he sent his dragon. It failed, but now the maelstrom is weak. She will restore, but it will take time, time that I pray we have. The dragon has since returned to its task with the dead creatures and the holy place beneath us. It seems, for now, Vankou fears you, Kealin, so he will not attack himself."

"I am an elf; he is himself. Why does he fear me?"

"That, too, I do not know for sure. But the Dwemhar blood may play into that fear. That is not the point; if the Itsu come as Vankou stated would happen, he believes that my defenses will not hold. He hopes the Itsu can breach this place and kill you and the others."

"Can the gates be thwarted?" asked Taslun.

"No, not that I believe, for no power exists to my knowledge that can break the gates once they are sealed, save my own words. I alone have the key to open the gates. But I cannot doubt that the enemy may be more resourceful than I know."

"Is not the path underneath, from the Saints of Dimn's holy place, a danger? Can it be breached?"

"That path is veiled. Though it is not of the gates, it cannot be found unless known."

"The beasts knew," said Kealin. "They fought us up to its door. I can see no reason why they would not tell their master."

Dimn looked toward the hallway and then began a quick walk that way.

"I do not have time for this." He turned from them. "That pathway was sealed with a multi-layered veil magic, and in the times it was used, I had no fear of it being a route into this place. A folly of my own. They cannot get in easily, but eventually, they could get in if they have some degree of arcane knowledge."

They went down the hallway and to the stairwell. They were not even down the first few stairs when it became clear all was not well. The dark passage was cold, much colder than it had been. At the far end of the hallway, where the furling veil was, there was a deep orange glow beyond the doorway.

Dimn lifted his hand, and clouds began to flow in

from above them, like rolling fog; they filled the hallway, before gathering together as a large gate between them and the doorway. He then went to the foggy mass and placed his hand. A wall solidified. "That will have to hold."

"Will it?" asked Taslun.

"I do not know."

Kealin was getting annoyed by the answers of the god. He followed behind the rest as they went back to the main hall. This 'god' was much more in line to what he had believed than what the priestesses of Urlas had proclaimed. The gods were powerful but not all mighty. This deity was clearly unsettled. A fact that even Kealin's siblings were catching on to.

"There is more," Dimn said to them. "The winds have spoken to me while I was within the other realms. The Itsu received a weapon from Vankou. I do not know if it is a weapon like the traditional type, or a bit of spell craft, but it is something that can kill a god, and in such, I must go south. I must warn my brothers, Kel and Wura. I believe the workings here were to keep me from intervening."

"What of the approaching Itsu, the shadow upon the northern shore?" asked Taslun.

"I will return, and I will bring Kel. Between the two of us, the Itsu stand no chance. I will hope to be gone no longer than I must. You will be well to stay in the temple. When I return, we will talk more of Vankou, and we will throw down the Itsu before we move to rid ourselves of that beast. Kealin, there is much to be discussed. I believe I know how we can halt

Vankou, but as of now, I have no time. Walk with me, Kealin. I would like to speak to you privately."

As Dimn left the temple, Kealin followed.

"I tell you this away from your siblings but do not hold you to remain silent."

"Very well," he replied.

"You four survived the way to Vankou, but I tell you, no other living soul could have done that, and to only escape with one suffering a wight's bite—"

"It is good sword work."

"It is unheard of in the realms of elves and gods."

Kealin fell silent.

"I fear your place in all of this, Kealin. The power that your shaman has is an old one. To speak to the land of the ethereal is not common, nor even rare; it is beyond that. You four were pulled into this plot, and you will have to be the ones to end it. The gods have fought each other longer than worth speaking, but Vankou has never taken a side so directly.

"I will get back to this place to help you, but know that the Itsu may take me before I can."

"Why do you not tell Taslun? He is the eldest."

"He is not you, and not the one who can converse using the power of the Dwemhar. Your sister could, but she is naïve in the ancient powers. Her own focus will be understood in time but for now, guard your mind and guard the winds. I will speak with you more on my return."

Dimn's form began to change from that of a man to wisps of clouds. In a white mass growing in size, he vanished beneath the cloud line.

16

SHATTERING OF THE SKIES

KEALIN RESTED his hands on the hilts of his swords and sighed. He wondered how he had become such a pivotal person in the events they had passed through. He had gone on this quest due to his siblings alone, and now, according to the maelstrom woman, they were going to die and he had made their situation worse because of some cursed gift. He didn't understand it and he didn't want to. His faith had always been strong in himself and them. Now, he felt marred by some affliction that made his speech strange. Sure, it gave him insight in some situations, being able to talk to Tulasiro had been of great assistance to them, but they didn't need that right now.

The clouds before him were stilled and no longer shifted, although their black color increasingly darkened. The wind blew across the grounds of the temple, and he shivered. He no longer felt any comfort here; Dimn had taken that from him.

Kealin turned, joining his siblings in the entryway of the temple. Taslun looked up at him.

"So, he will return?"

"Yes."

"Then I feel until then, we must prepare. I have already thought of our next steps. Alri can rest first. You can watch the cloud plains, I will watch the hallway, and Calak can bounce between the two of us. We can alternate resting, but assure we do keep watch."

Kealin looked down. "Brother, do you know we are beyond the help of any here?"

Alri looked to Kealin. "We knew we would be. Our parents have no help; we do not need help either."

"There is a difference," he said. "They have not only themselves but others, hundreds of Urlas elves, and even more from different regions. We four are the last line to this sacred place."

"You've never been bothered by thoughts such as this," said Calak.

"I do not feel good about it. Had I not been here, you three would likely not have found your way here."

"But," said Taslun, placing his hand on Kealin's shoulder, "that would mean we would be dead. You have helped us more than once with your ability. I do not understand it, and am thankful it hasn't gone to your head, but it is not by horrid deeds we have reached this place. We are here for a reason. I am confident in Dimn."

"So was the Saint in the chapel below; it served him well, I guess."

Kealin turned from them and heard his brother sigh but remain silent.

"Dimn told me we should all be dead," he told them. "That the wights of Vankou would have killed anyone else. I feel we are part of a plot, and one that is far beyond us."

"Have faith," Taslun said.

"I do not have faith in this god or any other."

"No, Brother, have faith in us. We will defeat any evil that assails us. I will stand beside you in battle, as will Alri and Calak. Do not despair, for that is what the Saint in the chapel below did. It is why he hid away. The last thing we will do is hide."

Kealin nodded as Taslun approached him. They embraced.

ALRI WENT TO LIE DOWN, still in the center hall just off to the side of the main hall. It became quiet throughout the temple. The footstep of Calak pacing between the gateway and the stairwell was the only sound other than a sudden gust of wind that periodically rushed through from the Mouth of Winds.

The sky was darkening, but Kealin had learned from before it never went completely dark. Sometime later, Calak and Alri switched spots, and now Taslun walked the path while Alri watched the doorway. Kealin remained where he was.

Taslun waited for Calak to be asleep and then went to Kealin.

"What do you know, Brother? You never despair as I saw a few hours ago. What else did Dimn tell you?"

Kealin stood. He had been slouched over his knees for a while, and his back cracked as he stretched.

"It does not matter," he told him. "Fate is not set; I do not believe that."

"So Dimn knows the future?"

"No."

"Then what troubles you? I may be older, and you may not agree with my ideals as a Blade, but we are brothers. I want to help and comfort you, if I can."

Kealin noticed that Taslun seemed genuinely worried for him. He knew his brother cared, but glancing at his eyes, he saw a look their father gave them when he was concerned. Which just so happened to be days where his training with Master Rukes had been particularly grueling and he was alone in his room meditating on his many injuries. But now, that felt so long ago. He felt that he had truly moved from being a Blade in training to something else. The thought that he would never return to Urlas crossed his mind.

"I am a key to this. It was me, my power, that led us to this fate."

Taslun laughed. "So then, we might have a fight ahead of us. We will fight, together. As it should be, if you ask me! Have faith, little brother."

"I am trying." He smiled to him, and his brother embraced him.

"Don't worry; if I drop my blade, I know you will be quick to grab it and defeat one hundred enemies before I can arise again. Just please hold on to it. Don't throw it like that time in the arena. We may not get it back."

Kealin laughed. Had it not been for the pillar of the arena, the sword would have likely flown into the lake. Kealin remembered, too, that he had beaten his brother that day.

"That is a good memory, but I am tired," he told him.

"Calak has slept long enough. Go wake him."

Kealin stood and looked over to his brother. He was on his back, mouth agape, and jerking occasionally as he snored.

"Calak," Kealin shouted.

His hands jerked; he partially drew his sword as he glanced around. "To arms?"

"Not quite. It is your turn to keep watch. I'm going to sleep."

Kealin lay down, curling up on the floor. The thin blanket Calak had felt quite warm, and he went to sleep fast.

It was a rush of wind, but not like a gust of the Glacial Seas. There was the rapid clamor of someone running past. Kealin's eyes jerked open to see Alri. Her staff was alight, and a silver blast of air flew from the tip.

He had been sleeping well, too well. He focused his eyes as Calak ran past him, his sword drawn.

Kealin jumped to his feet, drawing his blades, and Alri looked to him.

"Go, Taslun needs you."

He ran past Alri. A flash passed over him as she released another spell into the chaos ahead. Reaching the steps, he paused for a moment.

The sky was red. Lightning shot up from the portal in the clouds, which was now colored the deepest black he had ever witnessed. The entire surface of the realm was churning. White beasts, running on all fours like dogs with red eyes and burning fire upon them, had breached the temple grounds.

He ran forward, his elvish blades up, before he slashed into the nearest one, turning its form to ash. Calak was to his right, but Taslun was much further in already. They fought their way nearly to the platform they had arrived on just hours before. Moving down the walkway in a loose formation with his brothers, he engaged the wave of creatures.

There was a horn call, and it seemed that more of the beasts clawed their way up from every place they could. There was no order to their assault, no sense to it, just a continued rage.

Kealin fought through them with ease. With a single strike, the creatures would shatter, dissipating to light and then passing as dust down into the portal. He struck with his left sword then right and then back with his left. Each flash of Urlas fire shredding his foes one after another. He reached Taslun just as he cleared the platform. They both looked down and could see all the way to the sea.

"Has the portal been broken?" asked Kealin.

"I do not know. But I can see the sea. The maelstrom is no more. There is no protection here. I do see something else below; it takes them time to reach this place, but they do come in waves."

Away from them a good distance was Calak, moving from beast to beast, hitting each in an elementary fashion compared to the sleek and confident style his older brothers had.

Kealin and Taslun joined him, fighting side by side; their sister came, too, and it was no time before the small creatures were gone.

"Itsu?" asked Alri.

"I assume as much," said Taslun. "They come up the portal. I think we can keep them down there longer, or at least hinder their advance."

"Could we close their way up?" suggested Calak. "Could we wake the maelstrom?"

"I do not see it possible," said Kealin.

"Alri, do you know a spell?"

"I do not know. I know much of wind magic, but that may be beyond it."

"It is too bad you are not an archon," said Calak.

"She is the closest we have," said Taslun. "And this magic is of the gods, not our realm. Very well, stay and watch for them. We know they are coming now. I will go check the doorway, and then, I will try something, something to keep them from this realm."

Kealin looked at him with a peculiar glare.

He smiled to him. "Trust me, little brother."

. . .

As Taslun went into the temple, Kealin went to Alri.

"Stay safe. If you must, fall back into the temple and seal it. If we fall—"

"Stop, Kealin. I am with you three. If one of us falls, we all will remain until the last. I will not retreat while you die."

"I know I cannot convince you. I know how you are when your mind is set upon the task. You are like our mother."

"I am glad you know that." She shook her head in confidence.

The lightning began to surge near the portal. It was clear that whatever spellcraft had been used to break into the realm, it was upon the creatures crossing into the realm when the lightning began.

Creatures began to appear on the outer edges, and Kealin and Calak went forward.

"Taslun, they have returned," Alri shouted. Her staff up, she gripped it, looking at her prey just beyond her two brothers. She felt the buzz in her hands, her staff glowing white, and then she released the spell, striking two at once.

As Kealin prepared to strike, he heard a sound above. He glanced up just to see Taslun indeed had a plan. He now wore the Wind Armor of Dimn, and it was of no difficulty in skill for the elder elf as he flew effortlessly down the portal.

He tore down into the clouds, his wings flapping, with the spear and the sword. Kealin rushed to the platform, the only space that he could easily look down and watch as the mass of white creatures engulfed his brother.

Calak joined him, but he noticed Alri had gone back into the temple.

"Alri?" he asked.

Calak looked over the edge, seeing the speck of Taslun going from one side to the next, slashing and turning the Itsu to flashes, a sign of their demise.

"That is hellish," he said.

"Where is Alri going?"

"Oh, she thought of something. Had to go into the temple. This is a nice way to battle," said Calak, with his attention obviously taken by the happenings below.

Kealin shook his head. "Only a start, I fear. Keep your blade ready, Brother."

Winds from the temple blew toward them, cutting through the black clouds. Taslun seemed to be floating upward, and it gusted more, pulling him as it shot below him and then back up. The Itsu attack seemed to have died down. He flapped just above them and then landed with a thump a few paces away.

His armor smoked, and he was breathing heavily. His spear and his sword were both reddened from the heat of the Itsu bodies, and he had glowing scratches covering his armor. He took a knee.

Kealin knelt down to him. "Brother, are you well?"

"There are many. I do not know how long I have gained us. They are gathering again. Larger ones approach, but it seems they are doing such with a group of the smaller ones—" Taslun was out of breath. He took several breaths and then continued. "I will go again, but be prepared up here."

"Let me take your armor. I can go, Taslun," Calak said, placing his hand on the spear.

"No, little brother, I will handle this. You and Kealin must protect Alri. She is the youngest of us and most prone. She was not well not too long ago."

Kealin knew that was a poor excuse, but ignored it.

Taslun stood and looked over the edge. "Keep well, Brother," he said to Kealin.

As a mass of white began an ascent up, he plummeted downward. Kealin watched as he tore into the flock of Itsu.

"Kealin, I will check on Alri," said Calak.

"Very well, hurry. Stay alert to fight if needed; we do not know what other tricks the enemy has."

Calak sprinted up the hill as Kealin paced the platform. He watched Taslun, a worry growing in his stomach, seeing his brother at odds such as this. The larger creatures were going for him now, as the smaller ones flew upward.

The creatures were gripping the edge of the platform. Kealin swung his blade in repeated swipes downward, sending their ashes back to the sea.

A few moments later, and it was clear another assault wave came upon the grounds of the temple. The creatures swarmed again. Kealin was engaged with multiple beasts on the platform. Calak emerged from the temple with sword high, striking those nearest to him that had gone for the temple doorway.

A large Itsu beast had made it past Taslun, and its

clawed hand struck the platform. Kealin looked down at it, noticing it was nearly three times his size. He jabbed his blades into its hand, and it recoiled, grabbing with the other. Kealin went to stab this one, but the creature pulled itself up. He stepped back, holding his sword in front of him.

The Itsu creature was white like the other smaller ones, but this one had armor of gray crystal. In its hand was a sword, and it appeared less of a beast as it seemed to sidestep slowly, studying Kealin. It had white eyes, and a red raiment flew off its back.

It began to speak. "Half-elf, I call you. You are not pure. You will not taste as good to my soul to kill."

"My apologies, I care little to be a decadence to your soul."

Kealin stepped forward, feinting right before leaping to the creature's left and swiping his left sword into the creature's neck. The elven blade hesitated at first, caught in the energy of the creature, jerking Kealin from the smooth transition.

He swung himself into its back and kicked to pull his sword free. The creature turned, white glowing fluid pouring from his neck. It was the same as other enemies; it charged him, one hand on its gushing neck, the other haphazardly swinging his blade. Kealin dodged him and then swung through, cutting into its back and cracking its armor. The creature went to turn around again, and Kealin kicked it, throwing it from the platform.

Kealin checked his area and then looked to Calak; Alri was now with him, and they worked to push the creatures back. He looked over the edge of the platform; his brother came but had two of the larger creatures upon him. He flew high, missing the platform, flying toward the entrance to the temple. Landing with a rolling thud, he attempted to push himself up, but collapsed.

Kealin sprinted toward him. The two creatures were atop his brother, trying to rip at his arms and legs. Alri stabbed her staff into the ground. A blast of fire caught the first one, throwing it backward; it toppled and fell. The other rushed Calak, who parried the strike, but faltered, falling himself.

Kealin ran toward the one struck by Alri. It had begun to get up when, from behind, Kealin crossed his blades and severed its head. Alri smacked the one near Calak, and it turned its attack. Calak forced himself up and cut behind the knee of the creature; it was crippled. It fell to the ground and, by a well-placed blast of wind by Alri, broke its neck. Its ash flowed back down from the realm of Dimn.

Kealin ran to Taslun, who was struggling to stand. He pulled the armor off, unclasping the main components. From that, Taslun was pulled out. He pushed Kealin off.

"I am fine, little brother. I just need to catch my breath."

Taslun had a cut on his face and was trembling. Alri held her staff over him, speaking a healing spell.

"He is weak, but I think I can get him a bit better, at least. Kealin, I'm working on a spell to call forth the maelstrom again. I saw its writing earlier, and I have managed to learn part of the incantation."

"That is good," he replied.

He was listening to her, but his mind was on the application of the wind god armor. He had it fastened before Taslun noticed. He felt the armor as if it was his own body, not bulky like the armor he had felt before, freeing in a way. He thought of flying, and his wings flapped with ease, and he was off the ground. He landed and went to the spear and the sword, taking them in hand.

"Kealin, no!" protested Taslun. "Little brother, it is too much." He attempted to stand but could not.

"Let your body heal, Brother."

Calak nodded to him. "We will hold them here."

Kealin nodded back and flew toward the portal. He looked down at the circling mass of white preparing to come through. He closed his eyes and then dove down.

He felt himself falling. The wind rushing over his face burned near his eyes and mouth. He tucked his lips together, centering his sight on those below. He felt his sword and his spear, feeling them brim with power, a slight buzz in the air.

It was not the same as fighting on the ground; he pointed himself toward his enemy and barreled into them, feeling their forms roll off of him as, with his sword, he cut into their passing bodies. He had reached the bottom of the portal itself. The rush of cold on his feet was more pronounced, and he looked to see the night sky. He looked back down as more of the creatures ascended. He flew with swiftness, his spear at his head. He slashed those he passed with the blade and stabbed those ahead of him, ascending in an arc back up the funnel before dropping down again, repeating the same.

As he reached the lower portion, six of the larger beasts were upon him, grabbing his spear and his sword. He used what force he could muster and spun, ripping the hands of those that held him, but was caught by the next. He let go of the spear and grasped his sword, pulling it free before flapping as fast as the wings would to ascend back up.

He had lost the spear.

Several of the smaller beasts had made it past him now, but he trusted Calak and Alri to deal with them.

"He is not of pure elven blood; how does he fight as this?" he heard in the air.

"Half-elf, but he has a stench of something else, too," another said.

The larger ones that had attacked him before were on him again, with a laugh in the air. He did not care. He swooped downward, slashing his blade and hewing three heads in a single pass.

He reached down to his hip and drew his elven blade. He held them in a cross toward the remaining three, landing upon the body of the one and forcing it down. He then pushed off, throwing himself into another, which he jabbed his dual blades into. He swung the beast off of him, and then, for the finale, he parried before a follow-through stab of his blade before it, too, fell to the "half-elf."

He looked out into the darkness of his world. There was a dark shroud over the seas with no end to it. The flow of Itsu had halted, and a single form came out of the shadows. It was large, larger than the rest of them, and it was veiled in a dark coat. In its hand was a staff, unadorned but silver.

A voice boomed over the sound of the winds. "Folly you have been found in, to face the Itsu as this. You are no god. Why do you wear his armor? You have killed many of my brethren with ease, yet I hear you are a half-elf."

Kealin felt his head aching; from beyond what his eyes could see, he saw a figure in the veil. He felt himself weakening to its glare. He tried to use his new powers to curve his mind away. The figure's image grew in his mind.

"Dat is enough!" he shouted.

"Your mind speaks well what your mouth does not. You wish to see my form. Well, dear half-elf, there isn't one in this realm. Soon you will see me as I am."

The veil of the creature was pulled back, and Kealin saw, at first, a bright flash. Then his ears went silent, his eyes tunneled. He looked up to the red skies of the realm of Dimn, and flew as fast as he could. He closed his eyes; in his mind, he tried to hide from the creature as he flew and noticed his wings flapping less as winds from the temple had caught him and drew him up.

He looked down to see his siblings at odds with

some of the smaller Itsu. Taslun went to him as he landed. He was dizzy and worked to balance himself. His brother helped him.

"There is something else down there," Kealin told him.

"Fine," Taslun replied. "I will go after it. Out of the armor. Alri needs your help inside.

Alri ran up to them."

"Brother, there are words, written strangely, that speak as I try to read them. I feel you may understand them better than I. They are spoken like the shaman. "

He looked to the portal again and unlatched the armor.

"Are you sure you are well?" he asked Taslun.

"It will take more than some scratches to defeat me, little brother! Where is the spear?"

Kealin looked at him with a raised eyebrow. "I lost it."

"Ha! You just wanted two blades! I know it! Hmm, perhaps I should say something to Master Rukes when we get back to Urlas, I'll tell him that Blades should look into using two blades over one. You seem to be handling yourself quite well."

The two brothers shared a quick smile at one another.

Taslun got back into the armor and flapped his wings. Calak was near the entrance to the temple, watching for their enemy. Kealin turned and ran in that direction. Alri had already gone inside.

"Watch yourself, Calak."

Calak nodded.

Kealin continued inside. He didn't see Alri yet, but he went to the doorway toward the temple, past where the wind armor had been kept. Alri was against a far wall. Runes floated in the air above her.

"This is it here," she told him.

"I do not hear anything."

"Walk into the runes and you will hear it."

Kealin stepped forward; the runes surrounded him, and his eyes saw the seas. A faint voice came upon him, and he heard it, just as if Alri was speaking to him.

Waters churning, thirst and yearning,
Like siren calling, dead birds falling.
Twisting, pulling, ocean calling,
Winds of Dimn contrived, conjoining.

"DIS IS SIMPLE. IT SAYS DIS." His speech then returned to normal, and he repeated it to her.

"Then that is the spell. The words were twisted when I heard it."

"Does this mean you can summon the maelstrom?"

"Yes, I believe I can. This wall has an image high above." She pointed.

It was a golden engraving of what looked like the actual maelstrom.

"I thought I would take a look and, well, I saw signs like from my archon instruction back home." She smiled. "I wanted to really help you three."

He smiled back. "You have."

A scream pierced the air, shattering their moment of quietness. They both ran. Kealin drew his blades and leaped through the gateway.

He scanned, seeing no Itsu but Calak on his knees holding their brother. Taslun was down; his legs were bleeding, and his face was bloodied. Kealin ran to him, dropping his blades as Alri began trying to heal him again.

The bleeding wasn't stopping.

"Taslun!" shouted Kealin.

There was no response.

"Get the armor off of him. We need to stop the bleeding," Kealin said as he and Calak ripped at the fasteners, throwing the armor to the side.

A strike had landed beyond the armor and sliced his chest; a golden glow burned him, and his skin smoked. Kealin pulled his fingers through the wound. His fingertips burned, but the mark was cleared. Alri placed her staff on the wound, and it began to heal.

"I will return," Calak said.

Kealin looked up to find his young brother already in the armor of Dimn. At that moment, Taslun opened his eyes, gasping to breathe, and looked toward Calak.

"No!" he shouted.

Kealin jumped to stop him, but he was just out of reach.

"I will help you, Brothers. You've done your part."

With that, Calak flew straight up before twisting in the sky and shooting downward, his blade out before him.

"Kealin, that thing, that creature. It will kill him!"

Taslun worked to stand. His legs still bled, and Alri had begun to feel the effects of continued magic casting. Her skill was not fully developed. Her staff bounced, and her vision was blurring. Kealin pulled Taslun up.

"I will go to the platform. I can wait for him. I can see what happens and prepare."

"It is no good. There are too many. They've stopped coming at random. They have formed like a land army in formation. That creature with the staff, it is leading them. I know not what it is."

"Alri, can you cast the spell? Awaken the maelstrom?" asked Kealin. Before Alri could answer, the portal erupted with lightning, and thunder shook the temple. A mass of the larger Itsu emerged. They formed a line on the edge of the portal, instead of their instantaneous attack before. Kealin grabbed his swords and pointed for Alri to go left.

From the portal came blasts of green magic that shot high into the sky before turning and diving toward them. Alri grabbed Kealin and pulled him to Taslun, dropping to her knees and pushing her staff upward. A shield of white expanded from it, and the ground shook as she struggled to hold up her staff against the weight of the blast.

The shield lowered, and Kealin was back on his feet. The pathway to the platform, and most of the road now, was no more. The blasts had destroyed them. The creatures began to emerge in the largest wave yet.

Taslun stood and pointed. "Get to the stairwell of the temple."

Alri was ahead of them already, managing to jump a small gap in the path, and from her staff, she sent a flurry of red flames that struck each of the Itsu creatures one after another.

Kealin brought his brother to the edge.

"I do not think I can jump," he said.

Kealin picked him up and jumped with both of them, reaching the ground near Alri, whose entire body had been engulfed in flames. She turned and looked at them. Her eyes gleamed red, and her hair furled from the arcane energies flowing off of her. She set her eyes on the Itsu and began to force multiple ones back.

Kealin ran forward, his blades out. He jumped upon one and used it to go to the next. He slashed that one and continued on, dragging a third and fourth down to the ground before burying his blades in each.

Alri had stopped her spellcraft as smaller Itsu were now approaching Taslun, who was unarmed, dragging him away from the gates. Overwhelmed, he punched the ones closest as Alri ran for him. Kealin saw that more of the larger Itsu emerged. Another line ready to face the elves of Urlas. Calak was still below them.

ALRI STRUGGLED to control her breathing. She remembered her master's words, *Focus, Fracture, Fade*. She repeated the words, summoning her energies as more of the dead piled up around them. Kealin was overwhelmed, at least a dozen foes were moving in around them and her archon powers were not enough. Kealin had pushed back the Itsu surrounding Taslun.

She felt a tinge within her stomach, a pleasure in the dead around her. She tried to force the thoughts, her last necromantic attempt was beyond weak. But the more she tried not to think of it, to keep her focus on supporting Kealin and occasionally sending a blast of fire or ice, the more the desire to refocus her energy began to overtake them.

"Calak is still beneath us!" Kealin shouted. "We must hold them until he returns and then fall back."

Taslun wasn't moving. Kealin knelt down, his blades engorged with fire as he spun about in a circle. His blades crackled and sang, surging waves of energy upwards and through his foes as even more of them rose up to face them.

Alri lowered her staff, seeing the dead around them and focusing on one of the larger ones.

Focus, Fracture, Fade.

She closed her eyes, reaching out to the Itsu's corpse, opening her eyes as green fire erupted from her staff, striking the creature.

She could see from its eyes, she could feel a seething hatred for its reawakening.

"Serve me." She said plainly.

The creature seemed to acknowledge her, yet was resistant. It clamored forward, slapping at its kin. Kealin looked back to Alri with widened eyes as she moved her staff about, sending suggestions to the creature.

It cleared many of their foes but still more came. Kealin struggled to keep the path clear between him and Taslun and her. Alri called her summoning towards her.

"Defend us," she said.

The creature seemed to stumble before its form shredded into nothingness. The sudden dissolution of the spell threw her off as more Itsu now charged her. She lifted her staff, forming a ward just like back at Nidea Archo, deflecting the beast.

KEALIN RUSHED for Alri as more of their enemy overwhelmed them. Her ward shattered and he turned to try to shield her.

It was then one of the creatures grabbed him. He hacked at its arm, but he felt it fling him, tossing his body upon the steps of the temple. Alri was backing up as Taslun was shrouded and covered in the smaller Itsu. Kealin pulled himself up; his blades now lay a distance from him. The creatures were converging, and he saw Alri try to cast a spell but lower her head in weakness. Her last bout had taken all of her remaining energy. He grabbed her and pulled her up the steps, scanning a last time before dragging her into the temple.

Once inside a few paces, he lay her down. He looked back out. He prayed to see Calak but could see only more of the Itsu in the gateway. He turned and ran for the crystal at the Heart of the Winds. Smaller Itsu began to run toward him. He pulled the crystal, and a gust of wind struck the grounds, spreading out in all directions.

A slamming sound at the front of the temple followed, and a gate covered in lightning fell downward. The Itsu were sucked out, their forms annihilated by the gate as they were pulled into it. Kealin went to Alri. She nodded quickly and tried to catch her own breath.

Kealin went to the gate and looked out. The Itsu advance stopped, and the larger Itsu had formed a column, with packs of the smaller ones at their fore. It was then from the portal the veiled figure appeared.

Rising up, its hand grasped Calak's leg. It floated down to the steps of the gate and dropped him, the armor clanging on the steps. From the mass of Itsu, Taslun was dragged, still alive but moaning, beside Calak.

The veiled figure pointed the silver staff as it approached the gate. He was covered in white raiment.

Kealin stared at it.

It stopped at the gate and then spoke. "We need to speak to one another, Kealin Half-Elf."

17

TORMENTOR

KEALIN LOOKED out the gate at the figure.

"A hasty defense you threw up here against the many angels of the Itsu. I could not believe what my subordinates had told me. Four mere elves strong enough to stand against us? I had thought the old Dwemhar warrior Riakar and his siblings lived again! But, no, I would not have pushed them into a temple like cowering mice."

Its voice was like a strange cackle, higher in tone than Kealin heard before. It continued.

"You elves cost me many of my precious warriors. I would not have thought those who were like the others who came to face the Itsu with Kel would have put up such a fight. Why were you not with the others? Why did you not go to the Southern lands? You came here when you should have never been here!"

Kealin said nothing.

"I do not care myself. I only wish to know to whom

to tell that they were all killed. None can stop what we bring, a grand and glorious change is upon you!" It snickered and then began to pace back and forth. It set its staff against the wall of the temple.

"I went through much to assure a simple taking of this temple. I spoke with the one you know as Vankou, convinced him of lies, his own grandeur, and then let him attack this place first. Dreadful show he put on, but still, through one working or another, it managed to convince Dimn to leave his holy house and head so hurriedly to the south. The dragon also did well to damage the maelstrom, allowing me an easier passage.

"I care little what the one of death and his pet lizard wish with Dimn. I was going to come here, do what I must to take care of a small deed, but then the noble elves of Urlas remained to defend the holy ground."

The figure turned from the gate and grabbed Taslun by the arm. Taslun looked up at him, bleeding from the mouth.

"Do you think he will open that gate?"

Taslun spit at him. "Curse you."

The figure stepped back. "You cannot curse me!" It shouted the words loud and deep before stomping Taslun's hand. His fingers were broken, and blood ran red from the splintered bones piercing his skin.

Kealin struck the gate. "Creature! Over here! You want to speak with me, do it. Do not hurt them."

The figure bobbed its head back and forth. "How wrong you are. Hurting them furthers the will of the Itsu!"

It went to Calak. "Wake up, elf!"

Calak opened his eyes, and his head bobbed. He then spotted the figure and tried to punch him. The figure laughed and then stuck a curved finger into his eye, ripping it out.

Calak screamed. The Itsu Priest threw his eye on to the steps that led to the gateway. Calak tried again to attack the Priest but in a single motion, the Priest struck Kealin's brother in the chest, cracking his ribs on his right side, Calak coughed blood and collapsed back down.

"Bastard!" shouted Kealin. "Get over to this gate! Speak with me!"

The figure rushed up to the gate and placed his ear toward Kealin. "What would you like to say? That you will open the gate?"

"It does not open," Kealin replied.

"Wrong again, half-elf. Is that why you are not full elf? You cannot comprehend basic truths? How about you, young one? Can you open it?"

Alri was still on the ground and weakened from before.

"Hmm, no response. Well, here is the deal I have for you. Dimn is gone, and if he was here, I would deal with him, but since you are here, I offer you this. Free passage home. You can take your brothers here and your sister there, and you may leave. I will simply take what I came for and be on my way."

"You want to destroy the winds; I cannot allow that."

The creature knelt down and stroked its head.

"When did anyone say that?" It stood back up. "I have need for an item within there. Nothing more. Your winds will be fine."

"What is your name, creature?"

The figure laughed. "My name is my own. You shall never know it! Call me creature, for now. I am a priest of the Itsu, and I come in their name. I am both myself and they. I have memory of my own creation and that of my masters' vast knowledge but my purpose in clear."

"You command, though. You are not Itsu?"

"I am between realms, you might say. Like the one called Vankou. Although, I fancy the realm below. The people are more gullible than the deity types. Oh, how many ill happenings are caused by men corrupted to the lust of power. They are so easy to manipulate and betray."

Kealin stared at him, "So you admit you are untrustworthy. So why would I open the gates?"

"Because"—it spoke in a deep voice again—"you do not wish to see this."

It turned to Calak and crushed his hand just like Taslun. Blood now flowed from each of his brothers. Calak screamed.

"Stop it, creature!"

The figure placed its foot over Calak's broken hand and began to dig into it, smashing the bones and spreading them out over the stairs. Calak screamed and cried, slapping the foot with his other hand. Each strike became less and less forceful. Calak's strength was waning. The figure kicked him, knocking him out.

"I give you time. Time to think. Before I continue," the figure said.

Kealin jerked away from the gateway and walked toward Alri.

"What does it want?" she whimpered.

"For us to open the gate, but we cannot."

"It does not open, Kealin."

"I know. But our brothers—- we must do something!"

Kealin picked her up, and she glanced over at the gateway; the figure stared in.

"This way," he said to her.

He took her past where the armor had been, and they stood near the stairwell.

"Do you know any spells, any single bit of magic that can help us?"

"No. I do not. My last spell took much from me, and the maelstrom cannot help us now."

"It says it can open the gate. It tortures Calak and Taslun before our eyes. Should we try?" Kealin turned from Alri, clutching his forehead. "Sister, I do not know what to do."

They began to hear the sounds of rocks being thrown near the stairwell leading to the old shrine. They looked downward and noticed orange glowing through the wall that had been erected by Dimn. The wall he had crafted was beginning to crack, and from tiny holes, claws could be seen picking at the wall.

"The dead creatures of Vankou, they are close to being within these walls," Alri said. Her voice choked.

"I do not have enough magic to defeat them. I am sorry. I am no archon, I failed you. I failed them."

Kealin pulled his sister back up the stairwell, leading her near to where the armor was. He peered around the corner; the figure still stood waiting. He looked back to her. Alri looked horrid. Her eyes were sunken in, her skin was blanched. The necromantic spell had pulled much of her life force. He couldn't expect anything else of her.

"Could you move our brothers to the Heart of the Winds?"

"You mean into the Heart of the Winds?"

"Yes."

"I don't . . . don't . . . know. The gate would have to be down, but how long I could last to move them in . . . The Itsu would be upon us . . . Elves of Urlas would never do this."

"We are more than elves of Urlas. That I know, somehow, I understand it more now. The Itsu? Do not mind them. I will deal with them. You could move our brothers into the Winds and then escape yourself."

She shook her head. "Dimn said that was folly."

Kealin smiled. "He said it was 'gambling with fate.' I will take that chance."

"I will try. But I cannot promise I can."

"You can, Alri." He began to walk, but she grabbed him.

"What about you?"

He paused. "Once you have them and are gone yourself, I will join you."

She smirked and nodded. Kealin was glad. He

didn't want to tell her the truth of his intentions. He had always been different than his siblings. He would do what was needed for them. That was his purpose.

As he walked toward the gates, Alri stood by the Heart of the Winds, her staff in hand.

"So have you thought of my offer, Kealin Half-Elf?"

"Yes, and I will open this gate. You will let us go free."

"Of course."

"Then tell me how."

The figure laughed. "When you faced me below, above the seas, I felt something within you. I believe you could even hear the words of the Itsu, a gift, and you would make a great asset to them. Tell me, will you join us?"

"I am to open this gate, nothing more."

It laughed again. "Pity, then. Well, the gate cannot be opened with one using powers such as yours, but between you and me, we can force the locks. It is not just a matter of how rare your gift is but also the blessings of the Itsu upon us. I can show you power beyond. Tell me, will you not join me?"

"I said I will open this gate, but I will not join you!"

The figure stared at him. "Use your mind and join with my own power; envision it, and it will be. There is indeed a power beyond the gods. Now, we must make this gate open."

Kealin closed his eyes and saw the gate and the figure's form. He began to try to open the gate, but it only shook.

"More!" the figure bellowed.

Kealin tried but could not muster the strength. Concentrating, he began to shake. The gate lifted a small fragment and then slammed shut.

"Need more inspiration, half-elf?"

Kealin opened his eyes, and the figure took hold of Taslun's other hand. He chopped off his thumb and threw it.

"Angry yet? Angry?"

"Stop!"

"You can make it stop. Open the gate."

He closed his eyes again, concentrating on the gate. He could see the magic holding the gate shut through his mind's sight. Ripples of power flowed from the temple to this center point.

"Do it, Kealin!"

He struggled and then heard Taslun scream again.

"He only has three more fingers! Open it!"

The gate began to lift again. The power of the temple seemed to work against him. He could hear the wailing of winds within, blowing toward him, but still he tried. Taslun screamed again.

"One more, half-elf! One more finger remains!"

He tightened his eyes and balled his fists. His head surged with pain, and he saw the gate lifting more and then slamming shut again. His eyes jerked open to Taslun's wails. The figure cut off the final finger and then slashed his face prior to smashing his body with his foot over and over, blood splashed over the steps. Once the figure had finished, Taslun had stopped moving. He then went to Calak, who had just opened his eyes.

"You lost one brother! Open it, or I will kill the young one!"

Kealin closed his eyes. He made note of where his swords were between the Itsu Priest and the Itsu beyond. He knew he could force the gate. His heart thudded, and he sweated. Taslun, his elder brother, his friend since birth, was dead.

He would get to Calak.

The gate began to lift again, sliding quicker as a sharp southern wind struck him.

I am coming.

Kealin heard a voice in the wind. It was Dimn.

The gate began to slide down as he thought of Dimn's approach.

"Itsu, the god approaches. Do not let him near us! Open that gate!"

The figure drew a large curved blade from his robes and held it at Calak's neck. "Now, Kealin."

Kealin shook. He pushed the gate up but then felt the temple itself work against him. It began to fall again. He was failing. His mind could not keep up.

"Too late, half-elf! Open it. I will give you reason to open it."

The figure sliced into Calak's neck.

"Goodbye, Brot—" Calak's last words were gurgled in blood as the Itsu Priest cut through his throat.

"No!" shouted Alri.

Kealin cried out, and tears fell from his eyes. The gate shot up, fracturing the foundation of the temple.

A blast of wind followed, and Kealin shouted, running for his blades, rolling on the ground as he took one of his own and one of his brother's swords in hand.

The Itsu angels ran toward him, and he cut into each of them. One, two, three, four, five. He sliced their heads, turning them to ash. He turned to see the Itsu Priest running into the temple. Alri stood her ground. She held out her staff, but the Itsu Priest made a motion with his, and she flew against the Heart of the Winds, falling unconscious.

He ran into the temple. He went first to Alri. Grabbing her by an arm, he pulled her unconscious form up and held her above the Heart of the Winds. "Live on, my sister."

He dropped her in and watched her body disappear in the winds. From behind him, the Itsu angels were entering, the smaller ones first, sprinting toward him.

From the hallway, the dead creatures of Vankou had come wobbling in, pointing their blades at him. Against the distant wall, the Itsu Priest opened the vault containing the orbs. Kealin ran toward him. In a leap, he took to the air, flying toward the figure. It turned as he did and swung its staff.

The two fell into a duel, and Kealin spun, striking multiple times, the blades of the elves cutting his robes into tatters but not hurting the being beyond.

It struck Kealin with its staff, and he flew, rolling across the floor. He forced himself to his feet, still grasping his blades. Itsu and the dead creatures both came upon him. Within his mind, he heard the wails of Taslun and the last words his little brother had said cut short in a bloody gurgle.

He felt his heart surge, and his arms cut into all that faced him. He felt their blades burn his skin, slicing tissue, and his blood splattering their faces. His blades shimmered a brighter red, both from his bleeding arms and their natural elven glow. He broke through the throng of enemies and again went toward the Itsu Priest.

"I will kill you."

It laughed and evaded Kealin's strike. He smacked the half-elf to the ground with his staff. Kealin landed facedown. The Itsu and the other beasts held their stance as the Itsu Priest walked around Kealin.

He tried to push himself up, but he couldn't. His arms trembled, and his face lay in a puddle of his own blood.

The Itsu Priest laughed. He picked him up by his arm and dragged him along the floor to the very center of the temple.

"You cannot harm me, foolish elf, and soon I will be untouchable by all within the realms. This was a mere test for me by my masters. Now, I will leave your body as a gift to Dimn."

He flipped Kealin over, and the half-elf stared upward. He coughed, and blood shot up. He still gripped his blades but lacked the strength to swing them. The Itsu Priest lifted his staff high into the air.

Kealin inhaled. He knew this would be it. The old Kealin, the young pupil training to be a Blade of Urlas, was already dead. As his heart thudded in his chest, he felt something else within him. Something that had awakened even before he had left Urlas— something he sensed, somehow, around Valrin. He was more than what he believed but that had been only a short instant in his many decades of life. In truth, he had felt it growing with each passing moment, with every Itsu Angel he had destroyed he felt closer and more aligned to what he could become.

He thought of his mother and father, hoping that if they ever knew of his and his sibling's deeds, that they'd be proud.

He opened his eyes, waiting for the strike.

It was then a cyclone struck within the temple itself. The ceiling caved in, showering them in rubble. Kealin turned his head as rocks hit his face. A white mass flew in, blowing back all of the Itsu. The sounds were horrendous, and screeching winds tore into all. The priest cowered, and Kealin felt himself sucked into the air. His eyes scanned, and he saw the Heart of the Winds. His eyes went dark as he fell into it.

18

UPON THE SEAS

KEALIN AWOKE to the sun shining upon him. He could not move. His head still ached, pounding with a throbbing, dizzying pain. He was unable to do much but crack open his eyes. The sound of the sea with rolling waves was to his left. Something was over his eyes that made the already blinding sun worse to attempt to see through.

He could not remember what had happened, and for now, it was good. He wondered why his brothers and sister had not come to get him.

He fell asleep. Night came upon him, as it had many times since his arrival at this place. The sun came up the next morning, and then set again, although to him, he simply slept. Fairies visited the half-elf and continued to heal his many wounds.

He opened his eyes again, seeing the sunrise and now able to turn his head to witness waves rolling onto a black rock beach. He looked around but saw no one. Though someone was searching for him.

The days passed on, and still Kealin was weak. A crab walked near him, pinching his cheek, causing him to open his eyes in pain, but it was not with ill intent, for the crab sensed his weakness and offered him a slice of fruit to eat.

It tasted sweet and refreshing, and the crab remained with him, bringing him fruit unceasingly until he shook his head no more. It then crawled away. The next Kealin knew, the moon was up again.

His mind thought to the Urlas Woodlands and his siblings. He still did not remember the horror of the events, but he saw them all upon the *Aela Sunrise*, and he saw Vals at the helm, smiling. He watched them soaring above the storms and crashing back to the sea. Narwhals appeared, and it was then he awoke from his drifting dream and looked to his left.

Tulasiro had come, and with a strange black object in tow. He blinked and then turned back over. He felt cold, a deep sadness gripped him from within and a melody in his mind made him feel coldness across his body.

Vankou.

He then saw the image of the wights and the mouth of the maelstrom. He still felt the surge over his body as he was sucked downward into its grasp, and then he saw Dimn, his siblings standing beside the wind god. The image faded.

He rolled to his side. Thick hair fell into his face,

and he looked at Tulasiro. The narwhal had brought the boat he had used before. He had not seen it since the incident at the maelstrom. He was remembering now.

"Do you know if Alri was healed of her sickness, friend?"

The narwhal dove under the surface of the water and splashed him with its horn. Tulasiro then swam out and back toward him, releasing the bite line and letting the boat run up on the beach.

I have seen not sister . . . I found you. Others like me lost with the freezing sea.

I am sorry.

In time, a trio of fairies appeared. They floated over him, and he felt himself slowly healing. The cuts on his arms vanished; the pain in his back and neck ceased. When, at last, they floated away, he felt much better but was not perfect. He had been near death before. He was fortunate for the fairies.

Kealin sat up on the beach. The ground was barren and rocky. He was in some type of cove where the waves beat upon tall rocks behind him, casting sea foam high into the air. He felt his head. He had been here a while; his hair was longer than he normally kept it.

The crab that had fed him before brought him another piece of fruit, dropping it on his leg. He took it between two fingers and then watched the crab scurry into the thick bushes it had come from.

He ate it and then stood, wobbly but managing to keep his gait stable. His head still ached. He went to take a step, and his feet kicked something on the ground. He looked down and saw both his and Taslun's swords.

He reached down, picking them up. Looking at the sword of his brother, he saw his face at the gateway of the temple, the blood from his body. He then teared as he remembered again Calak and his throat being cut by the Itsu Priest.

They cannot be dead. They cannot be lost.

He began to pace, holding the swords. He then lifted them, driving them into the sand. He dropped to his knees, breathing fast and crying. To his side, Tulasiro beached herself and made a sound to him. He looked up to the narwhal.

"It is us now," he said. "We need to find Alri."

He grasped the hilts of his ruinite blades and tucked them into his belt.

I need to kill that Priest. I will kill that Priest.

It was then that a strong wind blew from the north. A parchment floated over him, and he snatched it from the air. It was a note, written in silver letters.

Kealin Half-Elf, you have escaped death by all degrees and have awoken where the winds wished.

Tulasiro has surely come to you by now.

I cannot say where your sister was sent, but the winds tell me she, too, is alive. The Heart of the Winds is safe, and my temple is once again secure. Of your siblings, I cannot say. Their blood remained, but their bodies were taken.

There was much confusion as to what transpired within the Glacial Seas. I will deal with what a god can, but your work is not done. The Prophecy of the Glacial Seas will come to pass, and though it is not understood by you, it will be in time. May the peace of Dimn be upon you.

Know that I am sorry that I failed to protect that which you loved.

He folded the parchment and placed it into a pocket. He climbed into the boat on the beach and sat down, shaking his head. Had this been the point of their quest, for him to find himself upon the sea with a narwhal, alone?

He had released a Lord of Death upon the Glacial Seas, watched his brothers be slain by a figure calling itself a priest, and lost his sister.

Tulasiro took hold of the lines, and they began out of the bay, turning into the open sea with no destination yet known. The boat flew across the water, headed south.

Kealin was deep in thought, wondering in his memories of the tranquil waters of the Urlas Woodlands, the moon high above as he stared out over the sheer surface. As a young boy, he had watched a swan take to flight and go to the heavens. He had wished to do the same so long ago, but that was then. He was no longer a young boy, but neither was he the Blade he was training to be, before the events that had passed in the past few days in his mind.

He was friend to Tulasiro, wielder of the blades of both himself and Taslun of Urlas, and in his heart, was a zeal for his siblings and a wish upon his soul for retribution on his brothers' murderer. First, he would find Alri, and then he would have his revenge on all that had set him upon this path. He no longer desired to be a Blade of Urlas and perhaps, he never really did. He did not know who or what he truly was but something within him had awakened and as he sought his sister, he'd discover who he truly was meant to be.

Kealin, the rogue elf of Urlas, would not stop.

THE END… for now. Book two in *The Rogue Elf* series can be found here:

https://mybook.to/Rogueelf2

AUTHOR'S NOTE

Welcome to the Dwemhar Realms! I'm sure if this is your first foray into my work, that this book was quite a shocking first look… I assure it gets a bit brighter. :)

****Join my mailing list if you haven't yet:**

www.subscribepage.com/therogueelf

As of the writing of this note, Seer of Lost Sands (Rogue Elf #2) is due for release in a few weeks. All of the books in this series up to book #8 are already ready for publication!

I won't leave you hanging for long. :) If you're wanting to know more about the Dwemhar Realms, I suggest you head to my website www.authorjtwilliams.com.

I'd also recommend my series the *Stormborn Saga* if you're wanting to know more about Valrin and his crew… that's a fourteen book series and leads right into the events of Half-Bloods Rising! … you may get a to know few secrets, too…

I look forward to seeing you in the next book. You're going to love it!

J.T. Williams

For a complete list of titles please go to:

www.authorjtwilliams.com/series-timeline.html